River of Love

The Bradens
at Peaceful Harbor

Love in Bloom Series

Melissa Foster

ISBN-10: 1941480314
ISBN-13: 9781941480311

Cover Design: Natasha Brown & Elizabeth Mackey
Cover Photography: David Hickey Photography

WORLD LITERARY PRESS
PRINTED IN THE UNITED STATES OF AMERICA

A Note from Melissa

I had so much fun watching Sam and Faith learn and grow and inevitably fall in love; they've climbed right to the top of my favorite couples list. I hope you love them as much as I do! In this book you will meet the Whiskeys, who now have their own series! Be sure to check out TRU BLUE, the first book in The Whiskeys: Dark Knights at Peaceful Harbor series.

Newsletter: Sign up for my newsletter to keep up to date with new releases and to receive an exclusive short story featuring Jack Remington and Savannah Braden.
MelissaFoster.com/NL

The Bradens are just one of the families in the Love in Bloom big-family romance collection. Characters from each series make appearances in future books so you never miss an engagement, wedding, or birth.

FREE Love in Bloom goodies

Series Checklist
MelissaFoster.com/SO

Free eBooks
MelissaFoster.com/LIBFree

Reading orders, family trees, and more
MelissaFoster.com/RG

Keep track of your favorite characters with the essential Love in Bloom Series Guide
MelissaFoster.com/books/love-in-bloom-series-guide

For Elise, because our crazies have such fun together

Chapter One

A MAN COULD take a wedding for only so long before he drank too much booze or left with a warm, willing woman to wash away all that purity. Sam Braden stood with a drink in one hand and a greedy itch in the other, debating doing both.

"I'll take the redhead if you want the brunette." Ty, his youngest brother, lifted his chin in the direction of the bar. In addition to being a world-renowned mountain climber and photographer, Ty was also Sam's carousing partner. "Unless you're double-dipping tonight, in which case I'll go for one of the Staley sisters."

Sam scoffed. *Been there, done them.*

He spotted two blondes slinking across the dance floor toward them. He'd hooked up with the one who was currently eye-fucking him last month, and the redhead Ty had been ogling moments ago had joined them in their hot, sweaty romp. His gaze shifted to the sexy brunette standing by the bar looking like she wanted to jump over it and hide behind it but she couldn't quite figure out how. *Faith Hayes.* He'd been trying *not* to look at Faith all night, but he was losing that battle. Faith worked in Sam's brother Cole's medical practice. She was sweet, and good, and smart, and… Sam should not be thinking about laying her on the bar and doing dirty things to her gorgeous body.

No. He definitely should not.

Every time he looked at her, every time he thought of her— *which was every damn day*—that feeling of wanting more than a few quick hookups resurfaced. He not only wanted to lay her down on the bar, but he wanted to take her home. That was bizarre, too, since as a rule Sam never took any woman to his cabin. But half his *visits* with Cole at his office were merely made-up opportunities to get a glimpse of Faith. He didn't fully understand his fascination with her, considering he usually preferred the kind of woman who wanted to jump *him* and damn well knew how, but there was no denying the stirring inside him every time she was near. He forced himself to look away and focused on the dance floor, where Cole, their eldest brother, danced with his new wife, Leesa, and just beyond, their younger brother Nate and his fiancée, Jewel, were gazing into each other's eyes. Weren't they always? Sam used to get hives just thinking about being tied down—*unless, of course, it was to a bed.* But he couldn't deny how happy his brothers seemed since they'd fallen in love, and lately he'd begun feeling as if he were missing out on something.

The tall blonde sidled up to Sam, blocking his view of Faith and blinking flirtatiously, while her friend joined Ty. "You boys look lonely."

"Ladies," Sam said smoothly, bringing his attention back to the pretty girls who definitely knew how to use their bodies for the good of mankind.

"Care to dance?" she asked, and like a puppy with a bone, Sam followed her out to the dance floor.

Music and dancing ranked right up there with white-water rafting in Sam's book. As the owner of Rough Riders, a rafting and adventure company, he rarely slowed down, but a strong beat calmed his internal restlessness. And Sam was always a little restless.

The blonde moved sensuously in his arms, reminding him of all the reasons a woman should win out over booze tonight. On that thought, his eyes drifted back to Faith, still standing by the bar, holding a drink he'd bet was soda, and nervously running her finger up the side of the glass as she...*watched him?* Sam's lips curved up and Faith's gaze skittered away. She became adorably flustered whenever he visited Cole at the office, and though he probably shouldn't, Sam got a kick out of flirting with her.

Cole stepped into his line of sight, blocking his view of Faith and casting a threatening look at Sam, sending the message, *Don't even think about it.*

There were no two ways about it, Sam loved women and

everyone around him knew it. He loved the way they smelled, the feel of their soft bodies against his hard muscles, their delicate features, the sounds they made in the throes of passion. But his mind refused to play the *any woman* game these days. It was drenched in thoughts of Faith, and he wanted to experience all those things about her firsthand.

"Sam!" Cole chided.

He shook his head to clear his mind, laughing under his breath, as he turned his attention back to the woman he was dancing with. His hands sank to the base of her spine. *Mm.* She felt good. His eyes were drawn to Faith again, who was staring into her drink. *Bet you'd feel even better*, was his first thought, but it was the second—*I wonder what you're thinking*—that took him by surprise.

I SHOULDN'T HAVE come to this wedding. Faith checked her watch for the hundredth time that evening. She'd told herself she had to stay for an hour after dinner. That was the respectable thing to do at her boss's wedding, even though she'd rather leave right this very second. Work obligations outside of the office were uncomfortable enough, but now she was not only surrounded by people she barely knew, but her stupid hormones were doing some sort of *I Want Sam Braden* dance. God, she hated herself right now. *Look at him, getting all handsy with the*

town flirt. He'd been dancing all night with every other woman in the place. They practically lined up to be near him. Why shouldn't they? He was not only nice to everyone, but he was tall, dark, and distractingly handsome. The kind of handsome that made smart girls like Faith forget the alphabet. His arm was the most coveted spot in all of Peaceful Harbor, and damn it to hell, she did *not* want to be there.

Too badly.

I seriously need to dive into a tequila bottle. Or leave. Since driving home after drinking a bottle of tequila posed issues, she decided leaving was a better option.

She had the perfect excuse to cut out a little early, too. She was hosting a car wash tomorrow to raise funds for WAC, Women Against Cheaters, an online support group she'd started for women who had been cheated on.

By guys like Sam.

Sam glanced up and—*Oh God, shoot me now*—caught her staring. *Again.* She turned away, hoping he hadn't really noticed, even though his eyes were like laser beams burning a hole in her back. Of course he saw her. How could he not? She was practically drooling over him. She didn't want to have this stupid crush on the man who, if she believed the rumors, had slept with most of the women in Peaceful Harbor. If she took away his devastatingly good looks, he was the exact opposite of the type of man she wanted or needed.

Unable to resist, she stole another glance, and like every

other set of female eyes in the place that weren't related to him, she was drawn in like a fly to butter. He was *gorgeous.* Manly. Rugged. And that smile. *Lordy, Lordy.* She fanned her face. His smile alone caused her toes to curl. All the Bradens were good-looking, but there was something edgy and enigmatic about Sam. *Dangerous.*

Too dangerous for her, which was okay, because she didn't really want him. Not in the *try to keep him* sense. A man like Sam couldn't be kept, and she wasn't about to be the idiot who tried. She'd be happy with leering and lusting, and pretending she wasn't.

Except, *oh shit*, he was coming over. He moved across the dance floor like he owned the place, confident, determined, focused, leaving the blonde, and a dozen other women, staring after him. If looks had powers beyond the ability to weaken Faith's knees, Sam would have eaten her up before he even reached her. His dark eyes were narrow, seductive, and shimmering with wickedness. His broad shoulders looked even wider, more powerful, beneath his expensive tuxedo. The top buttons of his shirt were open, giving her a glimpse of his tanned skin and a dusting of chest hair. He looked like he should be lounging on a couch with women fawning over him. Godlike.

Godlike? I am pathetic.

Faith was not a meek woman without a man in her life. She was single by choice, *thank you very much.* She stunk at choosing men, and besides that…men sucked. They cheated, they lied, and eventually they all tried to put the blame back on her. Ever since JJ, her last boyfriend, made good on the unspoken All Men Must Cheat promise their gender seemed to live by, she'd confined her dating pool to include only boring, slightly nerdy men.

"Faith."

Sam's deep voice washed over her skin and nestled into her memory bank for later when she was alone in her bed, thinking about him. She hated that, too. Why, oh, why, did he have to be a player? Couldn't he be like his brothers Cole and Nate? Loyal to the end of time?

He touched her arm, burning her skin.

"Oh. Hi, Sam." That sounded casual, right? He was so big, standing this close, and he smelled like man and sunshine and heat all wrapped up in one big delicious package.

Great. Now I'm thinking of your package.

"Would you like to dance?" he asked.

Yes. No! Stick to your boring-man rule, Faith.

Sam was anything but boring, taking every outdoor risk known to man and out carousing every night of the week. Nope, she wanted no part of that.

"No, thanks." She sipped her drink, wishing it were tequila instead of Jack and Coke. Wishing she were home instead of standing beside the human heat wave.

His brows knitted. "You sure? I haven't seen you on the

dance floor all night."

"Have you run out of girls already?" *Holy Jesus, did I say that out loud?*

An easy smile spread across his face, like he wasn't offended, but...*amused?* He looked around the room and said, "No, actually. There are a few I haven't danced with." Those chocolate eyes focused on her again. "But I want to dance with you."

She downed her drink to keep the word *Okay* from slipping out and set the empty glass on the bar. "Thanks, but I'm actually getting ready to leave."

"Now, that would be a shame." His eyes dragged slowly down her body, making her feel vulnerable and naked.

Naked with Sam Braden. Her entire body flamed, and he must have noticed, because his eyes turned midnight black.

"You look incredibly beautiful tonight, and it's Cole and Leesa's big day. You should stick around." He leaned in a little closer. "And dance with me."

It wasn't like her jelly legs could carry her out of there any-way. *Incredibly beautiful?* Faith had been told she was pretty often enough to believe it, but *incredibly beautiful?* That was pushing it. That was smooth-talking Sam, the limit pusher.

She had to admit, he had this pickup thing down pat. His eyes were solely focused on her, while she felt the gaze of nearly every single woman in the place on her like they wondered what she had that they didn't—or maybe like they wanted to kill her.

Yup. That was probably more accurate.

"The wedding was lovely," she managed. "I'm happy for Cole and Leesa, but I'm hosting a car wash at Harbor Park tomorrow afternoon. I should really get going so I have time to prepare."

Sam stepped closer. His fingers caressed the back of her arm, sending shivers of heat straight to her brain—and short-circuiting it.

"Harbor Park?" The right side of his tempting mouth lifted in a teasing smile. "Surely you won't turn into a pumpkin this early. You can't leave without giving me one dance. Come on. Think of how happy it'll make Cole to see you enjoying yourself."

He was obviously not going to give up. Maybe she should just give in and dance with him. She had no desire to be another in the long line of Sam's conquests, but it was just one dance, and then she could leave, and he'd go back to any of the other women there. That idea sank like a rock in her stomach.

Her stupid hormones swam to the surface again. *You did ask nicely.* Maybe she was reading too much into this dance. It was just a dance, not a date.

But his eyes were boring into her in that *I want to get into your panties* way he had. She'd seen him give that look to several other women tonight.

Several. Other. Women.

Ugh! Why was she even considering this?

It was his hand, moving up and down her arm, making her shivery and hot at once. And those eyes, drawing her in, making her feel important. She wasn't important to Sam. She knew that in her smart physician assistant brain, but her ovaries had some sort of hold on that part of her brain, crushing her smart cells.

Faith glanced at the dance floor and caught sight of Cole whispering something in Leesa's ear. They were such a handsome couple, and Cole was such a kind boss. Maybe she should stay a little longer. She didn't have to dance with Sam. She could just talk with him until he got bored and moved on.

Cole's eyes turned serious, and Leesa looked over, too. He said something to her and headed in their direction with a scowl on his face and an angry bead aimed at Sam. *Shit.* This was not good. He was her *boss*.

Oh my God. What was she thinking? She shouldn't dance with her boss's brother!

"Actually…" Panic bloomed inside her chest as Cole neared. Cole respected her, but she knew he'd noticed the way she got flustered around Sam. He'd seen her turn beet-red with Sam's compliments when Sam visited him at the office. She didn't need him seeing her all swoony-eyed over him now.

"I really have to go, but thanks for asking, Sam." She spun on her heel and hurried away before she could lose her nerve.

Chapter Two

"STOP BEING A rebellious kid and focus on someone or something else," Cole seethed at Sam as Sam watched Faith slip out the door.

Sam was baffled. Women rarely turned him down for anything, much less a dance, but Faith saying no did something funky to his gut. The urge to go after her was stronger than anything he'd ever felt, but he was hemmed in by Cole breathing down his neck.

And maybe his conscience.

"Chill, bro."

"Chill? Sam, she's my employee. She's a smart, professional woman who happens to be excellent at her job. The last thing she needs—the last thing *I* need—is you screwing up her career."

Sam scrubbed his hand down his face with a heavy sigh, wishing he understood all the reasons he was so consumed with Faith. Sure, she was hot, but so were plenty of other women.

Maybe he *was* just being rebellious, because the feelings gnawing at his gut were definitely out of character for him.

He glanced at the door she'd just gone through and wondered what had made her rush off. Was it Cole or was it him? Why did he care? There were plenty of other women in the room. Usually having so many options would steal his focus, but all he could think about was the look in Faith's eyes right before she turned to leave. It was a determined, almost frightened look, and that bothered him. He wasn't a scary guy by any stretch of the imagination.

Dude, really? Okay, maybe he was scary to a girl like Faith. He wasn't exactly the suit-wearing, relationship-committing type of guy she probably went for.

"Maybe you're right," Sam relented.

Cole's jaw loosened a little.

"I don't want to mess up her life. It's just that she...intrigues me."

"Half of Peaceful Harbor intrigues you, Sam."

He scoffed. *If you only knew the truth.* The women he went out with didn't *intrigue* him; they only turned him on. There was a big difference, one he hadn't even realized himself until this very second.

"There's something different about Faith."

"You're right there is. She's off-limits, and you've always wanted what you can't have." Cole draped an arm around Sam and turned to face the rest of the guests. "There you go. A bevy of women, all thrilled to have a shot at you. Take your pick. Just keep your zipper up around my employees, will you?"

Sam glanced around the room. His reputation had never bothered him before. In fact, he was proud of it. Sam was good to the women he hooked up with. He treated them with respect, tried to make them feel special in the few hours they shared. But as he met the glances of several pretty girls, he didn't get the same urges he usually did. He couldn't stop thinking about what Faith had said: *Have you run out of girls already?* Everything was rubbing him the wrong way now, including Cole's ribbing, which he'd heard his whole life. And though he could hardly believe it, even his reputation was rubbing him the wrong way.

The itch in his hands disappeared, apparently unwilling to be scratched by just anyone tonight. Sam turned back toward the bar, wondering how many drinks it would take for him to stop thinking about Faith.

FAITH DROVE STRAIGHT to her apartment. She threw her keys on the couch and stomped into the kitchen, opened the freezer, and stuck her head inside.

"If you're looking for the Chunky Monkey, I finished it."

"Not looking for it," she said to her best friend, Vivian, who was visiting for the weekend. "Just need to cool off."

Vivian scooted up onto the counter. "Oh, do tell. If you have to cool off, then the wedding didn't suck?"

Faith slammed the freezer shut. "The wedding was gorgeous, just what I expected. It felt like an intimate gathering of Cole's closest friends and family, and about six dozen single women swarming over Sam." She rolled her eyes.

"Hot and single tend to draw women," Vivian teased.

"Not helping. I told you I didn't want to go." Faith sighed. "At least it's over. I can check off that duty box for work and focus on tomorrow's WAC event." Two years ago, after a painful breakup and after too many shots and not enough sleep, Faith had started the online forum for women who had been cheated on. Vivian had been right there, egging her on. The next morning, hungover and still just as hurt by the breakup as she'd been before the alcohol, Faith had decided the forum was a solid idea, and a meaningful one. She'd set out to create a safe place for women to vent about the wrongs that had been done to them, and it had quickly grown to be a nationwide community of women supporting women. They'd since created chapters in different cities. Tomorrow's car wash would include women from all over Maryland, and the proceeds would go toward hosting fees and, at some point, site redesign.

"You should have put me as your plus one for the wedding, like I told you to," Vivian said. "I would have reminded you of how hot you looked. So, tell me what you're *not* telling me, because you look like you've been made out with and left hot and bothered."

I wish. "I didn't think we both needed to suffer through my work obligation." She went to her bedroom with Vivian on her heels.

"Sam asked me to dance." She took off her jewelry, gazing at her reflection in the mirror and wondering what Sam had seen when he was standing so close he could have crawled beneath her skin. She thought she'd been in control of herself and her responses, but now that she had room to breathe and air that wasn't full of *him*, she remembered she'd asked him if he'd already gone through all the women there. *Real cool, Faith.*

Vivian crossed her arms, her smile turning to a serious scowl. "You didn't dance with him, did you?"

"No, I didn't dance with him." Vivian had spent last summer in Peaceful Harbor with Faith, and she'd seen Sam in action a few times at Whispers, a nightclub. Over the course of that summer she'd scoped out his *super-sexy* brothers, too— Vivian's words, not Faith's. Faith had filled Vivian in on her fantasies about Sam but agreed with Vivian's assessment that Sam was not the man for her.

Faith changed into a pair of shorts and a comfy shirt, avoiding Vivian's gaze. They'd been best friends forever, having both grown up in Oak Falls, Virginia, where Vivian still lived. They'd bonded over skinned knees and Sadie Hawkins dances, broken hearts, and after Vivian's ex cheated, and JJ followed that same dickhead move, their bond grew stronger over renewed determination never to be cheated on again.

"Good, because as kind and generous as Sam and his family are, he takes *personal generosity* to a whole new level. And that's a level you don't need, Faith. It can only end in a broken heart." Vivian took Faith's hand and dragged her out to the living room. "Let's talk about tomorrow. It'll keep your mind off not dancing with him."

"I'm not interested in Sam. I just like to look at him. And smell him." *What is wrong with me?*

Vivian arched a brow in disbelief. "No one stops at looking and smelling." She sank down to the couch, bringing Faith down beside her. "You know I love you, but that man is not for you. You created WAC *because* of men like him."

"I know. Don't worry. I left, okay? I didn't dance with him. And, by the way, I can't believe you ate all my ice cream. How's a girl supposed to bury her lust in anything else?" Faith reached for the WAC event binder.

"It's called a vibrator, my friend, and you bury it *in* you." Vivian waggled her eyebrows. "It lives in your drawer, so it can't cheat. It has no eyes to gawk at other women and can't suck the life out of your self-esteem. And best of all? You get to come as many times as you want without worrying it'll blow its load before you're done."

All true, but..."Don't you miss being in the arms of a man?"

Vivian rolled her eyes. "Like those guys you've been dating

are real men? They're not. They're like placeholders, itch scratchers. They're foreplay for real men."

"They are not! They're nice and reliable and they would never look at another woman, much less cheat." She had dated only a few men since she'd moved to Peaceful Harbor, each of whom were the antithesis of Sam Braden.

"Boring." Vivian whipped her blond hair over her shoulder with a shake of her head. "Give me my three-speed, battery-operated boyfriend any day of the week." She took out her cell phone and smirked. "Let's ask Charley."

"Don't get my sister involved in this! She's probably busy dissecting a crab or something." She reached for the phone, and Vivian jumped off the couch with the phone to her ear. Charley was five years younger than Faith and studying marine biology. This summer she was working part-time for the Brave Foundation in Harborside, Massachusetts, where she went to school, and also working part-time at a bar. She almost never dated, and definitely wouldn't have time for this foolishness.

"Char! Hey, how are you?" Vivian smirked at Faith as she listened.

She covered the phone and said, "She's not dissecting a crab. She's at a bonfire."

"Really? Good for her. She needs a break." Faith opened the binder and added, "Tell her I love her and *please* don't tell her why you—"

"Faith said she loves you," Vivian said to Charley. "And she wants to know if you think the men she dates are boring."

Ugh! She and Charley didn't talk about their dating lives often. Besides the age difference, Charley was always so busy, she tended to only half listen when Faith brought up men, unlike Vivian, who could analyze a dating scenario for hours.

"She says they're smart," Vivian said with disappointment.

"Thanks, sis!" Faith yelled.

"And that you shouldn't let JJ the asshole keep you away from guys who don't wear ties."

"I'll keep that in mind," Faith said halfheartedly, but her mind clung to the advice and drifted back to Sam. They'd never spoken more than a few words to each other when he visited Cole at the office, *nearly every week*, until tonight. *A man like Sam doesn't need words.*

Unfortunately, he spoke the universal language of lust, aimed at every woman around him.

Chapter Three

AFTER A FITFUL night's sleep with Faith invading every dream—and every waking moment—Sam took off for a predawn run, then hit Rough Riders early to organize the paperwork that was piling up in the office. He could barely keep up with the company's recent growth. Ty had always helped him out when he was in town between mountain-climbing excursions and photography assignments. For years that had been enough. Last year he'd hired Patrick Fisher, the younger brother of Nate's fiancée, Jewel, part-time, and this summer he'd taken Patrick on full-time. A few weeks ago he'd had to hire another full-time employee just to keep up with the number of customers and boat repairs. Tex Sharpe was turning out to be a worthy investment, but Sam still needed to hire an office manager. His desk was littered with release forms, itineraries for upcoming adventure outings, invoices, and other paraphernalia that needed to be dealt with. Not to mention the administrative preparation for next month's annual Rough

Riders barbecue. He'd been trying to hire someone for weeks, but most of the applications were worthless, and there were too many other things that needed his attention to focus on finding a viable candidate.

He swiped his forearm across his sweaty brow and squinted up at the sun, guessing it had to be close to noon. Tex had met him around ten, and they'd been checking gear, cleaning boats, and organizing equipment while they hashed out details for the barbecue while Patrick handled customers. He'd hoped the physical labor would help take his mind off of Faith and what she'd said last night. *Have you run out of girls already?*

Chuckling under his breath, he dragged the boat he was working on back into the boathouse. She'd looked hot last night in that tight little dress. Faith was something, all right. Flustered as could be every time he saw her in Cole's office, and then she came up with *that* when he asked her to dance? *Have you run out of girls already?* Did she think he made the rounds everywhere he went?

That thought grated on him like nails on a chalkboard.

His cell phone rang and he pulled it from his pocket. "Hey, Ty. What's up?"

"You tell me. You cut out early last night."

"I wanted to get an early start this morning," he said.

Sam tapped Tex on his tattooed shoulder and motioned with his thumb over his shoulder up to the parking lot.

Tex lifted serious dark eyes and nodded.

Sam headed up to the parking lot, smiling when he saw his bike. Usually he drove his truck, but this morning he'd been restless and needed the freedom his motorcycle offered.

"Like that's ever stopped you from having a good time before," Ty said sarcastically. "Want to tell me what's really going on?"

"Not really," he mumbled, grabbing his helmet off the back of the bike.

"Cole was pretty annoyed last night. Did he get to you?"

Sam had chewed on his brother's comment all night. As if the women he slept with intrigued him? What was intriguing about women who threw themselves at a guy? Hell, they were after one thing. A good time, just as he was. They all played the same games. Different faces, different names, same overt come-ons. Not that he didn't appreciate them. Sex was better than any drug out there, but strangely, it hadn't been his drug of choice last night. He had yet to meet a woman who made him want to get to know her better, or seek her out.

As he straddled the bike, he thought, *Until Faith.*

"Dude, you still there?"

Ty's voice pulled him from his thoughts. "Sorry. Don't worry about Cole. He'll have plenty of time to get over it on his honeymoon. I'm sure by now he's lying out on the beach at Treat's resort in Tahiti with a drink in one hand and Leesa's hand in the other." Their cousin Treat Braden owned resorts all over the world and had generously offered Cole and Leesa a stay at the resort of their choice.

"Probably so. What're you doing now?" Ty asked. "Want to hit the trails for a while, or are you buried in paperwork?" He was home for a few weeks between climbs, and like Sam, he rarely sat still. In addition to women, hiking, biking, rafting, and climbing were just a few of the interests they shared.

"Can't. Sorry. I'm headed home to shower. I've got plans this afternoon. But I'll catch up with you tonight. Whispers? Around eight?" Although their brother Nate owned Tap It, one of the busiest restaurant and bars in town, Sam and Ty liked to hang out where there were live bands, hordes of single women, and less familial eyes keeping tabs on them.

An hour later, freshly showered and still confused about his rampant interest in Faith, Sam was determined to figure it out—and not to get blown off again. He climbed into his truck and drove over to Harbor Park. Two bikini-clad women held up signs for the Women Against Cheaters Car Wash and guided Sam into one of two long lines of cars.

What the hell? Women Against Cheaters?

He pulled up behind a blue sedan to wait his turn, his eyes searching for Faith. Girls wearing skimpy shorts with bikini tops, one-piece bathing suits, or tanks and shorts soaped, scrubbed, and hosed down the vehicles. Normally Sam would sit back and enjoy the view, only he wasn't seeing the view he wanted.

He wondered if he'd misunderstood when Faith had said

she was hosting a car wash at Harbor Park. When it was his turn, a big-busted blonde stopped by his open window and smiled up at him.

"Thanks for coming out to the car wash. You might want to close your window so you don't get wet."

"Thanks," he said absentmindedly, still looking for Faith. He finally spotted her across the parking lot, focusing intently on her phone. Faith's hair was pinned up in a ponytail, and she wore a pink bikini top and a pair of white shorts, awakening every inch of Sam's body. He stepped from the truck, wondering what she was so enthralled with. A text from a boyfriend? His muscles corded tight with the thought.

"What about your window?" the blonde asked.

Sam barely registered the question. He handed her the keys with an offhanded *thanks* and rounded the truck toward Faith.

THE CAR WASH had been busy since they'd opened, and Faith couldn't be happier with the turnout. She was glad to finally meet some of the other members of WAC in person after getting to know them on the forums. It was oddly beautiful that awful circumstances brought them together. The bonds they formed over their hurtful pasts were strong and lasting, and after meeting them in person, her desire to help them was even stronger.

It had been a long time since she'd had this much fun, and as she finished posting a few pictures across social media for the group, she was excited to dive back in with the girls. She shoved her phone in her pocket as Lira, one of the members from a neighboring town, approached with a worried look in her eyes.

"Everything okay?" Faith knew from their online discussions that Lira had suffered the kind of broken heart that not many people would easily bounce back from. Her husband of three years had not only cheated on her, but he'd cheated with her sister, who was also her babysitter. In exchange for babysitting, Lira had let her sister use her car. Now she'd lost her husband and her babysitter, and if that wasn't enough, as soon as her ex moved out, he stopped helping with their bills and hadn't been back to see their eighteen-month-old baby, Emmie, in weeks.

Lira fidgeted with the fringe of her shorts, which looked about as old as her paper-thin flip-flops. Her straight dark hair was parted to the side and fell over one eye. She tucked it behind her ear as she spoke. "Can we talk for a minute alone?"

"Of course." Faith led her farther away from the group. "Is something wrong?"

"I was wondering if you knew of any free therapists. I see my ex everywhere around town, and between that and barely having enough money to pay my bills, I feel like I'm getting a little lost. And it's more than just what happened. I can't stand thinking about Emmie growing up around my sister and thinking what she did was okay. I also don't want her to choose the wrong guys when she's older, like I did. I think talking to a professional might help me figure all that out."

"Oh, Lira. I'm so sorry you're going through such a hard time, but Emmie's a lucky girl. You want to break the cycle of destructive behavior, and wanting it is the first step to making it happen." She embraced her, mentally going through the names of therapists Cole's office referred their pain patients to. Unfortunately, they were all in Peaceful Harbor. "Have you talked to your insurance company about finding a therapist or a counselor of some sort?"

Lira's face reddened with embarrassment. "I don't have insurance. I had to leave my job because they paid so little I couldn't afford a full-time babysitter, and finding a job in my small town is like finding a needle in a haystack. I make enough with my part-time job to pay for health insurance for Emmie, but it's too expensive to cover myself, too."

It was one thing to hear about the WAC members' stories online, but to actually meet Lira, to see the fear in her eyes and hear the embarrassment in her voice, brought a lump to Faith's throat—and strengthened her desire to do more.

"Did you try Social Services? Can they help?"

She shook her head vehemently. "I'm afraid to. Even though my ex doesn't seem to want anything to do with Emmie, my sister works for Social Services, and who knows what she'd do with that information. I know she loves Emmie, but I can't take the chance of her using it against me in some way." A forced smile curved Lira's lips. "It's okay. I just thought you might know someone."

"Let me talk to my boss and do some checking. I'm sure we can figure this out." She embraced her again. "Is there anything else I can do today? Where's Emmie now?"

"My mom lives about an hour away. She came into town to visit my sister, so she's watching her. It's not ideal, but it was just a few hours and I had no other choice."

"And you're here? Shouldn't you be visiting with your mom? Can she help you financially?"

Lira shook her head again. "Where do you think my sister learned to be such a slut? And where do you think I learned to pick horrible men? My mom isn't exactly the picture of stability. But they both love Emmie to pieces. I know she's physically safe when she's with them. Besides, I needed this." She glanced over her shoulder at the girls laughing and washing the cars, then back at Faith. "The girls in the group have been my lifeline in so many ways. It doesn't matter what time I sign onto the forums; there's always someone to talk to who understands what I'm going through."

Faith's heart felt full knowing her little venture was helping. The members had pulled her through many desperate nights after her breakup, too, but hearing it from Lira made it even more real.

"I'm glad you came, and I'll reach out to see if I can get you a referral for a therapist. You're leaving right after the car wash, right? You're not going out with us tonight?"

"I can't. I have to get back to Emmie. The gas money alone to come out here was a stretch. Thanks, Faith. I hate to say this, but I'm glad you were cheated on, because if you hadn't been, then WAC wouldn't exist."

Lira headed toward the ladies' room, and Faith wondered how many of the other members could benefit from having a professional to talk to if they could afford it. An idea began percolating in her mind, and she turned back toward the car wash with renewed determination. When Faith got an idea in her head, she was like a dog with a bone, and when it came to helping others, she was even fiercer.

With a bounce in her step she headed for the truck that had just pulled up—and stopped cold at the sight of Sam standing beside it.

He smiled, and emotion climbed each of his features until it reached his eyes and turned molten. Faith's pulse—and mind—raced. What was he doing there? And why was he looking at her like she was one of *his* girls, one of the *chosen*? She swallowed hard, trying to keep her eyes from drifting down his body, but damn. He was a sight for sore eyes in his faded dark jeans and tight black tank top that hugged every frigging muscle in his thick chest. She tried not to stare, but his arms...Sam had the kind of arms that she imagined brought complete awareness of where his body ended and a woman's began, bringing with them a feeling of safety and belonging. The kind of feelings that made a woman feel warm and good all over. The kind of strength to take her hard and aggressive, deep and—

What the hell am I doing? She'd obviously gone far too long without satisfying that particular need if she was thinking about Sam that way.

She stalked across the parking lot, a little annoyed that he'd show up and use the event as a pickup spot. "Sam? What are you doing here?" Several of the girls were watching them with interest. She shot a look at his truck, where Hilary was sitting in the driver's seat.

"This is a Women Against Cheaters group, right?" His infuriatingly luscious lips tipped up in a devilish grin. "Can you think of a better place to hook up with chicks? Everyone knows a woman scorned has something to prove in bed."

"Ohmygod. You're—"

He laughed. "I'm kidding, Faith. Loosen up a little." He paused just long enough for her to silently question if she was too uptight. "Getting my truck washed would be the obvious answer." He stepped closer—and she stepped back.

"You're probably the reason half the girls in this town joined the group."

His eyes filled with confusion. "What are you talking about? I'm not a cheater."

"Ha! And blood isn't red, either. I've got work to do." She brushed past him, and he grabbed her arm, firmly turning her to face him.

"Faith, I don't cheat on women. Jesus, that's what you think of me?"

She looked down at his hand, wishing the electric shock traveling through her wasn't such a turn-on. "Come on, Sam. You don't have to deny it. It's not like I'm judging you." She twisted out of his grip, instantly missing his touch and hating how it felt to say those things to him. She didn't like thinking about Sam *any* way, because she shouldn't think about him. But he was always there, lingering in the back of her mind. The sweet man who flirted with her at her office, the sexy dancer she'd seen out on the town, and the man who'd implored her to dance with him last night.

The type of guy who would hurt me if I let him in.

His serious stare nearly leveled her. "I do *not* cheat. I would never purposely hurt a woman, Faith. That's not who I am. How could I, anyway? I haven't had a girlfriend since high school."

His anger took her by surprise, but it was the hurt and confusion in his eyes that made her stomach twist into a knot. Did he really think there was a difference between not having a girlfriend and sleeping around? Didn't he know that the women he slept with probably hoped for more? Or was this all a crazy facade he put on? A game he played?

Ugh! Of course it was, and she didn't have time for this.

"I'm sorry. I shouldn't have said that, but I have to get back to work so we don't fall behind." She forced herself to walk away, hoping her racing heart would calm the hell down.

In the next breath he was beside her, taking off his shirt and stuffing it in his back pocket, making her head spin.

"What...?" She swallowed the drool pooling in her mouth. "What are you doing?"

"Helping." He dipped his hand into a bucket and scooped out a sponge. With the other he slid his aviators from his head to the bridge of his nose, reflecting Faith's face back at her. She looked mesmerized by him.

Lovely. She needed those glasses, darn it.

"You're not part of the group," she said in an effort to dissuade him from whatever pickup scheme he had in mind.

"No, but you are, and I want to be near you." He shrugged and began washing his truck.

Her heart skipped a beat. *Stupid, stupid heart.* This was smooth-talking Sam. She was nothing but a conquest to him, something he couldn't have, and he wasn't used to that. Logically, she knew why he was acting like he was so attracted to her, but inside she couldn't help feeling warm and good to be wanted by the object of her late-night fantasies.

"Hey, we have a hunky helper! I'm Brittany." Brittany waved, but it was wasted on the back of his head.

"Nice to meet you, Brittany," he said without ever looking away from Faith. "Just thought I'd help out Faith."

"Lucky Faith," Brittany said, passing a knowing glance in Faith's direction.

There was no way Faith could work beside him when he was half naked, with all those glistening muscles on display. Her fingers ached to touch his ripped abs, because they were *that* beautiful. He had those muscles that formed a perfect V aiming straight down his pants toward the danger zone. *Pleasure zone?* Those were the muscles that didn't need a name beyond *muscles that make girls go stupid.*

Everything about Sam made her go stupid, from his smile that said, *I'm a really good guy*, to his eyes that said, *I want to feel you beneath me*, all the way to the dimple just below the left side of his lip that she wished she hadn't noticed.

She needed to escape just to get enough oxygen to her brain to function like a normal person again.

"I'm going to help the other team." Faith walked over to the other line of cars, feeling Sam's reflective gaze on her every step of the way.

She tried not to pay him any attention, but it was hard not to notice the laughter coming from the girls and Sam as they washed one car after another.

"What is he doing here?" Vivian narrowed her eyes.

"He said he wanted to help." She didn't know why she was covering up the rest of what he'd said, that he wanted to help *her*, but she felt strangely protective of those words.

"Right. He's a nice guy, but don't let him suck you into his orbit, Faith."

"*Please.* I'm not stupid."

"Uh-huh. Looking and smelling. And my vibrator *never* gets a workout," Vivian said with a sarcastic tone. She took Faith by the shoulders and stared at her with the kind of demand only a best friend could get away with. "Trust me on this. It starts with looking and smelling, but soon you're touching and kissing. And then he's buried balls deep and you're screaming out his name."

She felt her cheeks flame at the thought of being in that position with Sam.

"And then..." Vivian lowered her voice. "He starts showing up smelling like other women's perfume, getting less and less interested in sex with you. The man who once stole your heart has gotten bored. Meanwhile, you...*me*...whoever we're *not* talking about here, have fallen in love or lust or whatever. And it all ends badly."

FAITH SPENT THE next few hours replaying Vivian's words in her head, trying to remember all the reasons her friend was right and trying to ignore the way Sam was not only helping with the car wash, but having what looked like serious conversations with the girls, too. He'd been talking with Lira for the past hour while they washed cars. What could he possibly have in common with any of them?

What am I missing out on?

Embarrassingly, when she'd uploaded more pictures to Facebook, she'd searched for Sam's account. He didn't have a personal profile, only a Rough Riders fan page, which had little info about him. She didn't know why, but she'd pictured him as being all over social media.

Hilary sidled up to her. "Sam's been here all day."

He was going to a lot of trouble for a guy just looking to hook up, especially for a guy who owned the only rafting company around. She'd heard about the Rough Riders barbecue coming up in a few weeks. Everyone in town was talking about it. Shouldn't he be busy running his company today, or planning his own event?

"Hot guys usually lead me to trouble, but he's super cute," Hilary said, eyes on Sam.

"I guess. If you like that kind of guy." *You know, full of muscles, bedroom eyes, and probably wielding a magical, orgasm-producing ten-inch cock.*

"Um...?" Hilary laughed. "The kind of guy who makes you laugh and jumps in to help? Or the kind of guy with a body that could make a blind girl weep?"

She stole a glance at Sam, crouched beside a car scrubbing the bumper, the muscles in his back bunching and flexing with every move. His tanned flesh glistened beneath the afternoon sun. He turned in her direction, and she could actually feel his gaze even before he lifted his glasses. He smiled and lifted his chin, as if to say, *Hey, baby*—that was *her* harmless fantasy speaking, of course. Heat coursed through her body, but it was the butterflies swarming in her belly that gave her pause.

"Both, I guess," she said quietly, but Hilary had already moved on. Faith was alone, staring at Sam, who was staring right back. She felt herself smiling despite her misgivings, and as she did, his smile widened.

"Sammy!" one of the girls yelled.

He unfolded his tall, rugged body gracefully, like a snake uncoiling, unhurried and unflinching as Lira aimed the hose at his back and soaked him from head to toe. His eyes remained on Faith as a hearty laugh burst from his lungs and hit Faith square in the center of her chest. She could get lost in that laugh.

Sam turned away, breaking their connection, and chased the shrieking girls. He snagged the hose from Lira. Faith wanted to be Lira, or maybe she just wanted his big hands wrapped around her.

He had enough women chasing him. She turned away, feeling a little...*what*? Disappointed? Jealous?

Cold water drenched her back and she shrieked. Sam's laughter followed her as she jumped on her tiptoes in a futile attempt to avoid the water streaming from the hose as Sam soaked her from head to toe.

She was no match for Sam. He was too fast, too focused.

For a smidgen of a weak second, she wondered if she ever could be.

Chapter Four

SAM STUCK AROUND after the car wash ended, helping clean up and hoping to have a few minutes alone with Faith. He'd watched her throughout the afternoon. She was an incredible mix of determination and focus as she dealt with customers, took photos and posted them on Facebook and Twitter, and God only knew where else, and washed cars with the rest of them.

After the others left, he waited for Faith to finish her conversation with Vivian, a snarky blond who appeared to be closest to Faith. She'd been giving him less-than-friendly glances all afternoon, and now she and Faith seemed to be getting into something. Faith's face was pinched tight, and her whole body looked rigid. Sam ducked into his truck, not wanting to make Faith uncomfortable. He grabbed his checkbook from the glove compartment, and when he stepped from the truck again Vivian was hugging Faith, while Faith remained unmoved. When Vivian finally left, Sam made his way across the lot.

He'd caught Faith watching him at least a dozen times today, but now she was back to dropping her eyes as he approached, and he wondered if that was because of him or something Vivian had said.

"Thanks for letting me help out today."

"Are you kidding?" Her beautiful dark eyes finally found his. "You didn't have to stay all day. Thank *you*."

"It was fun." He pulled his checkbook from his pocket. "I'd like to donate to the group."

"Sam." She shook her head.

"What? I spent the day getting to know everyone. Did you know that Brittany found her boyfriend in bed with another girl just an hour after she left for work one morning?"

"Yes, but I'm surprised you do."

"Me too." That made her smile, and boy, did he love the way it lit up her eyes. "These girls have been through a lot. They said you're using the proceeds from the car wash to pay for the site hosting and a possible site upgrade."

"Well, that's the hope." Her voice went serious again. "It's hard when a guy cheats on a woman. It makes her feel small and unimportant. Like anything they may have had before that point didn't mean anything."

"That sounds like firsthand knowledge." Had some bastard cheated on her? Made her feel small and unimportant? His chest constricted with the ugly thought. Sam knew what that felt like. Though he'd been just sixteen, it had cut him to his core.

"I'm also thinking of trying to find therapists, career consultants, and other types of resources to donate advice, or maybe an initial consult, or something along those lines. Maybe they can offer a discount, or WAC can pitch in some amount. But I'm getting way ahead of myself."

The fact that she didn't respond to his comment about *firsthand experience*, and the set of her jaw, told him that she wasn't about to share that information with him.

"That's a big endeavor, and an important one." He opened his checkbook and began writing a check.

"Sam, please don't."

Her admonishing tone surprised him. He slid his sunglasses to the top of his head, trying to read her expression. Determination? Frustration? He wasn't sure, but it definitely wasn't the *I Want You* look he'd hoped for when he'd arrived.

"This is important, and real to me, Sam. I want to help these women and you just want to *do* them. I don't want something I've worked hard to build becoming part of your game for picking up women."

Her words stung. "You really do think poorly of me, don't you?" He shook his head, trying to figure out where to go from here. "Faith, I'm not the person you think I am."

"So, you haven't dated nearly every woman in town? Sometimes sleeping with two at once? Because those rumors seem pretty consistent to me."

For the first time in as long as Sam could remember, his

reaction to hearing his reputation thrown in his face wasn't to laugh it off. He cringed inwardly. Not because he was ashamed of a damn thing he'd done, but because for some reason he cared about what Faith thought of him.

"Faith." He didn't know what to say, so instead he took her by the elbow and led her over to his truck.

"What are you doing?"

"I want you to see something." He grabbed his phone from the glove compartment and handed it to Faith.

Confusion riddled her brow.

"Take a look. It's not password protected."

"Sam—" She held the phone toward him and he pushed it gently back toward her, curling his fingers over hers.

"Please, just…"

"No. Sam, I'm not going to look through—"

He took it from her hands and navigated into his call history.

"I don't want to know who you call. *God.*" She took a step away, and he grabbed her gently around the waist and pulled her back, bringing her firmly against his chest.

She went rigid in his arms and just as quickly seemed to melt against him. And maybe stop breathing. He wasn't certain, but it felt like she was holding her breath.

"Give me two minutes; that's all I want." He wanted a lot more than two minutes. "Then you can run away."

"Okay," she said breathlessly.

Oh yeah, she was into him. She was so warm and tempting, he lost his train of thought for a minute.

"Sam!"

"Sorry." He scrolled through the log. "Whose names do you see?"

"I feel like a voyeur."

"Just read the names."

"Ty, Shannon, Tex, Tempe…Sam, why am I reading this?"

"You'll see." He navigated to his apps. "What do you see?"

"Sam!" She wriggled against him, trying to free herself.

He tightened his grip. She felt too damn good to let go that easily.

"No Snapchat. No Facebook Messenger. Just regular stuff." He scrolled to the Internet and showed her his history. "No porn sites, no—"

She turned in his arms, and a current spiked up his spine at the look of lust and disbelief mingling in her eyes. While he was hanging in a fog, she took a step out of his arms, and he fought the urge to tug her back in.

"What do you expect me to learn from that?" Determination carried every word again. "It doesn't change who you are or what you do."

She was right, and that slapped something inside him down a notch. She wasn't a random woman he wanted to hook up with. She was smart, and she respected herself enough to keep her distance from the likes of him. That confidence, that belief that she was worthy of more, made her even more intriguing.

"I just want you to see that I'm not a pig who has booty call numbers on my phone or uses Snapchat to exchange naked pics, or any of that crap. I am who I am. With me, what you see is what you get. I'm not hiding anything from you, Faith, and I'm not trying to say I haven't slept around."

"Then what are you saying?" She crossed her arms, a barrier between them.

He remembered what Cole had said, and he knew his brother was right. Faith didn't need him screwing up her life. The look in her eyes, everything she said, every signal she was currently sending, told him that she might believe that, too. But a voice inside his head told him not to give up. He'd been drawn to Faith since they'd first met, but he'd put her in the too-sweet-for-Sam zone. Now he wanted to breach that zone.

Maybe Cole was right about him wanting what he couldn't have. How the hell should he know why he suddenly wanted to take Faith in his arms and kiss the concern off her gorgeous face? To get a taste of the sweetness he'd been trying to resist and prove to her he wasn't the person she thought he was.

But so much of what she'd said was true. How was he supposed to reconcile asking her to take a chance on him? Fuck, this was not the way he'd imagined today going.

"I guess I'm saying you might miss out on a really great story if you judge a book by its cover." He took one last long look at her before saying, "Thanks for letting me take part in something so important. It was an honor to get to know the girls. I wish them all the best."

"HE DIDN'T EVEN try to cover up the fact that he'd slept with so many women." Faith wriggled into her jeans and pulled on a silky top as Vivian chose earrings from her jewelry box.

"I don't know what you expected from him, but I have to say, I'm surprised. How many guys would stick around all day *and* let you see their phone?" Her eyes widened as she handed Faith the dangling earrings. "Ohmygod. That's probably his burner phone!"

"What's a burner phone?" She slipped her feet into a pair of heels. They were meeting some of the girls from the group for drinks in half an hour.

"A *burner* phone. You know, drug dealers use them so the cops can't track them."

"Vivian, Sam is *not* a drug dealer." She stood in front of the mirror, surveying her outfit. "Does this say sexy?" Sam had said she should loosen up, and she wanted to prove him wrong on that, too. She was plenty loose. In a non-loose type of way.

"No. You are *not* wearing that." Vivian tugged Faith's top over her head and threw it on her bed. "What did the womanizer say about our group?"

She gave Vivian a deadpan stare. She hated linking Sam to

the term *womanizer* after he'd tried so hard to prove that he wasn't one, but who was she to deny it?

"He joked that women who had been cheated on were the best in bed because they have something to prove." Her stomach felt queasy repeating that to Vivian. It had taken her half an hour to pull herself together after Sam left. When he'd held her against his chest, he'd felt like heaven. His big, strong arm wrapped around her waist, keeping her trapped against all his body heat, all those muscles. She'd almost started to believe that rumors about him were false, until he'd snapped those heady thoughts from her head by flat-out admitting to them.

"He's got that all wrong. We were the best in bed even before we had something to prove. Shows you how much he knows." Vivian dragged Faith into the guest bedroom.

"He was kidding, and hey! I'm not dressed."

"You're wearing my clothes. Tonight we're going to stir up every man in that bar and leave them all high and dry. And they can blame it on Sam Braden's stupid comment." Vivian grabbed a black leather miniskirt from the closet and tossed it to Faith. "Put that on."

"On what? My left leg?"

"On. Now."

As Faith stepped into the miniskirt, Vivian looked through her suitcase.

"Perfect." She held up a cream-colored, slightly see-through cotton shirt. "It's rock chic. The boatneck will show enough skin to look hot but not slutty, and paired with the leather miniskirt and wedge sandals, you'll look like you wear this shit all the time."

Faith pulled the loose shirt over her head and it immediately slid off of her shoulder. She kicked off her heels and glanced in the mirror.

"Wow. I feel good in this. *Hot*. No wonder you dress like this. It's insta-confidence in a slinky little outfit."

"Want to really kick up the sexiness?"

Faith looked down at her outfit. She was a little out of her comfort zone, but not so far that she wouldn't wear something like this. If Vivian wasn't there, she'd probably pair the shirt with her jeans, but the skirt definitely gave her a confidence boost.

"If I kick it up any higher I'll be showing my you-know-what."

"Wear your black-framed glasses. You look so hot in them anyway, and with this outfit? You'll look like a *smart* sex kitten."

"Do I *want* to look like a smart sex kitten?" She bit her lower lip, thinking about how she wanted to look. The glasses weren't even prescription. They'd bought them just for fun last summer.

"Yes, so you can be ogled by a club full of guys and forget about Sam." Vivian fluffed Faith's dark hair. "You could wear a Hefty bag and you'd look sexy. You're gorgeous. This outfit just amps it up. And your glasses give you an edge we normal gals don't have."

Faith laughed. "Normal? You're a dead ringer for Julianne Hough. I've got nothing on you."

"You have glasses that say 'back off' but a body that says 'climb on.' Plus, if we're getting technical about it, you're smarter and you have a better job." Vivian worked in the marketing department of a clothing store in Oak Falls.

"You could have bought the exact same pair," she reminded her. "You love your job, too, and I'm not smarter. I just spent more time in school than you did. Anyway, let's just say we're both hot, even though you're *hotter*." They played this one-upping compliment game all the time, as Faith assumed all women did. "None of that matters. What matters is that you and I make a great team, and because of our excellent planning skills, everyone had a good time today."

Vivian followed her into the bathroom, where Faith fixed her makeup and slipped on her sexy-librarian glasses. She'd only worn them twice last summer, but Vivian was right—with the outfit, they definitely gave her a little wicked edge.

"Lira asked if I knew of a free therapist, and I was thinking about expanding WAC's resources."

Vivian looked at her over her mascara brush. "You can't hire a therapist, if that's what you're thinking. That takes a lot of money. The kind of money you don't have. It's a *free* forum, remember?"

"Not hire one, but maybe we can connect with other groups

that help women and find therapists who might be willing to give one free phone consult and then offer reduced or group prices." Every thought sparked another angle. "Or maybe we can find a therapist who's willing to do Skype sessions, individual or group."

"You're serious?"

"I think so. I mean, not everyone can afford help. Poor Lira barely had gas money to come to the event, and she doesn't even have health insurance. I would really like to help her find a job."

"Now you're getting way ahead of yourself." Vivian put her makeup away and said, "How can you do any of that? She lives in another town."

Faith couldn't quell her excitement at the prospect of growing the forum into something much bigger and more helpful. "How can we *not* try to help? Imagine how many others on the forums are in the same situation, or worse? I'm not talking about making a big organization or anything, but maybe we can create a resource page on the site and offer listings for jobs in each state. I don't have it all figured out yet, but I think I'm onto something."

Vivian pulled her out of the bathroom and grabbed their purses from the table. "You have that 'I'm doing this no matter what Vivian says' look in your eyes. Let's talk on the way."

A night out with the girls and her new project might be exactly what she needed to forget about Sam.

Chapter Five

WHISPERS WAS LOUD and crowded, just the way Sam liked it. It was exactly what he needed to get his mind off of Faith. He hated the way they'd left things earlier. After making an online donation to her cause—because he was sincere in wanting to help the girls he'd met at the car wash and, equally as important, to help Faith—he'd spent the better part of the evening trying to convince himself that he should back off, that Faith didn't need him in her life.

It had been hours, and she was still front and center in his mind. The feel of her smooth skin remained on his palm, as if she'd branded him.

Sam tried to concentrate on the band playing at the far end of the dance floor. He and Ty had been there only a few minutes before they were barraged by a group of friends. Now, packed in a booth like sardines, Sam was squished between Jennifer, a mouthy brunette, and Tia, one of her equally mouthy friends. He was dying for a drink, but there was barely enough room in the booth for everyone, and his arms were stretched out along the back of the bench.

"Dance with me, Sam?" Jennifer ran her finger down the center of his chest.

He wasn't in the mood to dance with anyone but the one woman he wasn't supposed to be thinking about, which put him on edge, but it would get him out of that tight booth.

With an arm around Jennifer, Sam pushed through the crowd to a spot closer to the band. Jennifer wrapped her arms around his neck and swayed her hips, brushing against him, despite the fast beat of the music. Normally Sam would be into her seductive moves, but Faith had gotten under his skin. The things she'd said had punctured his gut like jagged little pills. *It doesn't change who you are or what you do.*

Goddamn it. What was wrong with him? She was one girl out of a million.

One sexy, smart, ambitious girl who'd probably used her pain to drive her to create WAC. He hated thinking about someone hurting her. Faith wasn't like Jennifer or Tia or the other girls he hooked up with. They put themselves on the line with no expectations. Offered themselves up expecting only one thing in return. Sex for sex. And they couldn't hold a candle to Faith.

Faith was classy. She valued and respected herself. She was the type of girl a guy married. The others were the types of women a guy fucked. Which was exactly why Faith was staying away from him. Marriage had never been on his radar. Yet since he'd seen her at the wedding he'd wanted nothing to do with any other woman.

Could he talk himself further into a frigging black hole? He was supposed to be getting Faith out from under his skin, not wanting her even more.

He wrapped his arms around Jennifer's sexy body and tried to lose himself in her. She was warm, soft, and curvaceous. But she had on too much perfume, and she was a tall woman, at least five ten, which normally wouldn't bother him. It put their mouths closer together, which was always hot. But after holding Faith, so petite, so feminine, so *perfect*, everything about Jennifer felt wrong.

Someone bumped him from behind, and he glanced over his shoulder, then down to the woman who had consumed his thoughts, in the arms of another man. Sam's gut fisted. She wasn't his to claim, but just knowing she was there, close enough to touch and looking hot as hell, made him want to do just that.

"Sorry." Faith lifted her beautiful dark eyes and gasped. "Sam."

Even her voice did weird shit to him. Made him *think*. About the things she'd said and what he felt when he'd held her. And she wore a pair of black-framed glasses, which might detract from most women's appeal, but on Faith? They looked rebellious and sexy as sin.

"Faith."

"I didn't mean to…"

Jennifer's hand crawled up Sam's cheek, drawing his face back toward hers.

"Sam, I'm over here."

He was all too aware of the woman in his arms as she forced his face away from Faith. He looked over his shoulder again, registering the back of the guy's head Faith was dancing with. Faith peered around the guy's shoulder, meeting Sam's gaze. He could barely restrain himself from cutting in on her dance. But Jennifer was in his arms, and Faith's guy—*Date? Boyfriend?*—turned, sizing him up.

Sam wasn't in the mood to piss off some dork or the clingy chick in his arms. When the song ended Jennifer continued swaying against him, which Sam would normally be totally into. But Faith was disappearing into the crowd, and he quickly lost the battle of trying not to care, boyfriend or not.

He took Jennifer by the hand and led her toward the table.

"I wasn't done dancing," she complained.

"I'm sorry, Jen." At the table he caught Ty's eye. "Ty, buy Jen a drink?"

"Sure. Slide right up there, honey." Ty nodded to the other side of the booth.

"Thanks, bro." He took a step away, then thought better of it and whipped out his wallet. He dug out a few twenties and handed them to Ty. "Just in case."

"Seriously? Don't forget lunch at Mr. B's tomorrow. Shannon's leaving Wednesday." Their parents owned Mr. B's, a microbrewery by the marina, and their youngest sister, Shannon, had returned from her job in Colorado for Cole's wedding.

"I'll be there."

Sam made his way through the crowd. At over six feet tall, it was easy for him to scan the sea of people in search of Faith, but his search was made even easier when her lovely laugh danced through the air. Sam followed the melody across the dance floor to a round table where Faith sat with several of the girls from the car wash. The guy she'd danced with was nowhere in sight. Maybe there was a God after all. Her sun-kissed skin shimmered against the dim lighting. Her hair was loose and tousled, flowing sexily over her shoulders, and those glasses...With that outfit she had on, she looked like a playboy model slash scientist, and the combo was smokin' hot. But it wasn't the twitch beneath his zipper he was focused on at the moment. It was the urge to get her alone, have her undivided attention, and *talk* to her again.

What the hell kind of spell was she casting on him?

He couldn't let her stay in that too-sweet-for-Sam zone. Maybe he should, but not without first proving to her that he wasn't the guy she thought he was.

"Hey, Sam's here!" Brittany jumped up from the table and hugged him.

He returned the embrace, wishing Faith had given him the

eager greeting instead. "How's it going, Britt?"

Faith looked up from her conversation. The air between them sizzled and burned, obliterating the sweet zone completely.

FAITH CLUTCHED THE edge of the chair, trying to make her brain remember that the stud standing in front of her wasn't the right man for her. But that smile, that dimple, and those fierce dark eyes were locked on her, bringing her back to the parking lot and the claims he'd made about not being a cheater. She'd said all those harsh things about him. How could she have been so brazen? He was her boss's brother. What was she thinking?

She'd felt cool and sexy in her outfit when they arrived, but now she tugged at the hem of her slinky little skirt. She was dressed like one of his entourage—would he see her like that? *Do I want you to?*

Her pulse quickened at the thought. He was making her go all sorts of crazy again.

Vivian leaned over and whispered, "No. Do not get pulled into his hotness."

Faith tore her eyes away from Sam and looked out at the dance floor. She'd seen the woman he'd danced with. Tall, stacked, *gorgeous*. Why was he here instead of with her?

"We're having a great time," Brittany said.

"We're having a girls' night," Vivian corrected her. "Right, Faith?"

Faith glared at her when she should be thanking her for trying to keep her in line. She loved Vivian to death, but she didn't need a babysitter. She could handle herself around Sam. *Probably.*

He strode around the table, openly studying her, pinning her in place with his smoldering dark eyes. She was barely breathing, barely thinking. Maybe she needed a babysitter after all.

He held out a hand. His beautiful, long, strong fingers beckoned her. "I won't steal you away for too long," he said confidently, as if she had no choice but to go with him.

She stared at his hand as it came down over hers, sending thrills up each finger.

"Dance with me?"

Silence echoed in her ears. The girls seemed to be holding their breath, too, as he lifted her hand with gentle authority, bringing her up beside him. She struggled to get her synapses to work—not an easy feat with that beautiful creature looking at her like he wanted to devour her. *Yes, please.*

His arm circled her waist possessively as he guided her to the dance floor with an enticing air of self-confidence. The crowd parted for them, and suddenly they were amid a swarm of couples grinding to the slow beat of the music. Sam's powerful arms drew her against his hard body. Lord help her, she was right. She felt feminine and protected in his arms.

He gazed at her from what felt like miles above. His dusky eyes glimmered with warmth and passion, making her feel like he'd been waiting all day for this moment. His olive skin was peppered with sexy scruff, and a boyish, and somehow also sensual and manly, smile split his lips.

She should say something. Anything. But she couldn't figure out how she'd ended up here in his arms. It was unimaginably easy to get swept up in him. *Just one dance.*

"You look gorgeous." His voice was deep and intense, like everything else about him.

"Thank you." She became aware of the feel of his firm, hot waist against her palms. The press of his thighs, the brush of his abs against her breasts. Her nipples tightened, and she pulled back slightly, but his hand splayed on her back, holding her close.

A knowing smile played across his face. "It's just a dance," he reassured her, as if he could read her thoughts. "I was surprised to see you here."

"Not my usual hangout," she answered truthfully. She had been there a few times, but she usually preferred clubs that felt less like meat markets. She should have known Sam would be there. Why hadn't she thought of that when they made plans? Probably because last month when they were planning the evening, Sam was in the untouchable, *do not think about* zone.

He was alone in that zone. Filling it up without even trying, and making it impossible for Faith *not* to think about the damn zone.

"My lucky night."

His hands pressed more firmly as they danced. His movements were graceful and virile at once. As they found their groove, one hand slid up her back, the other to the base of her spine. He danced like sex liquefied. If this was all she'd allow herself, one dance, a handful of minutes to be in his arms, she was going to enjoy it. She gave herself over to the music, soaking in the feeling of being in Sam's arms. She wound her arms around his neck, and his eyes darkened even more. His smile turned sinful. She closed her eyes, pretending she wasn't already damp and dipping her toes into dangerous waters. Resting her cheek against his chest, she listened to the sure and steady beat of his heart, refusing to feel guilty for a few minutes in heaven.

His hand slid beneath her hair to the nape of her neck. Yes, oh yes. That felt luxurious and *so, so* good.

He leaned down, his warm breath feathering over her ear, as he said, "Talk to me, Faith."

He said her name the same way he looked at her, like she was important and beautiful, and that made the butterflies in her stomach spring to life again.

"I'm trying to figure out how you coerced me into this dance."

"You want to be here in my arms."

Those eyes, she couldn't escape them. And hell if he wasn't right.

"Maybe," she admitted, "but don't get any ideas. As you said, it's just one dance."

"Why are you so against spending time with me?" His brows slanted, giving him a deadly serious look.

"I'm not going to be another notch on your belt, Sam."

He leaned back and tugged at the waist of his sexy jeans. Holy moly, *that* was a turn-on, too.

"No belt, Faith."

A soft laugh slipped out. "You know what I mean."

"Then don't become a notch. There's no reason we can't dance, or talk, or spend time together."

Why did he make everything sound so easy? Didn't he know that just dancing with him was making her insides melt, and because of that she hated herself a little bit?

"Sam."

He cupped the back of her head. Wow, that felt amazing.

"Faith."

Melt, melt, melt. There went her panties.

No. She refused to be another swoon-for-Sam-Braden girl. She drew her shoulders back and set what she hoped was a slightly professional gaze on him.

"We are dancing," she said. "And talking."

"Go out with me," he said in the same vein as he'd asked

her to dance—it wasn't a question at all, but a gentle, coaxing demand.

"No, thank you." Good. That was quick, succinct, and left no room for negotiation.

His brows quirked up in amusement. "You want to go out with me, Faith."

"No, I don't." *Oh, what a tangled web of lies we weave to keep our hearts safe.*

"You do," he said easily. "You will."

His dark eyes held her captive for an interminable span of time before he guided her head possessively back to his chest. She should be angry at his assumption, but he felt *so* good. She closed her eyes, the devil in her mind mocking her, as she flattened her hands along his shoulders, feeling his strength and noticing his lack of tension. He was calm and relaxed as a summer breeze while she was strung so tight if he let go she might spring off like a tornado.

When the song ended, Sam ran his hand down her arm and laced their fingers together. Without a word he lifted her hand and kissed it. Then he held it to his chest and pulled her against him.

"One more dance," he whispered against her cheek.

She was playing with fire. How could she do anything but melt?

Chapter Six

SAM DIDN'T WANT their dance to end, but as he knew it would, the beat faded, and all that was left was the thrum of desire flowing through his veins and the urge to get to know Faith better. She gazed up at him like a deer staring down a buck—intrigued and scared in equal measure. He knew she had to return to her friends; he'd promised them he wouldn't steal her for the night, although that was exactly what he wanted to do.

Their fingers were still laced. Before he could check his words, "Take a walk with me?" came out. *A walk?* He had no idea where that came from.

"What?" Her eyes widened with confusion.

"A walk. It's what people do with their legs to get them from one place to another. Let's get out of here and walk along the beach. I just want to talk to you, Faith. Nothing more." *Nothing more* would be torture, but he wanted additional time with her more than he wanted to make a move on her.

She stared at him like he'd lost his mind, and maybe he had, but he wanted to get to know her. Faith had that weird thing going on, where she said things that made him think, and he rarely slowed down for anything.

"I can't just leave, Sam."

"Half an hour. That's all." Whispers was located at the end of Dunes Landing, a dead-end street overlooking the ocean. "They'll still be here when we get back, and they can keep an eye on us from the deck if they don't trust me." Hope swelled inside him as consideration washed over her eyes.

She glanced in the direction of her friends' table. "I can't."

"You can." He lifted her chin so he could look into her eyes. "I do love those sexy specs."

"Ugh. You're just trying to hook up with me." She pushed away, but he still had her hand in his, and he tugged her against him again.

"Trust me, Faith. If I wanted to hook up with you, I'd never settle for half an hour—and neither would you."

She inhaled an unsteady breath, and he liked that. He liked it a whole hell of a lot.

"Sam," she said with slightly less determination.

"Sand between your toes. A little conversation. That's all I'm asking for. I promise not to try anything else." The urge to taste her luscious lips was so strong his mouth burned, but he'd gladly fight those desires for a little more time together.

She narrowed her eyes, and he reluctantly released her hand.

"No tricks, no pressure. Bradens' honor."

"Seriously?" She laughed.

"Seriously." Sam was raised by an ex-military father and a mother whose every word held lessons in love, loyalty, and honesty. He might go through women like water, but he had the strength and security of knowing that no matter what he or his siblings did, they would always be there for each other. As disbelief filled Faith's eyes, he had the overwhelming desire for her to feel that security, too.

The thought hit him with the force of a bullet train.

Faith looked down at their separated hands, and when she lifted her eyes to his, he was sure she was going to blow him off. His chest constricted with the need for her to agree to the walk. Nerves pricked his arms as he tried to figure out what else he could say or do to buy a little more time with her. And then she touched his fingertips with hers and looked up at him with a half-smiling, half-serious expression.

"Give me a minute." She headed over to her friends, leaving Sam a thread of hope to hang on to.

She leaned over the table, and all the girls leaned in, listening. Everyone nodded and smiled, except Vivian, who shifted a death stare to Sam. She turned that heated stare on Faith, and his legs flexed with the urge to protect Faith from whatever was spewing from Vivian's lungs. But that wasn't his place. He'd never come between Faith and her friends, and as Faith rose to her full, petite height and reached across the table to squeeze

Vivian's hand, he prepared himself for her refusal to go on their walk.

"IT'S ONLY A walk." Faith wasn't sure if she was trying to convince herself or Vivian. She felt guilty for even considering going, since she was here for a girls' night and Vivian was leaving tomorrow. But she *wanted* to go, and besides, before Vivian's last boyfriend and current hiatus from men, she'd left Faith plenty of times to be with a guy she'd met while they were out. Sam had piqued Faith's curiosity. How many guys had asked her to go for a walk in Peaceful Harbor? Exactly none.

"He's already promised not to try anything." Faith wasn't sure if she was disappointed or relieved by that promise.

"He's dangerous for you, Faith. You're too attracted to him, and let's face it, as I said before, it's guys like him that brought our group together. Why can't you talk here?" Vivian pleaded.

She thought about Lira and all the reasons the girls had come together in the first place. She knew Vivian was looking out for her, and she knew Vivian was right. Sam posed a risk to her emotions. But there was a whisper drawing her in the other direction. She couldn't get past the honest look in his eyes when he'd said he didn't hurt women, or the sincerity in his voice when he'd said he wanted to help by donating to their group. That hopeful, and apparently stronger than she knew, part of herself was clinging to those things, wanting to dissect them like she would an ailment, and there was only one way to do that. Her physical safety wasn't in jeopardy, only her emotions. Besides, if he did try something, well, wouldn't that tell her everything she needed to know?

"Oh, let her go," Brittany urged. "He's such a nice guy."

"You should have seen his face when I told him that my boyfriend invited his *other* girlfriend to a couple's dinner that he'd already invited me to." Hilary sipped her drink. "I swear he looked like he wanted to wring the guy's neck, and he doesn't even know me."

Vivian narrowed her eyes skeptically in Sam's direction. "Really? So maybe there is more to this guy than I'm giving him credit for."

"Yup." Hilary smiled up at Faith. "Go, but I want to hear all about it when you get back."

"You sure you guys don't mind? This was supposed to be a girls' night, and—"

"If you really want to go, which it seems like you do, then go." Vivian tapped her watch. "But you're on the clock, and I'm holding you to it. You don't want to waste that outfit on him all night."

Her outfit. Geez. She'd been so wrapped up in things she'd forgotten she was wearing the skimpy skirt and a shirt that hung too low off her shoulder.

She closed her eyes tightly and recalled the confidence she'd felt when she first left the apartment. She clung to that confidence and opened her eyes, surprised to feel a little thrill about her racy outfit. "Okay, back in thirty minutes." When she turned, bringing Sam into focus, her mind froze, and thoughts of anything other than the man before her—handsome, determined, *dangerous*?—fell away.

He fell into step beside her, his hand gently wrapping around her arm. Was she really walking out of Whispers with Sam Braden? The longing looks from the women she passed told her she was, and the tightening in her stomach told her maybe she shouldn't. She slowed, but Sam's insistent touch drove her forward.

The evening air was cool on her face, bringing her smart-girl brain back. Sam was just a guy, and this was just a walk. She tried to ignore the heat of his hand, his earthy, masculine scent, and the way he was looking at her, like she was all he ever wanted.

Her smart brain cleared that right up. Sam didn't want just *one* girl, no matter what came out of his tempting, full lips.

He knelt beside her at the edge of the beach, placing his big, hot hand on her calf and threatening the brain cells she'd just salvaged.

"Hold on to my shoulder and I'll help you with your shoes."

No girl in her right mind could deny a sexy man kneeling at her feet. She held on to his shoulder as he removed her shoes and set them aside.

"You have cute feet," he said as he toed off his shoes and placed them beside hers.

"I do?"

"I like your Skittles toes." His hand landed on its new home, the back of her arm, and they stepped onto the cool sand.

"Skittles toes?" She looked down at her multicolored toes, having completely forgotten that she had painted her toenails different colors. "Oh my gosh, they do look like Skittles."

"My favorite candy." A breeze came off the water, sending his thick dark hair into impossibly sexy tufts.

"It is not. You're just full of lines." She shook her head, laughing under her breath as they walked along the shore.

"That's not a line, actually. Skittles *are* my favorite."

They fell silent for a minute as another breeze swept off the water, but heat rolled off of Sam, keeping Faith toasty warm.

"So," she said nervously. "Now that you've got me out here, what did you want to talk about?"

"Everything," he said easily. "You."

"Me? I'm boring."

"You're anything but boring. Tell me about WAC. Why did you start it?" He looked at her expectantly.

"Oh, you know. A bad breakup, too much tequila, and a best friend urging me on." She tried to play it off casually, figuring he was just fishing for conversation.

"Actually, I don't know. I told you I haven't had a girlfriend in years, and I don't date, so I don't really get the whole bad breakup thing. What happened?"

She mulled that over for a minute. "What does that mean? You 'don't date'?"

"You tell me your secrets and I'll tell you mine." His eyes twinkled with playfulness, and the contrast to the heat his body was sending knocked her a little off-kilter.

"There's not much to tell."

"You started a group for women who had been cheated on. It seems like there would be a story behind that, but you don't have to share it with me. I, on the other hand, am an open book. Do you want to know why I don't date?"

No. Maybe. "Sure. Let's hear it."

"You've known a class clown or two, right?"

Totally not what she was expecting to hear, but she went with it. "I guess."

"Everyone does. There's one guy in every high school class, and when the reunion comes around, he's the same person he was all those years ago."

"O-kay."

"Well, I'm not that guy." He fell silent, and she looked up at him.

"That's it? That's your story?"

"No. I was just trying to figure out how to explain what I wanted to say, and I realized it made me sound immature, so I stopped." He gazed out over the water, the playfulness she'd seen slipping out of her grasp.

"So, you can't figure out why you don't date, or you're too immature to admit the truth?"

He turned to look at her with a hint of a smile. "Do you always call people on their shit?"

"I don't know. Maybe. I'm just trying to figure you out, but you're complicated. It's like listening to a handful of symptoms and trying to diagnose a new disease."

"That sounds horrible. I am not a disease. I've never had a disease, and...That's just awful." He chuckled, making her smile again.

"Not that *you're* a disease, just...Okay, yes, I don't put up with a lot of bullshit."

"Because you were cheated on?"

Her mouth dropped open, and he held up a hand in surrender.

"Hey, fair's fair. You called me on my shit."

"Yes, okay? Is that what you want to hear? That I, too, have been treated like shit?" The admission made her feel vulnerable, and that wasn't a feeling she liked.

He touched her hand, regret washing over his features. "I'm sorry. I didn't mean to upset you. I just want to get to know you better, and not just the here and now, Faith. I want to know how you became the person you are."

His confession was completely unexpected, softening her toward him. But the nagging question of *why* he wanted to get to know her played on in her head. Silence grew and expanded like a bubble between them, and she stifled the urge to ask, because this was Sam. He had only one endgame.

They walked in silence, broken only by the sound of the waves lapping against the shore and the faint sound of music in the distance.

After a few uncomfortable minutes, he said, "Let's see...why don't I date?"

"You don't have to tell me." She felt a little silly for her earlier outburst.

"I want to. I was a rascally kid, like the class clown, only different."

"I can only imagine," she teased.

He cocked a brow, and she couldn't tell if he meant it as a tease or a dare.

"I was always willing to stretch the rules, take risks. I'd sneak out and play my guitar down at the beach, or go to parties."

He fell silent again, and she didn't dare say a word. She wanted to hear more of his self-assessment.

"You know that old commercial, 'Give it to Mikey; he'll eat anything'?" he asked.

"Life cereal?"

"That was me. 'Ask Sammy; he'll do it. He'll do anything.'"

"That sounds like a convenient excuse."

"Convenient? Maybe. But hey, being that guy kept me from

woman, and here was Sam. He'd whipped out his phone to prove a point, and now he was opening up to her about who he was.

"Why?"

His brows knitted. "Why did it last so long?"

"No, I sort of get that. But why until recently?"

He shifted his eyes to the water, then back to her. The air between them pulsed, drawing them even closer together. She licked her lips, preparing for a kiss she was sure would come. Sam's eyes dropped to her mouth, hovering there as he wet his own lips, making all her girly parts twitch with anticipation. She couldn't kiss him, shouldn't kiss him, but as he leaned closer, she didn't give a damn what she shouldn't do. The closer his mouth came to hers, the louder the blood rushing through her ears became. When he said—"I think it's your turn to share"— it took a moment for it to register and to realize there wouldn't be a kiss.

"Faith?" Vivian's voice broke through the pulsing air. "Is that you?"

She whipped her head around, saw the girls traipsing toward her, and quickly turned back to Sam. "I'm sorry." *For almost kissing you? For looking like I wanted to? For my friends interrupting us?*

He reached for her hand, speaking fast. "Go out with me."

"I...I can't." She knew the dangers of going out with Sam, and Vivian was right. She was too taken with him to make smart decisions.

"One date."

She knew he wouldn't take no for an answer, but she didn't trust herself with him. "You don't date."

"I don't sit on the beach and talk either."

She heard her friends' voices coming closer and rose to her feet, brushing the sand from her legs, feeling shaken and shocked and tingly at the thought of going out with him.

"People don't change, Sam."

"What makes you think I need to change? I'm not a cheater. I told you that." He stepped closer, leaving her no air at all. "I like talking with you, Faith. One date."

Brittany jogged over to them, with Hilary and Vivian on her heels.

"You guys have been out here for an hour," Brittany said. "We were worried."

"They were worried. I knew Sam wouldn't take advantage of you," Hilary said. She smiled and added, "Unless you wanted him to."

Sam's eyes bore into Faith's. Her mind whirled and spun. *One date.*

Vivian looped her arm into Faith's and said, "Come on. I want to dance. Sorry, Braden. It's girls' night. We gave you double time. You're lucky we aren't kicking your ass."

They dragged Faith down the beach toward the bar. She

looked over her shoulder at Sam, still standing in the same place she'd left him, lifting his hand in a half wave—and she thought she saw a tiny piece of herself back there, too.

Chapter Seven

"FINALLY." SHANNON SLIPPED off her barstool and embraced Sam. "I thought you were going to blow us off."

He kissed his youngest sister's cheek. "Would I ever do that?"

Shannon raised her dark brows. Sam, Cole, Ty, and Shannon were dark like their father, while Tempest and Nate took after their fair-haired mother.

Sam went around the bar and kissed their mother's cheek. "Hey, Ma. You look nice." He loved his mother's style. She dressed like she was either on her way to a beach barbecue or a bohemian concert, with long, breezy skirts and colorful tops.

His mother, Maisy, reached up and stroked his cheek. "Thank you, sweetheart. I'm glad you're here."

Sam patted his father, Thomas "Ace" Braden's, back. "How's it going, Pop?"

"I've got most of my kids under one roof—that makes it a great day." While his mother's hair was a wild nest of curls, his father had never veered away from his tight military cut. "Ty and Tempe are in the kitchen getting sandwiches. They'll be out in a sec. Can I get you a drink?"

"Sure. Just Coke, thanks." He climbed atop a barstool and turned his attention to Shannon. "So you're going back to Uncle Hal's? How did your project go from a few weeks to a few months? Does it really take that long to research foxes?"

Shannon had been staying at their uncle's ranch in Weston, Colorado, the last several months, while working on a project monitoring red foxes in the mountains.

"So many questions. I didn't miss that while I was away. You know how it is," she said evasively as Ty and Tempest came through the kitchen doors carrying trays of sandwiches.

Sam looked at Shannon with a question in his eyes, and she smirked, making him wonder what the heck she was up to. "Does this have anything to do with Steve Johnson?"

"Oh, *please*. Steve? He's a recluse. Totally *not* my type of guy." She waved a dismissive hand, but the flush on her cheeks told a different story.

Sam and their brothers had always watched out for Shannon and Tempe, and he hated knowing she might be dating a guy he couldn't...*What?* Warn to be good to his sister? Christ, he was as bad as Cole was with Faith. Still, he'd been doing it for so long he couldn't stop himself from saying, "You two looked pretty cozy at Rex and Jade's wedding. Just be careful, okay? We're not there to kick the shit out of him if he crosses any lines with you."

"You do realize I'm an adult, right? What you just said is the *best* reason for me to go out with him."

"Shannon," he warned. *Damn it.* She'd always marched to her own beat, much like him, but now he had an inkling of what Cole must have felt like at the wedding. Man, did this feeling suck.

She ignored him, moving on to a conversation with their father.

"Hey, Sammy." Tempest set a tray of sandwiches on the bar and came around to hug him. She tucked her long blond hair behind her ear as she climbed onto a barstool beside him. "I'm working on a new song focusing on imperfect beauty. I think you'll like it, given your insistence that all things are uniquely beautiful."

Tempest was a music therapist, and she was always writing new songs. She was the quietest and most cautious of Sam's siblings. She was also the one who took his beliefs most seriously.

"I'd love to hear it when you're done." Seeing Tempest sparked an idea. "Hey, Tempe. Do you know any therapists who would consider donating sessions to women who are going through a hard time? Or maybe offer a discount?"

Her eyes rolled quizzically over his face. "I can ask around. Why?"

He wasn't about to open that can of worms. "For a friend."

"Sure. I'll ask around." She leaned closer. "More important-ly, is it true you've got the hots for Cole's assistant?"

Sam glared at Ty.

"Dude, it wasn't me." Ty laughed.

"I heard that, too," Shannon said. "Was it supposed to be a secret? Jewel told me that you left Whispers with Faith last night. I think Chelsea told her, so if it was a secret, it's not anymore."

"Christ," Sam mumbled. "I didn't leave with her. We went for a walk on the beach."

"A walk. Is that what they're calling it now?" his father teased, which made everyone laugh, and made Sam stew.

"What's so funny about going for a walk? And no, Pop, that's not what they call *it* now. It's not like that with Faith." Sam's jaw was so tight he feared it'd crack.

"Dude, you don't do *walks*." Ty shook his head.

"Cole's assistant Faith?" their mother asked with a spark of delight in her eyes. "She's such a sweet girl, Sammy. Be good to her."

"Yes, Faith. And, Mom, have I ever not been good to a woman?"

"Of course not, honey," his mother said. "I just meant, well, she is Cole's employee. You should be careful. That could get sticky."

"Didn't Cole tell you to back off at the wedding?" Tempest asked. "That's what he told me."

"Isn't anything sacred in this family?" *That's the problem.* Everything in their family was sacred. They protected one another and those they loved as if their lives depended on it. Cole obviously felt like Faith was family, as he did with all of his loyal employees.

"Honey, we're just watching out for you," his mother assured him.

"For *her*, Mom," Shannon corrected. "Sammy doesn't need looking after."

Sam gritted his teeth, unsure why he was suddenly bothered by their honesty when he'd heard it forever. He didn't like hearing his name tied to Faith *needing to be looked after*—unless he was doing the protecting.

"You're right, Shannon. I don't need looking after, but I'll look after Faith, don't you worry." Sam took a bite of his sandwich, mulling over, well, everything, while his family looked at him like he was from another planet. "What?"

Ty and Tempest exchanged a glance Sam couldn't read.

"It's been a long time since you've said something like that, honey." His mother reached across the bar and touched his hand. "You just took us by surprise."

"I've never heard you say anything like that." Shannon smirked.

Tempest looked at Sam, holding his gaze as she said, "You were too young, Shan."

Sam needed to change the subject. Nothing good ever came

from reliving the past. He was a firm believer that if a person wasn't moving forward, they weren't living, and hell if he was going to be that person.

"Where's Nate?" he asked.

"He and Jewel went to Krissy's dance recital, which reminds me. You're coming to her big recital, aren't you?" his mother asked.

"It's almost two months away, but don't worry. I wouldn't miss it." Krissy was Jewel's fourteen-year-old sister. The Fishers were like family to them. They'd lost their father in a boating accident, and a few years later they'd lost their eldest brother, Rick, in the war. Rick was Nate's best friend, and Nate carried the added burden of having given the order for Rick to go on the supply run that had taken his life. Though Nate had loved Jewel for years, survivor's guilt had nearly stolen her from him, too.

"Good," his mother said. "We're having dinner here afterward with Jewel's family."

The conversation turned to Shannon and her return to Colorado. She told them about the project she was working on and caught them up on their cousins from Colorado.

"Uncle Hal still has great barbecues," Shannon said. "It's fun to see our cousins from Trusty, Colorado, too. I still can't believe so many of them are married, having babies, or engaged."

"It's about time." Maisy glanced warmly at each of her children. "Your generation is so focused on getting more, more, more. I worry the whole idea of family will fall through the cracks."

Tempest waggled her finger at her. "Mom, we get together almost every week for lunch or dinner. How can you worry about that? We all love family."

Their mother reached for their father's hand. "Not our family, honey. Your own families. Nothing is more wonderful than coming home to the person you love, or having a family of your own."

Their father pulled her in for a kiss. "Your mother wants grandchildren."

Maisy laughed. "Is that so bad?"

"Don't look at me," Ty said, giving Sam the *no fucking way* look.

Sam was busy trying to figure out how to get Faith to go out with him and was only half listening to the conversation.

"I want kids," Shannon said. "Lots of them. Just not yet."

"Me too. When I fall in love, I hope it's as deeply as you and Dad," Tempest said to their mother. "I have faith that it'll happen for all of us." She bumped Sam's shoulder. "Even you and Ty."

Sam wondered about that. He could have almost any woman around—but the only woman he wanted didn't think he was worthy. That painful reality should send him sprinting in the opposite direction, but he was too drawn to Faith, to her honesty, her vulnerability, her intelligence. Damn, she'd gotten to him without even trying.

He looked around, feeling the love of his family, thinking of their taunts and the tough love they doled out like medication when they deemed it necessary. He thought about their unconditional support, their giving nature—to friends, family, strangers. He loved all those things about them and, he realized, those were just a few of the traits that had drawn him to Faith.

He looked out the window at the marina, and like the boats entering the harbor, felt himself changing course. Charting a new path, breaking free from the current that had been his guide for so long he'd forgotten he had a choice, and setting himself free to swim upstream. *Toward Faith.*

"One thing's for sure," their father said as he wiped down the bar. "When love finds each of you, as I expect it will, it'll change your whole world. Love is a lot like alcohol. You think you want just a little, but once you get your first taste"—he shifted his eyes to Sam—"your first *real* taste of adult love, the type of love that consumes your every thought. Once you get a taste of that, you'll do anything and everything for more. You'll want to drown in it."

MONDAYS WERE ALWAYS busy at the Peaceful Harbor Pain Management Center, and with Cole away on his honeymoon, Faith had even more patients to see. It was after three, and Faith had been running from one patient room to the next without a break since she'd arrived. She was famished. But even the growling of her stomach and the vast number of patients she'd seen hadn't been enough to distract her from thoughts of Sam. She'd hoped he'd return to Whispers last night, but he never did. After she and Vivian got home, they'd checked the site, and they'd received an anonymous five-thousand-dollar donation. She knew it had to be from Sam. Who else would throw that kind of money at their cause? Vivian insisted he was using it as a ploy to get her into bed. *A very expensive ploy.* But she wasn't buying it. Vivian hadn't seen how sincere he'd looked when he'd offered to write the check.

Conflicting thoughts of Sam had invaded her dreams, and she'd woken up hot and bothered and even more confused than ever. If saying goodbye to Vivian this morning, along with this insanely busy day, couldn't take her mind off of Sam, nothing could.

She tried to set those thoughts to the side and turned her attention back to her patient. "You can change now, Mr. French, and we'll see you back in three weeks for a follow-up."

"Thank you, Faith. I'll put a good word in for you up front." He winked, and Faith smiled and shook her head.

"You'd better be careful flirting like that. I doubt Mrs. French would like it."

He waved a hand. "My Betty knows I'm joshin'."

"Have a nice afternoon, Mr. French." Faith left the room, closing the door behind her. She scribbled copious notes and set the chart in the holder by the door.

"How're you holding up?" Dr. Jon Butterscotch was Cole's partner, and he was as full of energy at eight in the morning as he was at midnight. Faith had assisted in enough of his emergency surgeries to know. With a mop of blond hair that always looked finger-combed, an ever-present tan, and a smile at the ready for even the most trying of patients, he looked like a surfer playing dress-up in his lab coat. But beneath the youthful exterior was one of the finest brains around—the brain of a man who should be twice his age. Much like Cole, Jon took his job seriously, and he took pride in treating his patients as individuals, not *cases*, which made Faith respect him even more.

"A little hungry, but other than that, I'm doing great." Not a day went by that Faith didn't thank God for her job. She had always wanted to help people, and medicine intrigued her. Being a physician assistant allowed her to enjoy both of those things without the added years and debt of medical school. She'd always thought she'd graduate, settle into a career, and marry JJ, her cheating ex. But life had a way of upending even the best-laid plans.

"You didn't get lunch?" Jon reached into his pocket and handed Faith a chocolate PowerBar. "You should have told me. You know I always have these on hand."

"Thanks. I didn't want to bother you." She thought about

the list she'd started last night for expanding WAC, and her conversation with Lira. "Jon, do you know of any therapists who do pro-bono work? For charity, maybe?"

His brows furrowed. "Not off the top of my head. Do you need to talk with someone?"

"No, it's not for me." She didn't want to try to explain WAC when patients were waiting. "It's for a friend from out of town. She doesn't have much money."

"Oh, in that case, ask Brandy for our network referrals. I'm sure they can send you in the right direction." Reaching for the doorknob of another patient room, he said, "Good luck finding someone for her, and thanks for doing a great job. I'll be sure to mention it to Cole."

Faith couldn't stop grinning even after he disappeared into the patient room. She'd met enough snotty, egotistical doctors during her clinical rotations to know she really lucked out finding a job with Cole and Jon. She tucked away the compliment and ducked into the kitchen to quickly eat the PowerBar.

Brandy, the receptionist, peeked into the room a minute later. "Faith, you've got a walk-in. He said it was urgent and you were the only person he'd see."

Faith fought to keep her shoulders from slumping. She had patients every twenty minutes for the rest of the afternoon.

"Is he one of Cole's patients?"

Brandy nodded.

"Sure. Brandy, can you please pull the list of therapists from our referral database for me around the Pleasant Hill area? No rush."

"No problem," Brandy said. "Room six. Sorry." She disappeared down the hall.

I love my job. I love my job. I love my job. Finding the motivation to smile again, she headed toward room six. There was no chart in the holder. Great. She was already behind. Now she'd need to get caught up to speed, too? Pushing the door open, she began her typical spiel.

"Hi, I'm Faith, and I—" Her jaw gaped, her voice lost somewhere between her thundering heart and the heat radiating off the nearly naked man sitting on the exam table, wearing a pair of black briefs and a toe-curling smile. She was going to kill Brandy.

"Sam," she whispered, then covered her eyes. "Why are you here?" *Ohmygod. Don't look. Do not look again.* Her fingers parted and she snuck a peek. She couldn't help it! He was right there for her to gobble up!

"In your *underwear?*" She closed her fingers again and slammed her eyes shut.

"Brandy said you usually have your patients undress before you see them."

How could he be so calm and confident when she could barely remain standing?

"Yes, *patients*! And they wear *gowns*! Why aren't you wearing a gown?"

"And emasculate myself?" He laughed a little. "How would I ever convince you to go out with me after you saw me in a paper gown?"

Breathe, breathe, breathe.

"Come on, Faith. It's like wearing a bathing suit."

Men in bathing suits didn't look like *that*. Well, except *him*, of course. This was crazy. How did he fluster her so easily? She was a professional. She could handle this.

But can I handle him?

"Besides," he said. "I told you I have nothing to hide. What you see is what you get with me."

Lowering her hand, she looked at him again, feeling her entire body blush. There was a whole lot of him to see. He was gorgeous. Too gorgeous. Too comfortable with himself. His chest was pure perfection, tanned, with just a light dusting of hair, and defined so beautifully she wanted to study it, *with her mouth*. His scent was intoxicating and making her a little dizzy. His gaze moved slowly from her eyes, to her mouth, her chest, all the way down to her toes, and she felt the sensual inspection as if he'd touched every inch of her.

"God, Sam. Are you trying to turn me into a puddle of mush and get me fired?"

He reached for her hand and tugged her forward. Right. Between. His. Legs.

Holy mother of heaven and earth and anyone else willing to listen, please, please, please let me remain coherent.

"I turn you to mush?" he asked with a seductive spark in his eyes.

Faith breathed deeply. That was all he heard? What about the getting fired part? This situation was getting out of control. She had to *take* control.

Control of Sam Braden. Even the thought made her hot and bothered.

She forced herself to act like the professional her bosses relied on her to be. *My boss.* Panic spread through her chest. Drawing her shoulders back and lifting her chin, she forced herself to regain control.

"Where are you injured?"

A mischievous smile formed on his handsome face. How could a single look make her body hum with need?

"My leg."

"Calf? Thigh?" The words fell fast, and thankfully not breathlessly.

He quirked a brow. "Thigh."

With embarrassingly shaky hands she touched his muscular thigh. Oh, that was nice. Hot and firm and…She cleared her throat. "Here?"

"A little higher." His piercing stare held her captive as she moved her hand farther up his thigh. "Higher," he repeated.

She was going to hyperventilate. "Here?"

"A little higher." The man was pure sin and seduction, and she was a devil in the making, lapping it up word by word.

"Sam." *Aaaaand…*there was the breathlessness she feared. *Goddamn it.* She wasn't this swoony girl. "Sam Braden! Are you even hurt?"

He set one hand over hers, the other over his heart. "Very much so. You turned me down last night."

"*Ugh!* Get over yourself." She tried to pull her hand away, but he held on tight, his eyes never wavering from hers.

"I'd rather get over you."

Ohmygod. She was nervous and turned on and reveling in his attention way too much. She held his challenging gaze, but it was all too much. *He* was too much. Laughter bubbled up from her chest and burst out like an explosion. She covered her mouth, but there was no stopping it. She'd gone hysterical.

Chapter Eight

SAM KNEW HE'D taken a chance by stripping down for Faith, but he wanted to prove to her he was not who she thought he was. And what better way than to make her laugh? He'd thought she'd laugh from the moment she saw him and was surprised when she didn't, but this hysterical laugher was refreshing, coming from the cautious woman who currently held the strings to his carefully guarded heart.

He stepped from the exam table, not wanting to embarrass her any more than he already had, and pulled on his jeans. Faith watched him dress, bursting out in laughter every few seconds. At least she was looking at him now.

"I think I liked your first reaction better, the whole adorably sexy blushing thing you had going on." He pulled on his T-shirt and closed the distance between them, gazing into her tear-soaked eyes. He wiped a tear of laughter from her cheek.

She nervously licked her lips, clenching her jaw to stifle her laughter, and gazed up at him through impossibly long lashes that made her look both innocent and wise.

"I was wrong," he said. Laughter, anticipation, and embarrassment lingered in her eyes—making him aware of how fast his own heart was beating. He hadn't been this aware of that particular organ since he was a teenager, when his heart had been crushed. Memories of the day Keira had told him she'd slept with a guy from her hometown came rushing back, followed by the painful memory of the day he'd heard she'd moved away. He'd been a stupid kid, infatuated with a girl from the next town over. Thanks to his warped view of wabi-sabi, he'd buried that part of himself deep. He wondered if his art teacher had known she'd given him validation to shut off his feelings completely.

Something had clicked inside him the night of Cole's wedding. Maybe it was the things Faith had said, or maybe it was just Faith. Whatever the reason, there was no ignoring what he felt. He wanted Faith, and he wanted to be a better man for her.

"Your laughter is like a drug, and I want more of it."

"Sam," she said softly. "You're Cole's brother. He's my boss."

"That's true, and he adores you and loves me. We're a perfect match." He knew he was taking a risk where Cole was concerned, but Cole was worried about him hurting Faith, sleeping with her once and walking away. But walking away wasn't on his radar, not where Faith was concerned. If Cole knew what he was feeling, Sam was sure he'd be cheering him on.

"You don't date, and I don't sleep around," she said firmly. "We're not at all a perfect match."

"You have valid points."

"Right." She turned away, and he gently took her by the arm and turned her toward him.

"You're worried about being hurt. Faith, I give you my word that I'm not going to hurt you."

She rolled her eyes in response, and the dismissal stung.

"Sam, do you really think people go into relationships knowing they're going to hurt each other?"

"No," he answered. "But I think when it comes to cheating you have a choice. No one makes a person cheat. It takes a cognitive, willful decision—*am I going to hurt my significant other or am I not?* That's something you don't have to worry about with me. I won't cheat, and I will never purposely hurt you."

"Says the guy who hasn't had a girlfriend since high school."

"Says the *man* who knows what he wants." The words came out harsher than he'd realized he felt, but they were honest and so were the emotions.

Faith cracked a very small smile. "You're not used to being turned down, are you?"

"Christ." He ran a hand through his hair. "No, but that's beside the point. I don't pursue women, Faith. Usually if I get turned down, I walk away. But I'm pursuing you, and not just for sex."

"I'm a challenge." She lifted her chin, like she was sure she had him pegged. "You'll get bored with me, and I'll be left like one of your groupies, wanting a man I can never have."

"Not going to happen."

She crossed her arms, and he could see she was still nervous, still wanting to say yes, even though her better judgment told her to refuse him.

"I'm really late, Sam. I can't play games. We're just not right for each other. I like you. You can see that. You're hot and fun and smart and *way* too dangerous for a girl like me. I can't risk my heart again."

He ached at her confession. "Faith, after all I've told you, why do you still think so poorly of me?"

"Honestly?" she asked.

"It's the only way I know how to be—"

"Like your thigh injury?" she teased.

"I *was* injured." He patted his heart. "But how could I resist? It might be the only way I ever get your hands on me."

"God." She laughed. "Don't you even have a filter?"

"Yes. It's set to 'honest all the time.' Please, explain to me why you think I'm a cretin."

"I don't think you're a cretin." She sighed, as if she was reluctantly going to be honest, and Sam hoped to hell she was.

"I'm afraid to go out with you. I know we'll have fun, but I don't want to be one of the girls who says they went out with

Sam Braden. I don't want to experience what every other woman in the Harbor has. I'm worth more than a rerun of a hundred other dates. I worked too hard to rebuild my confidence after…" She swallowed hard. "I'm in a good place, Sam. I can't risk that. Not even for you."

FAITH BARELY HELD it together until Sam left, and even afterward she stared at the closed door for what felt like a very long time before finally taking a deep breath.

What the hell just happened? She'd been so caught off guard that she'd forgotten to ask him if he'd given the donation to WAC.

There was a knock at the door seconds before Brandy peeked into the room. Her dark hair fell straight past her shoulders. She was a petite little thing, sweet as pie and currently looking guilty and embarrassed.

"Hey. I'm so sorry. Sam asked me not to tell you it was him, and he's Dr. Braden's brother, and so nice, and—"

"It's okay, Brandy. I know he can be very convincing."

"He's so cute, and that voice," Brandy said dreamily. "Are you two dating? He seemed really intent on seeing you."

"No," she said quickly, to avoid any office gossip.

"Oh, I just thought…Sorry. Anyway, your patients are backed up, so what do you want me to do?"

"Nothing. I'll go out and apologize, and I'll see them all, no matter how late I have to stay."

Brandy gave her the list of therapists she'd asked for and left Faith to finish seeing patients. She worked straight through until six thirty. By the time she left the office, she was exhausted, mentally drained, and second-guessing the way she'd handled things with Sam. She didn't want to keep blowing him off, and yet when she was with him, she was afraid not to.

She crossed the parking lot toward her car and was surprised to see a notebook with a plain white cover tucked beneath her windshield wiper. She flipped it open and read the handwritten note.

Faith,

I wonder what you would see if you didn't know about my reputation? Without that cover, would you still judge me in the same way? Are you willing to bet your future on who you think I am? If so, ignore this note and carry on. I promise never to bother you again. But if you have a shadow of a doubt, if you feel what I feel when we're together, then take a chance on me and head over to Chelsea's Boutique.

—Sam

"Oh my God, Sam. What are you doing?"

She read it twice. He was relentless, and that made her curious, and excited. She drove over to the cute boutique she'd been in only a few times, and as she parked out front she realized that she hadn't even considered *not* going. Her nerves were ablaze as she pulled open the glass doors and walked inside, unsure of what she'd find.

"Hi, Faith," Jewel said from behind the register. She came around the counter with a large bag and a curious look in her eyes. "I'm supposed to give you this." She handed Faith the bag. "And this."

"Thank you." Faith took the bag and the envelope from her. She'd forgotten that Jewel, Sam's brother's fiancée, managed the boutique.

Jewel must have sensed her trepidation. "They're from Sam." She went back to work behind the counter, leaving Faith to open the envelope in private. Inside was another handwritten note.

Hi, beautiful.

Beautiful? She stifled a smile.

Thanks for coming this far with me. You're probably still in your scrubs, and want to get out of them as soon as possible. Since you chose to come here instead of going home, I thought you might appreciate something more comfortable to wear. Jewel will let you change in the dressing room. Pick out a pair of sandals, too. They're already paid for.

—S

You bought me clothes? She looked up at Jewel, and Jewel smiled and held up a key to the dressing room.

"I have to tell you," Jewel said as she led her to a dressing room, "I think I'm as excited as you are. What's going on with you two?"

"Nothing." The lie tasted bitter. Something was definitely going on, but how could she explain what it was when she didn't even understand it herself?

Jewel opened a dressing room door and tucked her blond hair behind her ear. "If you say so."

"What did Sam say?" She wanted to ask her what Sam was really like when he wasn't at a club or out partying. Was he the man she was getting to know, or was this all a put-on?

"Not much. He came in and picked out an outfit, which took him almost forty minutes. He *really* took his time. Then he gave me a few things to give you, and when I asked why, he said I'd find out soon enough if he was lucky." Jewel waggled her brows. "Is he getting lucky?"

"Not *that* kind of lucky." *Forty minutes?*

"Well, if it helps, I've known Sam my whole life, and I think the world of him."

"Even though he, um, isn't so selective about who he sleeps with?" *Did I really just ask that?*

"There is that little downside to him, but he's got the biggest, kindest heart. I don't know why Sam sleeps around, but I love him just the same. I mean, tons of people sleep around, right?"

"I guess," she said halfheartedly. "I don't," she said more to herself than to Jewel.

"Join the club. I had zero experience when I started dating Nate. I don't know what's going on between you and Sam, but I can honestly say I've never seen him make an effort toward any woman beyond, well, you know."

Unfortunately, she did. She slipped into the dressing room and read Sam's note again, feeling special despite her misgivings. Everything he did was unexpected, and she had to admit, well thought out, too. She pulled out the clothes he'd bought, and it wasn't a slinky little dress like she'd expected. He'd bought her a pair of jeans shorts and a pretty pink shirt that was soft as a cloud. How did he know her size? *Jewel.* She looked at her reflection in the mirror, feeling...*important* to him.

Oh my.

She sank down to the wooden bench for a moment, letting the thought settle in.

When she finally came out, wearing her new comfortable and cute outfit, she found Jewel waiting for her by the shoe display. "Sam already paid, so pick out any pair you'd like."

"Gosh, I feel like Julia Roberts in *Pretty Woman*, only in comfier clothes and without the whole prostitute thing."

"You mean you feel like you're being treated well?"

"Yeah," Faith said as she looked over the shoes. "Exactly that. Or more than that. No guy has ever done anything like this for me. I feel like I shouldn't accept this stuff from Sam."

"Normally I'd be right there with you on that, but this is so out of the ordinary for him. I think it means he wants more than *nothing* with you. Selfishly, I want to see what he's got in store for you. He was acting so mysterious."

"So you don't think I'm crazy for following his notes?"

"Not even a little."

That made her feel a little less like a stranger in her own skin. She wanted to see what Sam had in mind, too. She decided on a cute pair of beaded sandals.

"One more thing." Jewel pulled another envelope out of her back pocket, went behind the counter again, and brought out a Rough Riders zip-up hoodie that said *Faith* over the logo.

"I have to admit," Jewel said, "I'm a little jealous, and I have the best man in Peaceful Harbor." She gave Faith a quick hug and wished her luck.

As Faith left the store she wondered if Jewel had that wrong. She didn't know a single man who would go to this much trouble to get a woman to go out with him. That put Sam in the running for the best man in Peaceful Harbor, didn't it? Or would his past forever keep him down?

She hoped and prayed this wasn't just a game to Sam, because as she hurried to her car, wearing her cute new outfit and monogrammed hoodie, she was getting seriously excited. In the privacy of her car, she tore open the envelope and read the third handwritten note.

Hey, babe.

Babe? In the span of three notes he'd gone from *Faith*, to *beautiful*, to *babe*, and as much as she knew she shouldn't feel special from a few words and some pieces of clothing, Faith reveled in it.

I bet you look sexy, and nervous, and maybe you're even blushing by now. I wish I was there to see it. I know you've had a long day, so the rest is pretty quick. Head down to the marina—or go home and leave me hanging. Either way, I'm glad you've come this far with me.

Your date, I hope.

—Sam

Date? He didn't date. And how did he know she was blushing? He was just as irresistible in notes as he was in person. She tried to hold on to the knowledge that Sam was a player as she drove toward the marina. As she approached Harbor Overlook, a walking bridge over the road, she slowed to a near stop. A big white sign hung over the side of the bridge with SAY YES TO SAM! spray-painted in big red letters.

"Holy cow, Sam." She pulled over to the side of the road and snapped a picture with her phone. As she drove under the bridge, goose bumps rose on her arms. He'd gone to all this trouble for her, even after she blew him off. That spoke volumes about him. He was either willing to go to the ends of the earth to get lucky, or he was really into her after all. She was leaning toward the idea of actually going out with Sam when she came to the next stoplight.

Two signs marked the corner. One with an arrow pointing in the direction of her apartment that read, SAFE ROUTE HOME, and one with an arrow pointing toward the marina that read, HIGHWAY TO HEAVEN. Laughing as she took another picture, she turned toward the marina, and that's when it became clear just how far Sam Braden was willing to go to get her to change her mind. The illuminated sign for the marina read, F. MR. B'S PLEASE. S. She wondered what type of strings he'd had to pull to get that sign changed.

She drove through the parking lot to the road that led up to Mr. B's, wondering why he went through all this just to take her to his parents' microbrewery. At Mr. B's there were no signs, no lights other than the ordinary. Faith straightened her top beneath her Rough Riders sweatshirt and looked around the parking lot, suddenly feeling nervous. She was wearing clothes Sam had not only picked out but paid for as she went into his family's restaurant! He'd actually thought of her comfort. She loved knowing that, but it still felt weird. Exciting and romantic, but not anything she was used to.

It was loud inside Mr. B's. The hostess took one look at her and her eyes widened. "Faith?"

"Yes." *Gulp.*

"Follow me." The energetic brunette walked quickly toward the bar.

Sam was nowhere in sight, but she recognized Mr. Braden and smiled up at him, feeling even more embarrassed.

"Here you are," the hostess said. She turned on her heels and left Faith standing there looking at Sam's father.

"How are you, Faith?" He came around the bar, and his eyes dropped to the Rough Riders logo on her sweatshirt. His smile revealed the same dimple as Sam's, just below the left side of his lip.

"I'm fine, thank you. How are you, Mr. Braden?"

"It's a magical night here at Mr. B's. I'm happy you made it over."

"You are?" *Oh no. That slipped.* She was too nervous. She should just zip her mouth shut for the night.

He laughed, and it reminded her of Sam's deep laugh. "I am, young lady. Sam will be thrilled that you've come. He's been a nervous wreck all evening."

"Don't reveal Sammy's secrets," Sam's mother said as she came up behind Faith. "Hi, honey. Let me take you up to Sam."

Faith had liked his parents from the moment she'd met them at Cole's office last year. His mother was effervescent, with thick and wild blond hair, and she dressed like she was part gypsy, with long skirts and flowing tops, while his father was far more conservative and quiet, but always welcoming and kind.

"Up?" she asked, following Sam's mother through a set of doors and into the kitchen, then through a heavy steel door and up a flight of stairs.

"To the roof." His mother lowered her voice and whispered, "Sam's gone all out. I've never seen him so excited. I'm glad you showed up after all."

Faith felt like she was in a dream, floating from one thing to the next, with happiness and nervousness sprinkled like fairy dust. Everyone seemed so surprised at Sam's efforts, and she was right there with them. But nothing prepared her for the hug his mother gave her at the top of the stairs.

"Have fun, and, Faith?"

"Yes?" She held her breath, waiting for the shoe to drop, to hear something like, *Don't let him fool you. This is Sam, after all.*

"Please don't break my boy's heart. He's tough as nails, but he's also sweet as sugar." She patted Faith's cheek, like her own mother had done a million times, and descended the stairs, leaving Faith to stare at the door.

Just beyond the door was Sam.

Tough as nails and sweet as sugar, Sam. He'd gone *all out.* The man who didn't date and said he didn't cheat. The man who believed nothing lasted forever. The man who'd talked with her on the beach for an hour last night and had gone to a world of trouble to get her here. Sam, the man she dreamed about, fantasized about, and now was so confused over she didn't know whether she should open the door or run away.

She looked down the stairs. It would be easy to walk back down and out to her car. Much easier than facing the emotions storming inside her and the passion she was trying to pretend didn't exist. But easy was boring, wasn't it? Maybe she didn't like easy after all, because she liked Sam.

Turning back to the door, she gathered her courage and pushed it open.

White lights illuminated a waist-high brick railing that ran around the edge of the roof. Faith stepped outside, holding the door open as she took in the table set for two, complete with a red tablecloth, linen napkins, a bottle of wine, and several dishes covered with shiny metal covers. Three beautiful candles sat in the center of the table, flickering in the breeze. Sam sat with his back to her, playing his guitar as he looked out over the ocean. She listened for a moment to the peaceful melody flowing from his fingertips, and when she stepped closer, the door slipped from her hand, *clanking* loudly against the frame.

Sam turned, heat filling his dark eyes as he rose to his feet, looking devilishly handsome in his jeans and tight black shirt. He set his guitar against the railing. Music drifted up from the patio below, providing a sexy backdrop to Sam, who was moving fluidly toward her. How could that much harnessed power appear graceful and virile at the same time?

"Faith." Her name slid off his tongue smooth as velvet as he took her hand.

His touch brought an unusual sense of safety, as it had last night, taking her by surprise.

His lips curved up in a warm smile. "I'm glad you came."

Her body felt electric and liquefied at once as too many sensations collided inside her. In a few short days he'd shown her more parts of himself than some people had in a year.

"I'm glad I came, too."

Chapter Nine

SAM BRUSHED HIS thumb over the back of Faith's hand, unable to take his eyes off of her and hyperaware of the heat sizzling between them.

"You look even more beautiful than I thought you would."

A rosy blush flushed her cheeks. "I can't believe you bought me clothes."

"I was worried you wouldn't agree to meeting me without changing after work. And then I worried that if you went home to change you'd rethink coming at all, and I'd be left alone up here, missing you." He leaned in to kiss her cheek, soaking in her soft, feminine, inviting scent.

She inhaled a sharp breath as his lips brushed over her skin.

"I thought about getting you jeans or a dress," he admitted. "But when I think of you, I see comfort, sweetness, and your alluring confidence, and that's hotter than form-fitting jeans or a short skirt could ever be."

Her eyes widened a little. "You see all of that when you

think of me?"

"That's only a fraction of what I see. I never realized how personal clothing was until I was standing in the store trying to figure out what you would be most comfortable in. I knew you'd look great in anything, but it wasn't about that."

"You went to a lot of trouble." She rubbed her fingers over her name on the hoodie.

He'd called in a favor to have the sweatshirt monogrammed so quickly, but seeing her in it, looking sinfully sweet and incredibly sexy, made it worthwhile. Something had come over him this afternoon as he went from location to location, setting up signs and making arrangements. All that time he'd been trying to keep his distance from her, protecting her from himself, because after all, even his own brother thought she needed protecting from him. A few weeks before the wedding he'd noticed a change in himself. Meaningless connections no longer held his interest, but Faith? She was on his mind day and night, regardless of how hard he tried to push thoughts of her away. Today he let himself examine those feelings more closely and realized it was Faith all along. She'd gotten to him, and because he'd been so determined to stay away, he hadn't allowed himself to see it. Now he was no longer willing to ignore the one thing that felt right or the one person who made him feel things he never thought he would. He not only wanted to prove he wasn't the guy she—and everyone else—thought he was, but he wanted to go above and beyond. He knew he wanted more than a good time with Faith, and now he wanted *her* to want that, too.

"Actually, I don't think I went to nearly enough trouble." He stepped closer and took her hand in his. Reflections of the lights sparkled in her eyes as they walked by the table. All the trouble he'd gone to had been worth it just to see her magnificent smile.

"It's like our own private tower. You didn't have to do all of this."

"Actually, I did." He poured them each a glass of wine. "You turned me down flat when I asked you out like a normal guy."

"You're not a normal guy, Sam. You're my boss's brother *and* you're everything I'm scared of."

He lifted his glass in a toast, hoping she'd move past her fears. "To imperfect matches."

She smiled. "I cannot believe I'm toasting to that."

They touched glasses, and as Faith drank her wine, Sam drank her in.

"No man has ever bought me clothes before. Well, except my father, but he doesn't count."

"Then I'm privileged to be the first. It's only appropriate, seeing as you're my first real date." Before she could knock down the idea of this being a date, he took her in his arms and said, "Dance with me."

Her brow furrowed as her arms came around his waist.

Sam lifted her hands to his neck. "I like this better. We're closer." He gazed into her eyes as they moved in a slow, sensual rhythm.

"We're dancing," she said softly. "On a rooftop with lights and music and candlelight. Sam, this might be the most romantic thing anyone has ever done for me." She smiled up at him, but he sensed she was still on the fence about them.

"You said you were worth more than a rerun of what every other girl in the Harbor had done with me. I've never bought any of them clothes, or sent them on a mission to find me, or brought them to my parents' brewery. Just you, sweet one."

She blushed and pressed her forehead to his chest. "You called me 'sweet one.'"

He laughed. "Yeah, I did."

"I can't help it. I have to ask." Her face turned serious. "Do you call all your girls that?"

He knew his reputation had bothered her, but he hadn't realized how it infiltrated her every thought. All he could do was answer honestly. "No, Faith. And I don't have 'girls.'"

She nodded, brows still furrowed. "What if I hadn't shown up tonight?"

"That would have totally sucked, and think of how much hell I'd have caught from Nate after Jewel told him what I'd done."

She laughed, and he was glad to see her guard come down a little.

"Did you have any more naked men in your office this afternoon?" He loved the flash of embarrassment that lit up her eyes, but just as quickly, she blinked it away.

"You weren't naked, but thankfully no."

She licked her lips, making him want to follow the path of her tongue with his own, but he promised himself they'd take things slow. He was determined to prove to her that he wasn't after only one thing—but the more he tried not to think about it, the more he noticed their thighs brushing, the press of her breasts against his chest.

"You're looking at me like *I'm* naked," she said just above a whisper.

"Am I? I'm sorry." He twirled her around, and she laughed, a sweet, musical sound that he wanted to hear more of.

She came back to him, wrapping her arms around his neck, and said, "No you're not."

"I am sorry if it makes you uncomfortable, but I can't help looking at you. You're gorgeous."

"Sam." She dropped her eyes. "You're embarrassing me."

He lifted her chin and gazed into her eyes, lured like metal to magnet past the invisible line he'd drawn to keep himself in check. His hand moved to the base of her spine. In his mind she was already his, but in his heart he knew it wasn't going to be that easy.

"I don't want to embarrass you."

Her lips parted on a sigh, and he fought the urge to cross

that damn line and finally kiss her, taste her, *brand* her. He'd spent the last three days thinking of her, and now here she was, in his arms, and he couldn't even kiss her.

"Tell me something about yourself, Faith. Do you have any brothers or sisters?"

"I have a younger brother and sister. Mack lives in Oak Falls, Virginia, where we're from. And my sister, Charley, is studying marine biology in Harborside, Massachusetts." She moved more fluidly, more relaxed.

"Ah, you're the oldest. That's why you're so careful and focused."

"Because I'm the oldest? Then where does a naughty beast like you fall in the massive Braden clan?" A hint of playfulness sparkled in her eyes.

"I'm the troublemaking second child. Can't you tell?" He ran his hand up the length of her back and felt her shudder against him. "Maybe you should tame the beast in me."

"Wouldn't that be a shame?" She held his gaze. "All those girls left without a naughty beast to play with?"

"You are a sexy little thing, aren't you?" Heat flamed inside him. "Would that be such a shame? Leaving them beastless?" His hand slid back down her back to the curve just above her ass.

Her breath came faster, her hips rocked forward, and her words came out low and seductive. "You tell me. What do you want?"

"You." *In my bed, on my lap, on my boat.* He wanted to be with her, share space, hold her, talk to her—and make love to her. The first of those were new emotions, the type he'd been wrestling with since the wedding, and they got stronger with every word they spoke.

"Why?"

He met her curious gaze. "Because you're smart and careful, and you keep yourself in a safe little bubble so you don't get hurt." He placed his hand over her heart, feeling it beating frantically against his palm. "But you want to be touched and loved and cherished. And I like when you come out of that safe world of yours and tiptoe on the Sammy side."

She smiled and trapped her lower lip between her teeth.

"Because I've resisted you for all this time," he said, holding her gaze. "And I don't want to do that anymore."

She leaned back a little. "I'm not jumping into bed with you."

"That's not what I want." He smiled. "Not tonight, anyway."

"Sam!" She halfheartedly pulled away, but he held her in place, needing her to hear the truth. "So all of this is just a means to an end?"

"Not the end you think, Faith. Not just sex."

"Right." She shifted her eyes away.

He silently cursed himself for screwing this up, but how could he hide his attraction to her when it was the last thing he wanted to do?

"I'm trying to be honest. How can you expect any man to look at you and not want to touch you, to kiss you? You're the sexiest woman I've ever met, the way you're careful one minute and confident and challenging the next. And you drive me insane in the most exquisite way, running hot one second and then scared in the blink of an eye. But mostly it's the way your eyes devour me but your words slay me."

"Sam," she whispered. Her hands slid down his chest to his waist, hot and seductive as they swayed almost imperceptibly to the music, their bodies touching at every possible point.

"Your eyes are so full of want and worry. I want to ease your worries and savor your *wants*."

She swallowed hard. Knowing he was affecting her as wickedly as she was affecting him spurred him on.

"I thought we could have dinner and get to know each other without doing anything more tonight, but I honestly can't stop thinking about kissing you. It's not that I'm trying to get you in my bed tonight, or tomorrow, or next week. But…"

Her heart pounded wildly against his chest. Her fingers dug into his waist, sending bolts of lust to his core. She blinked up at him, her eyes dark as the night sky, sending pinpricks of awareness down his spine. He couldn't hold back a second longer. He had to know if she was right there with him.

"What do you *feel*, Faith?" His voice was rough with restrained desire. "Right now, what do you want? Does any part of you *not* want to be here? Do you want to talk? Or do you want to stop worrying, stop craving, and finally get a taste of *us*? One. Single. Kiss."

Her eyes widened with surprise and quickly narrowed again, filling with untamed desire. Without a word she went up on her toes, and he claimed her, crushing her sweet body to his. The kiss was hungry and messy, demanding and urgent, as their tongues crashed together in an effort to taste more, *take* more. She tasted of night and lust and unnamed things that made his heart swell. Her luscious curves pressed against him, making him hard and hungry for more. His hands slid down her spine, earning a wanton moan from deep within her. He fought for control, but his hands itched to feel her hot skin, to hear that sexy moan as he came down over her naked body and buried himself deep inside.

Her hands moved up his chest, pressing against his pecs, while her hips wreaked havoc against his hard length. He slid one hand beneath the back of her shirt, needing the connection with nothing in between. A sinful sound escaped her, pulling a groan from deep within him. How was he supposed to resist her? How could he protect her from him when she consumed his every thought, drove his every move?

SHOCKED AT HER own eager response to the force of

pleasure one kiss from Sam was bringing to every inch of her body, Faith tried to pull back. But her brain didn't get the message, and she went up higher on her toes, trying to get closer, to take the kiss deeper. His hands were big and hot, branding her through her clothes and making her swell and ache between her legs. More, she wanted *more*. She clung to his neck, fighting the urge to climb him like a mountain and devour him limb from limb. But his parents were right downstairs, and if her legs wrapped around his waist she'd never want to let him go.

Oh no, no, no. She needed to slow down. She couldn't go there with him. He'd fried her brain cells. *Again*. This was becoming a habit, first his glances, then his words, then his touch, and now this...this delicious, incredible, perfect kiss. She didn't want to be his plaything for a night and know he'd be right back on the trail of some other woman a day or two later.

But his glorious, talented mouth was too delicious to resist. His tongue moved roughly over hers, and as if he knew exactly what she needed, he eased his efforts. Kissing her softer, slower, and bringing a whole new meaning to the word torture. His tongue moved sensually over hers, his hands pressed against her bare back, holding her possessively but not controlling her. Pleasure radiated out from every point in her body—her knees, her hips, her breasts—with the tantalizing tenderness of the kiss. He took control without force or domination, and without severing their connection, making the kiss that much sweeter.

His hands slid beneath her hair, and then his big, strong hands framed her face as he drew back, placing a series of shivery kisses on her cheeks, her chin, and finally, on her mouth once again.

"*That*, was…" he whispered against her lips, before pressing his mouth to hers again. "Open your eyes, Faith. Look at me. Be with me."

His intimate request brought her eyes open, and the way he was looking at her, like he'd been waiting his whole life to kiss her, to hold her this close, was dizzying. She sank back down to her heels. Her legs felt like wet noodles, but her body felt like it was on speed. Wanting, craving, aching for another kiss.

He touched his forehead to hers, and a satisfied smile curved his lips. "Do you want to leave?"

"No."

A flash of heat sprang into his eyes, and just as quickly they warmed with an emotion less urgent, less sinful, but just as powerful, and he touched his mouth to hers again.

"Thank God." His voice was thick with desire.

She wanted this—his kiss, his touch—but she'd almost lost control with him, and she needed him to know her limits. "But I can't do more."

"No more," he repeated.

She shook her head, and he wrapped her in his arms and held her tight, his cheek resting against the top of her head, and she thought she could be happy staying right there in his arms forever.

Her stomach growled and she groaned.

"Guess I can't pretend that was because you're hungry for me," he teased.

That would hardly be pretending.

After another sweet kiss, they sat down to eat. Her heart was still going a little crazy. Sam lifted the lids from their dinners, unveiling a delicious meal of salmon, steamed vegetables, and baked potatoes.

They talked and ate, and Faith remembered to ask him if he'd made the donation to the group.

His fork stopped midair. "Yes. You wouldn't take a donation directly, and I want to help."

"But, Sam, you gave too much."

"I don't think there is such a thing." He speared a piece of salmon and popped it into his mouth.

She had no idea how to play this game. Was it a game?

He set down his fork, sipped his wine, then took her hand again and moved his chair closer to hers.

"Faith, what good is success if I can't use it to help others? You did. You started the whole program. That had to take time, energy, and money."

"It did, but I did it because of what I'd gone through."

"Why can't you accept that I want to help?" His reaction was so visceral it compelled her to listen more carefully. "You told me that those women were in the group because of guys like me. I don't cheat, and I think I've made that pretty clear, but even so, I want to help them. I can't stand thinking about what Brittany or Hilary, or you or Vivian, or the other girls went through."

She wanted to deny his sincerity, but she realized she was fighting against herself, against what she was afraid of, instead of taking Sam for his word, and that wasn't fair to either of them.

"I'm sure you know Lira's life is a bit of a mess right now, too," he said, taking her by surprise that he knew about Lira's situation. "I think we can help each other out."

"Oh?" Hearing the curiosity in her voice made her realize that earlier today she might have responded with a sarcastic, *I bet.*

"She has a lot of office management experience, and I need someone to handle the admin work and help organize sponsors and coordinate things for the Rough Riders barbecue."

Her eyes widened with hope. "You think you might be able to give her a job?"

"We're talking about a long-distance trial run. We'll see how it goes. If she's as good as her experience indicates, she's been underpaid for so long, and I'm not sure she realizes how much she's really worth. But don't worry. If it works out, she'd be well taken care of at Rough Riders with full benefits."

He'd already spoken to Lira about this? "You really do care."

"Yes, I do. I was brought up to help others. I've done it all my life. I'm not sure why that's so hard to believe."

"Maybe because you didn't go to the car wash intent on helping." She arched a brow, and that earned her a sexy smile.

"You're right, but that doesn't take away from how strongly I feel about helping. If I didn't care, I wouldn't have given it a second thought."

It was hard to admit what she wanted to say next, but after all he'd done for her tonight, and for the group, she owed him the truth—even if it was embarrassing.

"I was judging you by what I knew about you, Sam. I'm sorry. That wasn't fair."

"Then get to know me better. Find out who I really am." He looked at her expectantly. "Go out with me, Faith."

"We went over this. You don't date, and—"

"And you don't sleep around. I get it. I'm not asking you to sleep around. *I'm* making a change. I want to *date* you. I've spent my life avoiding anything remotely close to emotional connections, but I can't avoid it with you. You've gotten under my skin, and I don't want to ignore what I'm feeling."

"You want to date *only* me? Sam, I can't—"

Suddenly she was in his arms, their bodies colliding, his mouth capturing hers, kissing away her worries. He took the kiss deeper, as if he needed her to feel, to taste, how much he wanted her. He was holding her like she was already his, making her feel desired and sexy and incredibly safe again, softening her resolve.

"Sam," she whispered, touching her stinging lips. She probably should be annoyed that he'd cut her off with a kiss, but she wasn't in the least. She'd needed that kiss.

He held her face in his hands. The look in his eyes was pure, unadulterated possession, and unexpectedly, *hope*.

"Don't overthink this." His eyes bored into her. "Don't pick it apart and put me into a box where I don't belong. *This* is right. I know you feel it, too. You won't go out with me unless I'm faithful to you, and I want that for you, for me. I want that with you. I want *you*, Faith. I don't want my mouth on anyone else, and I sure as hell don't want yours on some other guy."

"You're such a big risk, Sam. And I know that's a horrible thing to say." The honesty came without thought, and she couldn't stop the words from tumbling out. "If you cheat on me, it will completely humiliate me, and I have to live and work here. I can't just pick up and run from it."

She paced, remembering how much it had hurt to catch her ex-boyfriend out with another girl, and weighed the risks of getting involved with Sam against the thrum of desire raging through her.

"I won't hurt you," he promised.

"I believe your intentions are sincere, but you might make a mistake. And my job, my life, everything is so good right now." She continued pacing, too conflicted to look at him.

As if he knew she was fighting eye contact, he closed the gap between them, framed her face with his hands again, and forced her to look into his all-consuming gaze.

"I will never make the very poor choice of hurting you. Trust me, Faith, and I promise I won't let you down. Have faith in me," he whispered, and God help her, she wanted to. "I will not only make sure your life remains on solid ground, but I'll make it better."

"You're quite a salesman. Full of promises." Her words were teasing, but inside she was on the verge of jumping out of her safe little world and into the arms of the biggest risk she'd ever taken, and she didn't want to have to claw for purchase. "I need complete transparency, Sam."

"Crystal clear." His unwavering confidence made her want to believe every word he said.

"Do you even know what that means?"

"I'm serially a non-committer, not an idiot." He took her hand and led her to the railing overlooking the ocean, sliding his arm around her waist. She fit perfectly against his hard body, as if that spot were made just for her.

"What do you see when you look out there?" he asked.

"The reflection of the moon in the ocean. It's peaceful."

"It *appears* peaceful. But the minute you step foot in a boat, you're in the hands of Mother Nature. She can batter you in the blink of an eye. For me it's a risk worth taking, because I know I can handle anything she throws at me."

He turned his attention, and his piercing stare, back to Faith.

"When you look at me, you're afraid to step in the boat. But you don't have to be. I know you can't handle squalls or heavy winds, and *I'd* never risk losing the way you look at me in those moments when you see past my reputation. I see flashes of clarity, and in the next breath your eyes cloud over and you put your life jacket on. You don't need a life jacket, Faith. I'll keep you afloat."

Everything he said struck her heart. No one could fake the depth of emotion she heard in his voice.

"Doesn't it scare you, Sam, to suddenly *want* to commit to a girl like me? To someone so scared of being hurt?"

"Wanting to commit scares the shit out of me, but wanting to commit to you? Faith, you're the only girl I want to commit to. It took me thirty years to figure that out." His lips lifted in a warm smile.

"Don't you want to be with someone who parties every night? Someone who's wild, maybe brings another girl into the mix? Because I'll never do that. I don't share well."

He looked up toward the sky, cursing under his breath, but not angry. It was more like he was admonishing himself. When his eyes met hers again, they were dead serious.

"I'm not ashamed of anything I've done in my past, Faith. Everything I did, every choice I made, every tryst, brought me to this moment. Those girls I hooked up with are not the kind of girls I'd want to call mine. Can't you see what's going on?"

See? She could barely breathe.

"I want to be with *you*. I want to feel what I feel right now, and more, and that's only possible with you. You are the only woman who interests me, not anyone else. And if you think I'd ever share you with any other man *or* woman, you're wrong. Most importantly, I don't want you to worry that I'm with anyone else. Ever. I want you to know in your heart that I've given you my word. And my word is stronger than steel."

His honesty shattered her vow to remain uninvolved. She drew in an uneven breath, wanting to be closer to him, wanting the confidence he portrayed to be real and true, and pushed aside her fears. Vivian would have her head on a platter, or worse, have *his* head on a platter, but Faith couldn't live her life in fear of what might happen, and she couldn't make decisions based on what others believed.

As she gazed into his eyes again she saw another layer of the man he was unveiling. *Taking off his cover.* And she liked that man very much.

"Okay."

"Okay?" His eyes widened.

"Okay, yes, but—"

He picked her up and spun her around, kissing her fast and hard as she laughed.

"No buts," he said.

"Sam." Smiling, she wound her arms around his neck and he guided her legs around his waist. "I'm not easy."

"No shit." He kissed her again.

"I'm also jaded."

He kissed her again, still smiling. "Good thing I'm patient."

"If you hurt me, I'll castrate you."

"Baby, if I hurt you, then I deserve it."

Faith couldn't resist kissing him again, and as their mouths came together, she felt buffered from the world, safe and special in the eye of a hurricane.

Chapter Ten

SAM AWOKE TUESDAY morning feeling like he could tackle anything, which was a good thing, considering the workload on his desk. He texted Faith, then spent the morning getting his arms around his work at Rough Riders. Feeling more in control of his life than he had in years, he made a solid dent in no time and then Skyped with Lira to bring her up to speed.

"The annual Rough Riders barbecue is a major event for us. Corporate sponsors provide equipment for our high-adventure tours. Sometimes they provide lodging, too, depending on where we're going, with hopes that our clients will purchase their equipment in the future. We invite previous, current, and potential sponsors to the barbecue to secure their business. I guess it's like wining and dining in the business world, but for outdoorsmen. We invite everyone. Just as we do with sponsors, we invite previous and current clients, as well as potential corporate clients we hope to reel in," Sam explained. "It's also a great opportunity for community building. So hopefully, if this all works out and you don't quit before the event, you can come and meet the people you'll be speaking with."

"Oh, I'm not going to quit," Lira said. "I'm excited to get started. But I have to admit, I didn't realize there was such a big market for this type of thing in the corporate world."

"Corporations are doing everything they can to keep their executives on board, and lavishing them with high-end adventures is quickly becoming a go-to bonus. We want Rough Riders to be the only company that comes to mind when they're ready," Sam explained. "You'll be contacting previous and potential sponsors and clients who haven't yet responded to the invitation to the event, as well as coordinating the mess of financial work I've left undone."

Lira's dark eyes widened with excitement. "I can't wait to dive in. I looked over the documents you sent last night, and I've got a few good ideas of how to better organize the finances. I'll put my thoughts on paper and send them over and get started on contacting people right away."

"You sound as excited as I am to hand all this off."

"I am. Thank you so much for this opportunity, Sam. And for allowing me to work from home for now. You can't imagine how much this means to me. I won't let you down."

Based on her references, he had a feeling she was right.

After the call, Sam pushed away from his desk, thinking about Faith. She hadn't responded to his text yet, but he knew she was probably focused on her patients, as she should be. Too keyed up to sit still, he headed outdoors and surveyed the crowd of twentysomethings who had appeared en mass over the last hour. There were already a dozen boats in the water, a typical summer afternoon at Rough Riders. Except for one detail. A week ago Sam would have been right in the thick of the bikini-wearing and crop-top-clad girls, eating up the attention they were currently lavishing on Tex. But his mind was immersed in thoughts of Faith. Her sweet voice, her enticing scent, and the trust she'd placed in his capable hands last night were all he could think about, and he wasn't about to mess that up.

He stood on the sandy shore watching women fawn over Tex. They ran their fingers over Tex's arms and shoulders, *ooh*ing and *aah*ing over the colorful ink and throwing out flirtatious giggles like scraps of meat to a hungry bear. As Sam watched, he realized he wasn't checking out their bodies or wondering which one he might see later at a club, as he might have before Faith had agreed to go out with him. He was cataloging the number of customers to the number of available boats. He continued watching with intense curiosity and disbelief at how quickly his mind-set had changed. Tex draped an arm over a blonde's shoulder and nodded at Sam with a big-ass smile on his face, pulling him from his thoughts. Tex had come to Rough Riders on the heels of his own adventure company disbanding. He was used to these types of perks of the business and obviously enjoyed them.

Better you than me. The thought was so foreign, it gave Sam pause. Seconds later he thought it again, with more vehemence this time, and something inside him clicked into place, as if it hadn't realized it was off-kilter until the thought jostled it free.

With a satisfied smile, he turned to check on Patrick, who was helping a group of teenagers into kayaks. He had been tall and lanky when Sam had hired him last summer, with a shock of blond hair and youthful, unshaven cheeks. The last year had manned him up. He wore his hair closely cropped on the sides, a little longer on top. He'd broadened and filled out, gaining a manlier shape, patchy whiskers, and a set of car keys. *Sixteen.*

At sixteen Sam had lost his virginity, fallen in lust, or infatuation, *or both*, with a girl in a neighboring town, and she'd broken his teenage heart. He rarely thought of that time of his life, but now that he was, he wondered if that breakup had more to do with the way he'd lived his life than he remembered.

"Dude." Ty's hand landed heavily on Sam's shoulder, pulling him from the memory. At twenty-six, dressed in board shorts and no shirt, with his long dark hair falling over his eyes, Ty fit right in with those carefree, flirty girls—as he should— magnifying for Sam that at almost thirty-one, with a burgeoning business and one woman feeding his heart, he'd turned a corner and he was finally on the right path.

"Hey," Sam said. "I didn't hear you arrive."

"My stealth ninja skills." Ty lifted his chin in the direction of the women dipping their toes in the water and giggling while Tex helped them with their life jackets. "Why aren't you over there helping those lovely ladies into their life jackets? Every year they get hotter."

Thinking of Faith, he said, "She sure does."

"She?" Ty cocked a brow.

Sam headed toward the boathouse with Ty on his heels. He grabbed one end of a rowboat. "I'm seeing Faith. Grab the other side of this, will ya?"

They carried the boat out to the water, and as they headed back in, Ty said, "*Seeing?* Sammy, you're going against Cole just to get laid? What's wrong with you? He'll have your ass the minute he gets home."

Sam's muscles corded tight at the way he referenced Faith. He picked up another rowboat and motioned for Ty to get the other end. "It's not like that."

"What's not like that? Cole's coming back next week, so if you're making a move, you'd better be damn quick about it."

They carried the boat out and set it by the water. The boats didn't need to be moved, but Sam needed the distraction. He'd had an incredible night with Faith, and by some miracle she'd agreed to go out with him—only him. They'd hung out on the roof for hours, and after she left they'd texted until nearly one o'clock in the morning. Sam was up half the night thinking about her, and he'd woken up with her right there in the forefront of his mind again. In a few hours, which felt like a lifetime, he'd see her again. The last thing he wanted to do was talk about the guy who'd warned him away from her.

"Ty, I'm not out to get laid with Faith, so don't say that again. I like her a hell of a lot, and you know what it means to hear me say that. I'm not going to fuck that up, much less let Cole fuck it up."

His brother scrubbed a hand down his face and blinked a few times, as if he'd seen a ghost. "You're serious? I mean Faith's hot, but she's not your usual type."

"Dead serious, and exactly. She's nothing like the girls I usually hook up with, because I'm *not* hooking up, Ty. I'm seeing only Faith, and I'll deal with Cole when he gets back from his honeymoon." Sam heard his name and looked over at the girls getting in the boats. He sort of recognized the brunette waving at him. He couldn't remember her name, but he'd partied with her a time or two. He waved and turned his attention back to his brother.

"Anything else?" Sam crossed his arms, feeling edgy and protective of Faith.

Ty paced for a minute, shaking his head. "So you're what? Out of the game completely? Sam, think about this. I'm sure Faith's great, but how are you going to go from a different meal every night to the same one day after day? Aren't you worried you'll get bored?"

Sam clenched his teeth. "Bored? Hell no. I can't explain it, but something happens when I'm with her. And when I'm not? Like right now? I'm carrying freaking boats around because I can't sit still. I can't wait to see her. When have I ever felt like that?"

"Never that I know of. Shit, Sam. First Nate, then Cole, now you? Y'all dropped like flies."

"I didn't *drop* like anything. Look, I know this comes as a shock. It does to me, too, but what I feel for her is…" He searched his brain for the right word—*huge? powerful? all-consuming?*—and finally went with something he knew Ty would understand. "You know that feeling of reaching the peak when you climb?"

Ty nodded, his dark eyes skeptical.

"Indescribable, right? But too powerful to ignore. And, Ty, I don't want to ignore it." He smiled, thinking of the time he told Nate to get his ass in gear and go after Jewel. At that point Sam couldn't ever imagine being on the other side of the fence. Now there was no place else he'd rather be.

FAITH WAS RUNNING on too little sleep, too much adrenaline, and still reeling from Sam's early-morning text— *Good morning, beautiful*—which he'd followed up with, *Miss your sweet smile.* Even his texts made her heart go wild. She knew she had to be cautious and try to keep her head on straight about Sam, given his history with women, but that wasn't easy when everything he did and said turned her inside out. She'd been blown away by his confessions and his determination to win her over, but it was her own emotions that bowled her over. Just thinking about the way her body had sparked so hot she feared she'd combust when they were together got her hot and bothered again.

Work was insanely busy again, but at least Brandy had scheduled a lunch break for her today and had offered to order food to be brought in so she could do some research for WAC.

"Brandy," she said into the intercom. "I'll be in the break room if you need me."

Faith set her laptop on the table, pulled out her notebook, and began poring over the list of women's organizations she'd jotted down.

"There's my sweet girlfriend."

Her head snapped up at the sound of Sam's voice and his use of the word *girlfriend*, which made her stomach flutter. "Sam? What are you doing here?" He came around the table with a bag from Jazzy Joe's Café and a smile on his luscious lips. Oh, how she loved his lips!

She'd heard girls say that one kiss could move heaven and earth, but in all her kisses, until Sam, no one had ever come close. He kissed like he did everything. He was confident and commanding with a little finesse and a whole lot of seduction.

"Having lunch with you." He leaned down and kissed her. "Mm. I missed your kisses."

I missed your everything. "Sam," she whispered. "We can't make out at my work." *No matter how much I want to.* She'd relived their kisses so many times she was sure she was grinning like a lovesick fool, and because of that she'd avoided Jon as much as she could. That man had a romance radar. He'd known one of their billing clerks was in love before she did, and she wanted no part of trying to explain that she was seeing Cole's brother. She was worried enough about how Cole might react when he found out. Either way, kissing Sam in the break room was definitely pushing the envelope.

"Who's making out? I was kissing you hello. It's a common greeting among people who are dating." He sat beside her, unwrapped a sandwich, and set it in front of her, as if he hadn't just thrown the most enticing loop into her chaotic day.

"What about Jon?" Her mind spun in too many directions to make sense of Sam, at her work, having lunch.

"Butterscotch? I just saw him in the hall." He reached for her hand. "Are you worried about him finding out that we're going out? That we're *dating*? Because I dare anyone to stand in our way."

God, she loved that arrogant side of him in ways she probably shouldn't.

"Sam, this is my job."

"I'm kidding. Jon's cool. It's not like we're having sex on the lunch table." His eyes went volcanic. "Unless you're into that."

She covered her face with her hands and let out a breathy, "Ohmygod." Heat spread up her chest at the thought of having sex right there on the table. With Sam! How could she ever look at that table the same after this?

"What's the big deal? Should I have called you first? I'm not very good at this dating stuff yet, but I'll get there." He sat back and his eyes went serious.

"Actually, you're *very* good at this dating stuff. I'm just a little uptight about work. I love my job, and I don't want anything to ruin that. I'm sure it's fine. Or at least I hope it's fine. Jon knows I wouldn't do anything like…what you said."

At least not when other people are in the office. Sam definitely had a magical power that made her mind go places it never had.

His lips quirked up in a devilish smile. "Whatever you're thinking about, keep going." He moved closer, bringing her legs between his. His hands moved up her thighs, as he touched his cheek to hers and said in a gravelly, seductive voice, "You look so hot right now. I'd like to tear those scrubs off of you and feast on your body."

Melting. Melting. Melting. She gripped the edge of the chair, hoping she wouldn't slither to the floor in a hot and bothered mess.

"Oh, wait," he whispered. "We're behaving ourselves." He pressed a kiss to her cheek, then sat back and picked up his sandwich while she tried to remember how to function.

"You should eat. You only have"—he looked at the clock on the wall—"another forty-five minutes."

"Right." Her voice cracked. She cleared her throat, and Sam

handed her the drink he'd brought. "Thank you." Three big gulps later she was breathing normally again, but her mind was still playing over what he'd said. Would she ever get used to this? To him?

"What's all this?" He pointed to her notebook and laptop.

Another big drink, and she forced those dirty thoughts to the side enough to speak like someone other than a horny mess. "Remember I mentioned that I wanted to find resources for the WAC members? I've been putting together a list of women's organizations that have therapists, career advisers, even legal resources." She flipped the page and showed him another list. "These are therapy practices that work with charitable organizations throughout Maryland."

"Is WAC a nonprofit?"

"No. When I set up the forum, I never anticipated we would be doing anything other than hosting the forums." She pulled up the website on her laptop and showed him the monitor. "It's free to join, and we get a handful of donations. Nothing like yours, just enough to cover some of the hosting costs. We've only recently begun holding in-person events like the car wash. I haven't had time to think it all through, since the idea of doing more really just hit last weekend, but I feel good about trying to offer more for our members."

"It looks like you've already made great progress. If it's not a nonprofit, is it an LLC?"

She nibbled on her lip and shook her head. "I haven't even

gotten that far."

"So you bought the domain and hosting, but you never registered WAC as a business?"

She shook her head, cringing inwardly.

"Well, there are things you need to do to protect yourself from being sued. Do you have a business attorney?" He suddenly sounded very businesslike, very unlike the sexy seducer who was looking at her like she was lunch a minute ago.

And she liked this side of him very much.

"No, not yet. But now it's on my list." She picked up a pen and scribbled *business attorney*.

Sam took out his phone and scrolled through his contacts. "Faith, you definitely need to establish WAC as a business entity, not only because you take donations, but you're probably liable for all sorts of things under the eyes of the law. I don't know if you can get in any legal trouble giving out online advice, or referrals to other services you haven't personally vetted, but we need to make sure you're protected."

His use of *we* made her stomach flutter and her heart do a little happy dance. She couldn't believe she hadn't thought about the legal side of things. It made sense to form a business entity, especially since Sam had donated so much money. Usually donations came in increments of a few dollars. His donation was beyond generous and would go a long way, especially now that there were going to be legal costs involved. But what he was doing, making sure *she* was legally protected, meant even more to her.

"I'll hook you up with my buddy Brent Holloway. We grew up together and his office is right in town." He held up his finger as he called. "Hey, Brent, it's Sam." He paused. "Yeah, I got that paperwork, thanks. I'm a little behind, but I'll get right on it. I need a favor. My girlfriend's got an online forum…"

As he explained Faith's position to Brent, Faith reveled in how easily he said *girlfriend* again.

"That's great. Hold on." Sam moved the phone to his side and asked quietly, "He can fit us in Thursday at six thirty. Will that work?"

Us? "Yes, absolutely. Thank you."

He leaned forward and kissed her. With a tease in his eyes he whispered, "Girlfriend," then tugged her into another quick kiss before turning back to the call.

After he ended the call he said, "You're all set. Why don't I pick you up after work Thursday, and we'll go over together. You'll love Brent. He's a great guy."

"Sounds good. Thank you."

"No problem. You need business insurance, too. We'll talk to Brent about that. Our buddy Phil D'Amato can make sure you get whatever coverage you need at a fair rate." He searched her eyes, which were probably wide as hard-boiled eggs. "Are you okay? Am I being too pushy?"

"Pushy? No. Sam, you're a force to be reckoned with, but in the very best way. You brought me lunch, and in twenty minutes you've got my business going in the right direction. I'm a little embarrassed that I didn't think of all of this myself. I'm usually so good at making sure every box is checked and evaluated, and then you walk in and in mere minutes see that I've dropped the ball."

He smiled and touched her face. "You didn't drop the ball. You're focused on the aspects you should be focused on, helping others. I have a lot of experience with businesses and the liabilities you face as an owner. Rough Riders is a different type of business, but the framework of every business begins with certain elements."

"You should be my business manager." She was only half kidding.

"This is all you, baby. Your business, your forum, your ideas. I'm just giving you a helping hand."

"I just can't believe how much you're helping me." She leaned in closer, feeling too far away.

He slid forward on his chair, so close she could kiss him if she leaned in an inch.

"Believe it, Faith. I've wanted to be close to you for so long, and once that barrier came down, it opened the floodgates. You're stuck with all of me now, and if I overstep my bounds"—his eyes darkened seductively—"you'll have to restrain me."

His nearness, his words, and his piercing stare sent a rush of passion through her. He leaned so close she could see gold flecks in the center of his eyes. She would never make it through the rest of the day until their date later without one more kiss to hold her over. Her heart was pounding, her mind was begging, *Kiss me*, and her employee brain was losing the battle to remain in control. Sam's tongue slicked over his lower lip, and she heard an embarrassingly needy sound stream from her lungs. What happened to the levelheaded woman she'd always been? She felt like an addict, wanting more of her best addiction.

"Kiss me quick, Sam, before someone comes i—"

Her last word was smothered as his mouth pressed roughly against hers, fierce and urgent. She clutched his shirt and held on for the scintillating ride. Just when she thought, *This is so worth getting in trouble for*, Sam slowed them down to a series of languid, mind-numbing kisses. She touched his scruffy cheek and pushed her fingers into his hair as they drew apart. She was dazed, her lips still tingling, like the rest of her overheated body.

"Sorry," she said, slipping her hands from his hair. "I love your hair and I've wanted to do that for so long. I couldn't help myself."

He was looking at her as no one else ever had, as he seemed to do so often. Like he wanted to fall into her. *Breathe, breathe, breathe.*

"Don't apologize for touching me," he said warmly. "I want you to touch me."

And boy do I ever want to touch you. She shook her head, trying to clear the dirty thoughts and focus on Sam. Despite everything he'd said, she needed him to know she didn't expect him to keep doing so much for her.

"After everything you did last night, I feel kind of guilty. I hope you don't feel like you have to keep doing more for me because I was afraid to go out with you. You've got me, Sam. You can stop doing all these things for me and just be yourself."

He slid his hand to the nape of her neck and tugged her in closer. "I think for the first time in my life, that's exactly who I am."

Chapter Eleven

SAM CLIMBED THE steps to Faith's apartment later that evening sporting a ridiculous grin. Their second date felt like a milestone, maybe because for him it was. He knew he was coming on strong, but he couldn't help it. She really had opened up some sort of floodgates he never knew existed, and he was rolling with it. Just like he was rolling with coaxing sweet Faith out of her safety zone, and hopefully earning her trust, by showing her that he could have fun without debauchery. *Although a little debauchery is always nice.*

Faith answered the door, flashing the smile he loved so much, the one that instantly lit up her beautiful dark eyes and made her breathe a little harder. The one that made his heart take notice.

"Sam," she said dreamily.

Her voice, along with her smiling eyes, brought him silently closer. They'd just seen each other a few hours ago, and already he was starved for her. His arm circled her waist, and in the seconds before their mouths came together, her eyes fluttered closed. He loved those unguarded seconds, when he could see she wasn't thinking about his past and how it fit into his present, but of how much she wanted to be with him. He drank in the sweetness of their kiss, fighting the urge to take it deeper, to let her feel everything he was holding back. It was a kiss of divine ecstasy, a kiss full of promises of what was to come—trust, he hoped, and more. He needed to put space between them to keep from going further, but his body pressed forward. Everything about him had been moving forward since he'd given in to his feelings for Faith, which was a huge change for the man who moved from one woman to another, always on the same level, in the same realm, year after year.

His tongue swept over hers, her touch searing into his skin.

Moving forward with Faith was a million times better than anything he could have imagined. He felt alive, focused, driven. As their lips parted—his aching, burning, for more—he gazed into her eyes and somehow knew that only Faith could have this effect on him.

"Hey, sweet one," he said as her eyes came open. "How are you?"

"Better now." Her fisted hands trembled against his chest, and he covered one with his own.

Her eyes dropped to their hands and she whispered, "Sorry," as she unfurled her fingers.

He kissed her again, tenderly this time. "No apologies for

touching, remember?" He raked his eyes down her body, noticing that she'd worn the Rough Riders hoodie he'd given her over a clingy white V-neck shirt. She shivered against him. "Cold?"

"Hot. *Hot, hot, hot,*" she whispered.

He laughed. "I'll take that as a compliment. You look really sexy."

She looked down at her outfit, fidgeting with the long necklace dangling between her breasts. "You sure this is okay? I wasn't sure, but you said to wear jeans and dress comfortably."

"I'm sure." He gave her another quick kiss. "Ready to go?"

She cleared her throat and looked down at his hand, which was still wrapped possessively around her waist.

"Guess I need to let you go. Damn, I hate that."

She laughed and playfully pushed at his stomach. After another quick kiss he reluctantly released her. As she grabbed her purse from a table by the door, he glanced around her living room. It was exactly as he'd pictured it, neat and feminine, with floral pillows on the sofa, a bookshelf full of medical and fiction books, *for your smart, sexy brain,* and a few leafy green plants in front of the balcony doors.

"Okay, ready." She put her purse strap crosswise over her body, which pressed her shirt down between her breasts.

"I like that purse," he teased.

She rolled her eyes as they walked out the door. "Such a man." His hand circled her waist and she said, "Afraid I'll disappear?"

"Staking my claim. You're the one who wanted exclusivity. Rethinking that now?"

"Not on your life, Mr. Braden, but fair's fair." She slipped her arm around his waist as they descended the stairs. "You showed up at my work twice. Now you have to deal with the fallout when your brother comes home and fires me for fraternizing with his sibling."

"I'm pretty sure that's not an appropriate reason to be fired."

"We'll see."

"I already sent him a text telling him that we needed to talk when he returns. Don't worry. I'll always have your back."

She gazed up at him with a curious look in her eyes as they walked toward the parking lot. "Even if I dump you? Or will you ask him to fire me just to get back at me?"

"If you dump me?" He leaned down for another quick taste of her luscious lips. "All of the above."

"You're impossible. Where are we going?"

"You'll see. On my 'things I've never done with a woman' list is going for a ride on my bike." He nodded to his motorcycle.

"We're taking your motorcycle?" She took a step backward. "Sam, I've never ridden one."

He drew her against him again. "Not to worry. You'll just have to hold on to me."

"What if I let go?"

"Why would you *ever* want to do that?" He grabbed a helmet from the back of the bike and slid it over her head. "Jesus, Faith. You just got even hotter."

"I'm sure helmet hair will do wonders for my looks."

"Trust me. Your looks are not in jeopardy." He lifted her by the waist, making her squeal as he set her on the bike. "Seeing you straddle my monster like that? Babe, you've just reached the danger zone. Good luck keeping me off of you tonight."

"WE'RE BEHAVING, REMEMBER?" Faith said as Sam straddled the bike in front of her, although behaving was the last thing on her mind. His gray shirt stretched tightly over his broad back, outlining every muscle all the way down to his waist. Even his black belt looked hot on him. And his bike? His *monster*? Sam wasn't kidding. Seeing his powerful legs straddling it definitely turned her on.

"Behaving. Yeah, I remember. It's torture, but I remember. Now put your arms around me."

"So bossy," she teased as she wrapped her arms around him. He grabbed her by the forearms and tugged her forward, until her thighs were spread wide against his hips, her breasts mashed to his back.

"Perfect. Hold tight. Don't let go and you'll be fine."

The bike roared to life, sending the most thrilling vibration between her legs, up her chest, and everywhere in between. She had no idea where they were going, and she was scared to death of actually riding on this thing. But holding Sam, feeling the rumble of the bike hum through his body to hers, was like foreplay. When they pulled out of the parking space and onto the road, she clung tightly to him, and when he hit the open road, that vibration was even stronger, and her fear turned to excitement.

Holding tight as they flew through town, Faith felt every one of Sam's muscles. His abs jumped and flexed against her hands, and she couldn't resist spreading her fingers so she could feel more of him. Sam was right. There was no way she was going to let go of this scrumptious man. She felt exhilarated and freer than she ever had as he drove past Chelsea's Boutique, the marina, and Mr. B's. The signs Sam had hung just for her were gone, but the memory of that night would never fade.

Faith didn't care where they were headed as they left town and Sam kept going. This was already the most exhilarating ride of her life.

A few minutes later they pulled into Whiskey Bro's, a shady-looking bar just before the bridge that led into Peaceful Harbor. Faith had driven by it plenty of times. There were always motorcycles out front, as there were now. The windows were dark, and she'd never looked close enough to see if they were curtained or painted, but now she could see that they'd been purposely blacked out. *Gulp!*

Two men with long beards stood out front, both wearing jeans, boots, and leather vests. Faith had never seen anyone wear a leather vest other than in movies. Sam pulled his long leg over the bike and set his helmet on the back, smiling down at her.

"You okay?"

"Um, no." She looked at the bar, then looked back at Sam. "We're going in there?"

He helped her take off her helmet and set it on the back of the bike, smiling like this was the best date ever. He cupped her cheeks and gazed into her eyes. She was still sitting on the bike, and if she had it her way Sam would be in front of her, driving back to the part of town she was more comfortable with.

"Yes, we are." He slid his hands beneath her hair, fluffed it up, then tucked a loose strand behind her ear. "Gorgeous as ever."

He took her hand to help her off the bike, but she tightened her legs, refusing to budge.

"Sam," she snapped. "I can't go in there. That's the kind of place my father would drive ten miles to avoid."

He lifted her by the waist as she squirmed against him.

"Stop! Put me down."

He did, and immediately trapped her against his infuriatingly solid body.

"Remember that whole judging a book by its cover thing?"

She looked over her shoulder and shuddered at the thought

of going inside. She imagined the types of guys who might sell women for…she didn't know what. A bike? She knew that was a gross generalization based on nothing more than bad rumors, but still. She was a smart girl, and smart girls weighed risky situations. Her father had warned her away from places like this, and she trusted his judgment. She was thinking about that as Sam lifted her chin and kissed her tenderly, calming her with his gentle touch, which upset her, too, because smart girls didn't get lost in kisses. Did they?

When he took the kiss deeper, she felt her body going boneless, one bone at a time melting into him. *Oh yeah, smart girls get lost in kisses, and the feel of your rough hand on my cheek, and your scent of seduction.* Her eyes came open with that thought, and she tore her mouth away.

"You can't entice me with your panty-melting kisses!"

He laughed, still holding her close. "Faith, do you think I'd ever take you someplace unsafe?"

"Not on purpose."

"Right. And if we ever went someplace and it turned unsafe, what do you think I'd do?"

"Throw me to the wolves and run?" She knew that wasn't true, but she was so nervous, the tease came out lightning fast. Sam's eyes narrowed, clearly not amused. "I know you'd protect me, Sam, but…" She glanced at the two guys again, who were lost in conversation.

"Trust me?"

She drew in a shaky breath. "I do trust you. But what kind of place blacks out the windows?"

"The kind of place I hang out when I don't want to be bothered by the outside world." He laced their fingers together and kissed her knuckles as they crossed the parking lot toward the entrance. "Besides, you said you didn't want a rerun of what I'd done with other women."

"Do you really have to take me to this type of place in order to find somewhere you haven't slept with every woman under the roof?" The thought made her queasy.

"No, babe. I'm taking you to one of my favorite places because you mean enough to me to want to share it with you. It just so happens to also be someplace I've never hooked up with anyone, which was one of your requirements."

Requirements? Had she really come across like that? Like she needed special treatment? She stopped walking, feeling uneasy with the thought.

"Sam, when I said that I meant in general. I didn't want to be one of the long list of women you'd picked up, slept with, then moved on from. I didn't mean that you had to take me places where you'd never been with them."

"I know." His gaze was warm and thoughtful. "Faith, I know it's going to be hard for you when we go out in town, which we will do, because I'm not going to hide our relationship. But this place really is special to me, and until I know that when you look at me you see the real me, and not the guy you thought I was when I first asked you out, we're going to stay away from those places."

"You're worried about what will happen when we go out in town?"

He sighed, but his gaze was dead serious. "Right now you look at me with more clarity than you did two days ago. You look at me as if you *like* who I am and you want to be with me. I love that. I crave it. But I know that when we go out in town women will probably flirt with me regardless of if we're together or not, because they know me as the guy who did those things. I'll handle that appropriately, but I don't want you reverting to seeing me as *that* guy because of how some meaningless people might act."

What could she say to that? He was painfully honest, and that made him even more irresistible. She went up on her toes and kissed him.

"Thank you for thinking about my feelings. I've been trying not to think about that, and it makes it a little easier knowing that you're so self-aware and so in tune with me." She glanced at Whiskey Bro's again. "Okay, I'm in. Let's go visit your special place." He tucked her against his side, her new favorite place. "Do I get a cool biker chick name?"

"Not beyond the one you have."

She looked up at him. His gaze turned possessive as he said, "Braden's Girl."

Chapter Twelve

SAM WASN'T SURE what reaction he'd expected to see from Faith when he'd said *Braden's Girl*. A snappy denial maybe? Certainly not the eager acceptance it was met with. The combination of the delight in her smile, the passion brimming in her eyes, and his mounting desire to publicly make her *his* sparked a visceral reaction of his protective urges surging forward. He tightened his grip around her waist as they headed inside Whiskey Bro's.

"Gentlemen," he said to the two men standing out front.

They nodded in greeting, and the taller of the two opened and held the door for them. Sam inhaled the scent of testosterone, leather, and camaraderie, with an underlying fierceness of competition. Damn, he loved this place. This was where he came to talk shop, bikes, sports, or anything else, without the expectations of being the *it* guy.

Music, laughter, and the din of conversations greeted them, along with about twenty sets of curious eyes. Faith stiffened against him as they stepped inside. He leaned down and kissed the top of her head.

"I've got you," he assured her. Though he wasn't worried, he imagined the bandana-wearing, leather-clad, tattooed crowd was intimidating as hell for sweet Faith.

He led her across the scuffed and marred wood floors to a table by the rustic, unkempt bar, wondering what she'd think of the place, and pulled out her chair. He gave her shoulder a reassuring squeeze as she settled into the chair. He had to admit, this was a far cry from anyplace she was used to, but Faith wasn't a prima donna, which was one of the things he really liked about her. She was *real*, and she spoke her mind. If she let herself, he had a feeling she might end up liking the place, and the company, as much as he did.

"Braden, how's it going?" Bullet Whiskey's voice sounded as rough as his name as he slapped Sam on the back. Before Sam could respond, Bullet smiled down at Faith and said, "How're you doin', sweetheart?"

"Faith, this is Bullet Whiskey. He and his family own the place."

"Hi. It's nice to meet you." She smiled up at Bullet, her eyes drifting along his colorful tattooed sleeves to the tip of a snake's head creeping out of the collar of his shirt. Her eyes narrowed quizzically, but Sam recognized a hint of mischief that set his stomach in a tizzy every time he saw it. "Bullet is an interesting name. Have you killed many people, or do you drive fast?"

Sam laughed, but inside he was full of pride, because he knew how intimidated she was. Still she'd found the courage to taunt a man who stood three inches taller than Sam and outweighed him by at least fifty pounds.

Bullet stroked his beard, his smile stretching across his face. "Sweetheart, I think the only answer you really want to hear is that yes, I drive too fast." He winked. "What can I get y'all?"

"Faith? Wine, beer, soda?"

She touched his hand, still resting on her shoulder. "What are you having?"

"Just Coke for me. I've got precious cargo on board tonight." That earned him another warm smile.

"I'll have the same, please."

"Coming right up," Bullet said.

Sam pulled a chair close to Faith and sat down.

"Wow, this really *is* a biker bar," Faith said over the music, looking a bit wide-eyed.

"It really is," he said with amusement. He watched as Faith took in the rough wood walls littered with license plates, biker logos, flags, and odd paraphernalia like a banjo, old black-and-white pictures of the Whiskey brothers' relatives on their bikes, and flyers for upcoming rides. Her eyes lingered on each item before moving to the bar, where neon lights brought shocks of bright, colorful light. There were about thirty men and women sitting at tables and milling around the pool table toward the back of the bar. The band members were probably pushing fifty, three guys dressed in faded jeans and black boots, and one woman wearing leather pants and spiky boots. They all wore black shirts with a red and white logo.

"I like this place," she said casually. "It's definitely different, but Bullet seems nice, not at all like I expected. I thought he'd be cold, or *something*. That sounds bad, doesn't it?"

"No, it sounds honest." *And I love that about you.*

"Do you come here a lot?" she asked.

"Not a lot. Every few weeks." Sam had stumbled upon Whiskey's when he'd first graduated from college and returned to Peaceful Harbor. He'd been out for a bike ride, looking for a place to clear his head, and he'd been coming ever since.

"Why? I don't mean that in a bad way, but why so far out of town when there are so many places near home?"

"Everyone needs an escape." He took her hand in his, loving that she seemed more at ease. "Except from you. I don't need an escape from you."

She dropped her eyes shyly, then met his gaze and tilted her head, as if she was trying to figure him out. "Your life seems full of fun, with your adventure company, friends, your family."

"My life is full, and it's great, but sometimes it's too much." He never would have admitted that to anyone else, but he wanted Faith to know who he really was, and that meant not holding anything back. "It's nice to come here where no one expects me to do anything but kick back, talk, or chill."

"Funny. I can't imagine you relaxing. You're always on the

go."

"Not always on the go," he said. "The Rough Riders barbecue is coming up, and I was assuming you'd be my date, but I should formally ask, right? Will you go with me? Hopefully we can enjoy some downtime together." He leaned forward and couldn't resist adding, "Would you like to get down with me, Faith Hayes?"

The space between them sizzled, drawing his emotions to the surface. He loved the caged tigress look simmering in her eyes, like she wanted to play but felt like she shouldn't. He was feeling her out, pushing her limits a little at a time. Letting her know that even though he was behaving himself, it was goddamn hard, because she was sexy and enticing and he wanted her more than she probably allowed herself to believe.

"You don't like naughty talk?" He held her gaze, loving the hitch in her breathing.

She lifted a shoulder in a half shrug, half *please don't make me answer*, and looked sinfully adorable. He slid his hand to the nape of her neck, which already felt familiar. He couldn't wait to nuzzle against it, to kiss it, to trap it between his teeth and suck until she begged for more. *Down boy.*

"Don't worry," he reassured her. "I won't take your sweetness away."

She stared into his eyes, exuding femininity and lust, all behind some kind of invisible cloak of forbidden fruit. Just when he thought she'd turn away, she broke the silence.

"I'm not that sweet." Her tone was pure temptress. "I say those things...*in my head.*" She touched his lower lip with the tip of her finger in a slow, alluring swipe. He knew she was as lost in them as he was.

"If you try hard enough, I bet you can hear it, too." She pressed her mouth to his, taking him by surprise, and *oh, hell yes*, her tongue parted his lips eagerly. The kiss electrified, sparking through his body like a dozen live wires. She pulled away in one sharp move, leaving him hard and desperate for more.

Touching her finger to her lips, as if they were burning for another kiss, just as his were, she asked, "Did you hear it?"

Before he could get the blood to move north and feed his brain, Bullet brought their drinks and leaned down, speaking low in Sam's ear. "Bear wants to take you in darts. That cool with your girl here? I'll tell him to bug off if you want to hang."

Faith blinked several times, her smile spreading wider, her eyes never wavering from his. "I love darts. You should play, or play teams and I'll be on your team. I mean, if you don't mind. I'm pretty good."

Bullet looked as perplexed as Sam was. "You play darts?"

She nodded excitedly. "My dad taught us all to play, and I played all the time in college."

"Damn, Braden. Where have you been hidin' this sweet little lady?" Bullet nodded at Faith. "You want to play, sweetheart, we'll put a game together."

BY THE SURPRISED and still heated look in Sam's eyes, Faith was sure she'd actually turned into some sort of vixen. She had no idea where that kiss had come from, but the urge to take control had hit her like a gale-force wind. It felt so good to break free from her own mental confines and kiss the hell out of him. And that kiss—Jesus, every kiss with him—made her whole body come to life. The atmosphere in this dimly lit, out-of-the-way bar where no one knew her felt dangerous and edgy, amping up her desire to *be* that way.

"I'm sorry. I hope I didn't embarrass you," she said to Sam.

"You've got to be kidding." He leaned closer and said, "I heard every naughty word circling that pretty little head of yours."

"Ohmygod. I can't believe I said that." Laughter burst from her mouth, making Sam laugh, too. "It's this place. No one here knows me, so it's easier to...*play*."

"We're not so different, you and I." Sam's eyes turned serious. "I spent my life playing around because it was what was expected of me, and I was too lost in it to realize I was playing a role. You've spent your life being cautious, because it's been who you are. Maybe Whiskey Bro's is the perfect place for both of us."

She looked around at the muscular guy behind the bar, with tatted-up biceps and a five-o'clock shadow as dark as Sam's. He was watching the band, his head bobbing to the beat. He could have easily been a bartender at Whispers. She shifted her eyes around the room, taking in the jeans- and leather-clad people. A couple sat at a table near the band, as focused on each other as she and Sam were. To their left was a table of burly guys; one guy was completely bald, sporting a thick beard and mustache, another had closely cropped hair and tattooed shoulders, and the others were pretty nondescript. Other than the nodded greetings she'd noticed—to Sam, to Bullet, to *her*—everyone kept to themselves. Her father had drilled into her head that bikers were dangerous, and she'd wrongly assumed he was right. There was no denying the contented look in Sam's eyes or the newfound feeling of freedom whirling inside her. She'd sorely misjudged this place, and the people in it, the same way she'd misjudged Sam—based on other people's opinions and her own skewed views.

"No wonder you like it here," she said. "I get that now. It's nice to be able to let down your guard."

"No more book covers?" He arched a brow, his eyes alit with his secret message.

"No more book covers."

"Bones!" The guy behind the bar hollered, startling Faith. He nodded toward the short-haired guy with tattooed shoulders. "You're with me. Dixie!" He lifted his chin toward a waitress Faith hadn't noticed. She wore tight jeans and a half shirt that read WHISKEY BRO'S. Her flame-red hair cascaded in gentle waves nearly to her waist.

"Yes, brother dearest?" she said with a smirk.

"You're with Braden and Braden's Girl," the bartender answered.

Her heart leaped. *Braden's Girl.*

"Faith," Sam called out to him. He stood, bringing Faith up with him, and tucked her beneath his arm.

"I liked Braden's Girl," she said quietly.

He leaned down and kissed the tip of her nose. "Just making sure everyone knows who you are beyond being *mine*. I'm getting you a sweatshirt that says 'Braden's Girl.'"

Bam! She fell a little harder for him for that.

"The bartender's name is Bear. Bear, Bullet, Bones, and Dixie are siblings."

"Where did they get those names?" She'd heard of biker names, but she was curious about how they came up with them.

"Bones is a doctor," Sam explained. "Bullet was in the Special Forces." He stopped talking as Dixie set her eyes on them.

She had a mouthful of bubble gum and popped a bubble as she set a serving tray on the edge of the bar, then made a beeline for Faith. Her hips swayed like a model on a catwalk. She wore black boots with spiked heels that *tapped* with each step, and when she reached Faith she crossed her arms over her chest and openly eyed her from head to toe. Faith's nervousness returned, and she was glad for Sam's arm around her.

"How's it going, Dix?" Sam asked.

Dixie shifted her pretty green eyes to Sam, back to Faith, and then to Sam again. "How long have I known you, Braden?"

"Couple of years," Sam said casually.

Her eyes narrowed. "How many women have you brought in here?"

Oh God. Here it comes. This isn't really a special place, is it?

"None," he said with the same cool confidence as he did everything.

Dixie set those green eyes on Faith again and stopped chewing the wad of gum long enough for a wide, radiant smile to form across her lips, showing her perfectly straight pearly white teeth. She was stunning despite her rough demeanor. Faith held her breath, waiting for the shoe of reality to bonk her in the head.

"Damn, girl," Dixie said. "You must be something special to be under this man's arm in this place." She pulled Faith right out of Sam's arms and hugged her. "Welcome to Whiskey's. It's about time someone livened up this man's life. He's been wasting it for too many years."

Faith couldn't imagine Sam wasting one minute of his life. He was too effervescent, too interested in going, doing, seeing.

"Dixie Whiskey," Sam said. "Let me formally introduce you to my girlfriend, Faith Hayes."

"I think I got the whole girlfriend-boyfriend thing by the way you were sucking face at the table and that 'stay away from my girl' thing you got going on." She pointed to his arms, then his face. "You two are real cute together."

Faith warmed at the compliment. Sam was an intense and enigmatic person, and she wasn't either of those things. She was confident, and she liked to believe she was a fun person. But her fun and Sam's lifestyle were so different that she was sure people would wonder what he was doing with her, just as she had. Although, the better she got to know him, the more she realized they weren't that different after all. And now, as she left Dixie's arms and saw the pride in Sam's eyes, she realized that it wouldn't matter what anyone thought of their relationship.

Dixie hugged Sam. Then she put an arm around Faith and dragged her away from him. "We're teammates. You, me, and Sam against my cocky brothers. We'll kick their butts."

"Sounds good to me."

Dixie glanced at her name above the Rough Riders logo on her sweatshirt. "He's claiming you well and good, isn't he?"

Faith couldn't suppress her grin.

"Sam's one of the good ones. They're hard to find."

Yes, they are. Faith heard Sam laugh and their eyes connected. His gaze conveyed his earlier words: *Good luck keeping me off of you tonight.* But in her head it was *her* saying them.

"Girl, you two've got it bad," Dixie said in a low voice. "You need to take that man back home and tear his clothes off before you do it here on the floor."

Faith tore her eyes from Sam, the image of them having sex on the floor of Whiskey's seared into her mind. First the break room table at work, now here. Was no place safe from their fictitious sex life?

She sensed Sam's presence behind her before she felt his arm claim her waist. She leaned in to him, feeling safe and happier than she'd been in a long time. She loved that Sam wasn't trying to win her over like guys usually did on the first few dates. He was just *Sam*, and that was so much more than enough. The others gathered, and Sam introduced her to Bear while Bones and Dixie gave each other a hard time about who was going to lose.

"Hey, sugar. Good luck," Bear said with a lift of his chiseled chin. He had a rugged, handsome face and deep-set honey-colored eyes that Faith was sure bought him a ticket just about anywhere.

"Okay, let's see what you've got, sweetheart," Bullet said to Faith. "What do you know how to play? Shanghai? Killer? Legs? Baseball?"

"I can play all of those, or Cricket or Round the World." Faith noticed Bear and Bones trading glances, then giving Sam a look she couldn't read. He pressed a kiss to the top of her head. *Staking claim again?* A little thrill jogged through her.

"Shanghai," Bones said, now openly staring at Faith.

"Faith?" Dixie motioned for her to go first.

"Show them what you've got." Sam patted her on the ass.

Between Bones watching her intently, Sam's ass pat, and going first in the game, Faith's nerves were on fire. She drew in a deep breath, mentally going over the rules of Shanghai. The goal was to hit the numbers in sequence, one, two, three, and so on, but only one number was in play during each turn. She needed to hit number one with all three darts to gain the highest score.

"You've got this, sweetheart," Bullet encouraged, making her more nervous.

Faith closed her eyes for a second, centering her mind and letting her shoulders relax. *I can do this. I can do this. I can do this.*

There were two ways to win: either having the highest score at the end of the game or scoring a Shanghai—hitting the single, double, and triple of the number in play. The thin outer doubles ring counted as twice the number scored, and the thin inner triples ring counted as three times. That was Faith's specialty. She was *that* good. But now, with her nerves on fire, she wasn't sure she could hit one, much less three.

She should have had a drink. *Or three.*

She opened her eyes and focused solely on the board, tuning out the music, the ass pat, and the conversations going on around her. The slim dart felt comfortingly familiar as she drew her hand back and released it. It sailed through the air in a perfect line, landing directly on number one.

Before she could stop herself, "Yes!" came out, and she jumped into the air. As soon as her feet hit the ground she wanted to curl into a ball with embarrassment.

"That's my girl!" Sam pulled her into a kiss, alighting her nerves for a completely different reason.

Bullet nodded appreciatively. "Damn, sweetheart, you nailed it."

Sam pressed his scruffy cheek to hers and said, quietly enough for only her ears, "You're so adorable I want to play darts with you in my cabin. Naked."

She gasped a breath as her entire body reacted, from her pert nipples to the heat simmering between her legs.

"Just trying to give you something else to think about."

"Why?" she whispered. "Do you *want* to lose?"

His eyes smoldered. "No. I want to win—*you*."

He stepped away, leaving her to try to act like he hadn't just rocked her world.

Chapter Thirteen

WHEN IT CAME to Faith, Sam couldn't behave. At least not entirely. He was completely, utterly taken with her. When her cheeks pinked up or she did something out of character from her normally in-control personality, he couldn't resist bringing out more of her playful side. After the first round of darts, when his comment about playing darts naked had thrown her so off-balance that her darts barely made it to the dartboard, she'd started firing innuendos back. Every furtive glance, every heated word, every sensual touch, made Faith *temptation overload*, testing Sam's control to the very edge. He'd been sporting wood ever since. Thank God his shirt hung low enough to cover it.

Faith stood beside him now, her hand shoved deep in his back pocket, her fingers making slow strokes over his ass. Her other hand rested on his abs beneath his shirt, two fingers hooked into the waistband just above his zipper.

They were down to the final round. The guys and Dixie had been joking and chatting with Faith all evening. Sam had wondered how he'd feel, revealing one of his most private lairs to Faith, but he didn't feel like he'd lost his privacy. Being there with Faith made it better.

She gazed up at him with a look that said, *I want you*, warring with another look he'd come to know so well—*I need to behave.* He wondered if she could read him as easily—*Be with me. I'll be good to you.*

Torture.

"I just figured out where I know you from," Bones said to Faith.

Faith swallowed hard and half smiled at Bones. Sam could tell she was too entrenched in the lingering sexual tension between them to give Bones her full attention.

"Where?" Sam asked, coming to her rescue.

Bones was about as clean cut as they came, and when he wore shirts that covered his ink, with his businesslike haircut and serious eyes, he looked as out of place as Sam knew Faith had felt when they'd first arrived. But now, with his five-o'clock shadow, wearing a faded black tank top, jeans, and black biker boots, with his tattoos on display and a beer in his hand, he fit right in.

"The hospital," Bones answered. "You work with Jon Butterscotch, don't you?"

"Yes." Faith snapped out of her Sam-trance and pulled her hands from his body. He knew she worried about her professional image, and he could see that worry filling her eyes. "How do you know him?"

"I'm an oncologist. 'Bones' sounded better than 'Doc.' I must have seen you there."

"I sometimes assist him in surgeries." Her eyes darted to Sam, then back to Bones.

Bones must have caught her nervousness, too, because he smiled and said, "Don't worry. There's nothing wrong with being here. Butterscotch wouldn't care if he knew."

"Oh, it's not that." Her voice quivered with the fib.

Sam put his arm around her, hoping to calm her nerves.

Bones laughed. "I became a doctor so I wouldn't have to worry about what my bosses thought of my lifestyle. I get it. But, really, I know Jon, and unless you're out causing trouble, the guy doesn't care what you do in your spare time."

She let out a relieved breath.

Bones turned to Sam and said, "But I bet your brother will have something to say about you bringing Faith here. He's pretty conservative."

"I'll handle Cole," Sam assured Faith more than Bones. He felt her entire body stiffen and lifted her chin with his finger, gazing into her eyes and wishing he could take her worries away once and for all. "I've got this. I promise." He lowered his lips to hers as Bones turned away, and kissed her again, until her body relaxed in to him.

"Okay, lovebirds," Dixie said. "Faith, you're up."

"Thanks, Dixie." Sam's eyes were still locked on Faith.

"Don't worry about Cole. I promise you, he's going to be fine with us. Okay?"

She nodded and stepped away. Sam pulled out his phone and sent another text to Cole as Faith threw her first dart. *Need to talk. Please call as soon as you're back in town.* He hated that Faith worried about anything, especially a job she loved so much, but in his heart Sam knew that Cole wouldn't care what she did with her spare time either. He was too professional to go down that road. Sam was proud of his brother, and he knew that aside from his previous lifestyle, Cole respected him equally. One phone call would ease Faith's worry, and he'd make a point of it taking place before she had to face him at work.

"Your girl's got a single and a double," Bear said to Sam.

Sam shoved his phone in his pocket. Faith's eyes were focused on the board. Her breathing was calm, her body angled slightly to the right, her right foot a few inches behind her left, and her shoulders were parallel to the floor. Everyone's eyes were on her as she drew her hand back, her eyes narrowing even further. With the grace of a dancer, her arm came forward, her right foot slid up to her toes, and the dart sailed through the air, landing on the triple twenty.

Everyone yelled, "Shanghai!"

Bullet swooped Faith into his arms and spun her around, laughing as Dixie and Bear joined in the group hug. Faith's eyes sought Sam's, full of pride, and as Bullet broke free of the crowd, carrying Sam's smiling girlfriend to him and placing her in his arms, all thoughts of Cole disappeared.

Faith gazed into Sam's eyes as she pressed her hands to his cheeks, looking happy and sexy as she lowered her mouth to his. It wasn't a kiss of unbridled passion, or a kiss that said *take me now*. It was an unfamiliar kiss, one he wanted to experience for infinity. It was the kiss of a couple sharing a moment, building history, minute by minute, hour by hour.

When their lips parted, she was still smiling. "See what I can do when you're not making me hot and bothered?"

"You never fail to amaze me." He lowered her to her feet and whispered in her ear, "I'd love to see what you can do when you *are* hot and bothered."

"Then maybe you should heat me up when we're alone, *Braden*."

Invitation accepted.

Sam settled up with the guys, keeping a firm arm around Faith. They said their goodbyes, and a few minutes later the fresh air touched his warm skin, doing absolutely nothing to cool Sam down. Before the door even closed behind them, she was in his arms. Sam backed her up against the building, their mouths fused together, their kiss ravenous. She clung to his back as his hands moved over her ribs, his thumbs brushing the underside of her breasts. She moaned, making him ache to fill his palms, his mouth, to feel her nipples taut and eager against his tongue. Her hips rocked forward, making him harder than he'd been all night. If he didn't get them out of there *now*, he wouldn't be able to focus enough to drive.

He reluctantly pulled away. "Let's get out of here."

She put her arm around his waist before he even got his around her. Man, did he ever love that. *Claim me, baby. Make me yours.*

At the bike, he took her face in his hands and gazed into her eyes. Unbridled passion brimmed back at him. He took her in another rough kiss. His lips were hard, his tongue searching, his body desperate, and when she pushed her hands into his hair and held on tight, he groaned. He kissed her mouth, her chin, her jaw, and buried his face in her neck, kissing, sucking, *wanting*.

"Sam. *Oh God*, Sam."

A tiny voice in the back of his head told him to regain control, but when she dug her nails into his back, it sent currents of fire through his veins. He kissed his way back up to her ear, running his tongue around the rim, then sucking the lobe into his mouth.

"*Ohmygod.*"

She panted as he nibbled and sucked, licked, and teased the sensitive skin just beneath her lobe. When her hands shoved beneath his shirt, hot and eager, clawing at his back, he reminded himself they were in a public place—and he'd promised to behave. He was so far past wanting to behave he couldn't even spell the damn word. He fisted his hands against her hips to keep from tearing her clothes to shreds and drew back from his delicious appetizer.

"Faith." One look in her ravenous eyes stole his next words. "Home. I'm taking you home." His hands shook as he lifted her onto the bike.

She clung to his forearms, her eyes pleading for more. He was powerless to keep his distance. He straddled the bike, facing her, and took her face in his hands.

His emotions poured from him like liquid. "How many times have I held you like this in the last twenty-four hours?" He didn't wait for an answer, and he had a feeling she couldn't have answered if she wanted to. She was flushed and had a lustful, dazed look in her eyes.

"I've never held another woman so possessively. A kiss was the last thing on my mind with anyone else. Your kisses consume me, and holding you like this, eye to eye, feeling your beautiful face in my hands, brings us that much closer together. If all we ever had was kissing, it would be torture, but I could live with it."

"God, Sam," she said breathlessly. "Kiss me."

He claimed her eager mouth in a series of hard kisses. The sound of a bike roaring to life jerked him back to their sur-roundings. Their lips parted, but neither looked toward the noise; the current between them was too magnetic. Sam touched his forehead to hers, cupping the nape of her neck and trying to calm the adrenaline coursing through him.

"Home, baby. I've got to take you home."

THE NIGHT AIR did little to clear Faith's mind on the ride to her apartment. Being pressed against the man she wanted so badly, combined with the vibration of the bike, didn't help her think any more clearly. By the time they arrived, all she wanted was more of Sam, and she could tell by the tightness in his jaw and the way he fell silent on the way up to her apartment that he was fighting the same internal battle.

The silence pressed in on her as she fished out her keys. She wanted *Sam* pressing in on her. The restraint in his eyes made her heart swell. He was behaving because it was what she'd wanted, but now, as they each waged their silent battles, she wished she'd never made such a big deal out of not doing more than kissing the other night.

She pushed the key into the lock, and Sam's arms came around her waist. His hot, glorious mouth lavished her neck with openmouthed kisses, stimulating her every ion. She pushed the door open but rested her head back against his rock-hard frame, giving him better access to anything he wanted. His hand slid up the front of her shirt and over her rib cage, causing a full-body shudder. His other hand turned her chin toward him, and he claimed her in a full-on assault of her senses. He plundered and took, kissing her roughly and filling his free hand with her breast. His thumb brushed over her nipple in a slow circular motion with master precision, just hard enough to send tingles of lust straight down between her legs. She tried to turn and face him, but he held her in place, his hard length pressing against her backside as he deepened the kiss, consuming her—body, mind, and soul.

When he finally turned her in his arms, he didn't break their connection, kissing her heartbreakingly slowly, dreamily, as if he had all day just to enjoy this closeness. The sound of a car door slamming jerked Faith's mind out of her lusty delirium, and she reluctantly pulled back. Fisting her hand in his shirt, she pulled him into her apartment. He closed the door with his foot, his primal stare making her feel sexy and exposed at once as he openly studied her. His powerful body moved in silent persuasion, closing the distance between them. Faith stood motionless, nervously licking her lips, trying to keep from jumping his bones, because *boy, did she want to jump his bones*. His sexual magnetism made him so attractive to everyone in his path, and she was right there with all the women before her. Jealousy dug its claws into her heart, vying for blood. She tried to tamp down the ugly emotions, and one look in his eyes tore those claws from her skin. Sam was hers now, by his own volition, and he'd done a lot to get her to agree to be his. He closed in on her, sucking the oxygen from the room.

His hand came heavily around the nape of her neck, drawing her to him, a devilish curve to his mouth, wicked and alluring. She loved anything he did at her nape. He could nuzzle it, kiss it, suck it, or brush his thumb over her sensitive skin, as he was now, while looking at her like she was a goddess: beautiful, sexy, and oh so tempting. She didn't see herself that way, but Sam made her *feel* that way. His desire was inescapable, emanating from his face, his body, his hands as they slid beneath her shirt again and up her back. His fingers curled over her shoulders and he held her tight against him.

The anticipation was merciless. She was wet and panting, fisting her hands in the back of his shirt so tightly she was sure she'd leave marks on his skin. His heart was beating as rampant as hers, and he searched her eyes so intensely she wondered what he was looking for. *Reassurance?* She went up on her toes and kissed the center of his chin. His scruff was rough against her face, and his intoxicating musky scent overwhelmed her. So masculine, so *Sam*. She lingered, placing more kisses along his jaw, feather-light kisses and openmouthed kisses. He made a sexy, wanton sound deep in his throat, and she wanted to hear more of that sound, to feel it rumble in his throat and through his chest. She nipped at his lower lip, then slicked over it with her tongue.

His fingers tightened around her shoulders as he hissed out a breath and swept her into his arms, taking her in another exquisitely torturous slow kiss as he carried her to the living room and lowered her to the couch. He came down over her, kissing her lips, her neck, her mouth again. His hips ground sensually against hers as his arms enveloped her.

"So beautiful," he whispered against her cheek. "So sexy. How am I supposed to behave myself?" His hand moved over her ribs and palmed her breast.

Faith sucked in a sharp breath with the intense pleasure of his touch, combined with the friction between her legs as he ground his arousal against her swollen sex.

She didn't want him to behave and forced herself to respond. "We'll just behave a little."

His lips curled up, but his brows slanted together. "I'm not sure what that means."

"Me either," she admitted. "But I don't want to stop."

She pulled his mouth to hers and surrendered to the passion burning inside her, pushing her hands through his hair, over his shoulders, down his back, wanting to feel every inch of him. She tugged at his shirt, lifting it up so she could feel his flesh. He reared up and pulled it off, staying above her long enough for her to get an eyeful and then a mouthful as she rose and kissed his chest. He leaned on one hand, the other still toying with her nipple. His pecs jumped and flexed against her tongue. She ran her hand over his chest, lingering over his nipples, and followed her hand with her mouth, stroking the hard tips with her tongue.

"Christ," he growled.

His eyes were closed, his jaw tight, neck muscles straining. She loved knowing she was the cause of all that restraint. What would he be like when he let loose? She kissed his neck, dragging her tongue along the length of it. Another growl vibrated through him. His head dropped forward and his eyes came open, pleasure wading in their dark pools. He rose onto his knees with a predatory look in his eyes. She was his most willing prey, panting as her eyes dropped to the thick erection pressing against his jeans. His eyes turned serious, roaming over her—*all of her*. He closed them for a beat, as if he were trying to regain control, and she sat up and pressed her hands to his sides, kissing his stomach. She felt every breath against her tongue, felt the restraint in his muscles.

His eyes locked on her. She reached up and played with his nipples, continuing to taunt him with her mouth.

"Faith." He clenched his jaw tight.

She lifted her eyes but didn't stop kissing, licking, or touching. He reached down and gathered the sides of her shirt, lifting it slightly.

"Okay?"

She nodded, unwilling to give up even a second of tasting him. He lifted her shirt over her head. Her necklace fell between her lace-covered breasts, and he carefully removed that, too, setting it on the coffee table beside the couch. He moved painstakingly slow, his normal confidence hindered by her self-imposed limits. She loved that he respected her enough to take things slowly. She desperately longed to feel him untamed and wild, but not now. Now this was perfect, and somehow he must have known that.

He eased her lace bra strap down her arm. His eyes locked on hers as he kissed first one shoulder and then the other, as he lowered the other strap, unhooked the clasp, and tossed her bra to the floor. Her breasts fell heavily against her skin. She waited for her skin to flush with embarrassment beneath his carnal stare, but there was no room for that wasted emotion when her body throbbed and ached for the breathtaking man before her.

Chapter Fourteen

FAITH LAY BENEATH Sam, unguarded and trusting and so beautiful she made his heart stutter. Her dark hair fanned out around her. Her eyelids were heavy with desire. Her full, perfect breasts were untouched by the sun, creamy, silken against her tanned skin. The dark peaks beckoned him. He lowered himself to her, savoring their first skin-to-skin contact, feeling like he'd been given a gift.

"Feel that?" he whispered. The answer was in her quickening heartbeat and the look of entrancement in her eyes. "That's *us*. So right. So perfect."

Their mouths came together with a sense of urgency belying his tender tone. Tongues tangling, breath mingling, lips burning. He'd never get enough of kissing her, touching her. His hands moved feverishly along her curves, from her hip to her breasts, then back again, feeling her body tremble. He caressed her breasts, their hips moving together in perfect harmony, his arousal aching for release. He drew back, giving her lower lip a gentle tug and earning a sexy moan from Faith. He rained kisses along her jaw, her neck, and finally—*finally*—her breasts, her body bowed beneath him. He drew the tight bud up against the roof of his mouth, and she fisted her hands in his hair, holding him in place. *Oh yeah, baby. Show me what you like.*

She arched against him, urging his mouth open wider. Taking more of her luscious breast in, he cupped it with both hands and loved it fully.

"That feels so good." Her words came fast and heated.

He gave the other breast the same attention, adding a teasing graze with his teeth. Her hips bucked with pleasure. He wanted to taste every inch of her gorgeous body. He dragged his tongue in slow circles around her nipple, avoiding the peaks, even as she tried to lower his head to them.

"God," she hissed.

He laced her hands with his, holding them beside her head, and continued teasing her. Her eyes closed, and she bit her lower lip. He moved up and claimed her again in a rough kiss.

"Don't hold back." It came out as a command, and he softened his tone, meeting her heady gaze. "I'm greedy. I want to hear every little noise you make for me."

She bit her lip again, and he used his teeth to tug it free.

"Only I get to bite that lip tonight."

Her eyes widened a little with the demand. He kissed her softly, then traced her lips with his tongue.

"Okay?" he asked, giving her control again.

"Yes," she whispered.

He lowered his mouth to her breast again, swirling his tongue around her nipple while grinding his cock against her core. He sucked her breast hard, and she gasped with pleasure. As he sucked he lifted his eyes to hers, loving the look of untamed passion in her eyes. He released her hands and moved down her body, licking and kissing each of her ribs, the curve of her waist. He rolled her nipples between his fingers and thumbs, squeezing just hard enough to hear her gasp with pleasure again. He ran his tongue around her belly button, dipping inside slowly and sensually. She moaned, her hips bucking with each stroke of his tongue. He gave her nipples another squeeze as his tongue dipped inside again and she fisted her hands in his hair, sending exquisite shocks of pain through his scalp. He lifted his eyes to make sure they were on the same page, and hers were slammed shut and her head was back as she panted out each breath.

Using his teeth, he unbuttoned her jeans. Her body stilled and her eyes came open.

"Tell me to stop, baby, and I will."

"Don't stop," she said quickly.

Fuck. She was so damn sexy. He moved swiftly up her body, framed her face with his hands, and kissed her greedily.

He moved down and unzipped her jeans, carefully taking them off. His mouth went dry at the sight of her in nothing more than black lace panties. Her skin was flushed, her lips glistening from their kiss, and her hands—those delicate, feminine hands—were pushing her panties off. He helped her slip them off, then came down between her legs. He ran his hands over the tops of her thighs, then brushed his thumbs over her damp, dark curls. He kissed her inner thigh, noticing her hands fisting in the couch cushion as her hips bowed up. God, what she did to him, wanting him so much it made him ache.

His thumbs slid to the creases between her legs and her sex, opening her for him. Her flesh glistened, and the scent of her arousal was intoxicating. The first stroke of his tongue brought her sweet, divine taste. She moaned, her thighs falling open further. He teased her with his tongue, tasting and taunting, reveling in her quickening breaths and arching hips. He licked circles around her swollen clit and slid two fingers deep inside her velvety heat. A long, low moan escaped her lips. He sucked her sensitive nerves into his mouth, his fingers furtively seeking the pleasure point that would send her over the edge. Her heels dug into the cushions and her thighs tightened. He pushed them open wider with his elbows, allowing him to use his fingers and mouth more adeptly, stroking her *up, up, up.*

"Sam!" she cried, her body thrusting and shaking.

Her sex pulsed around his fingers as she rode out her climax. As it began to ease, he replaced his fingers with his tongue, and teased over her clit, sending her right back up to the peak.

"Sam!" she cried again—and he fucking loved hearing his

name sail uncontrollably from her lungs as she shattered against his mouth, drenching him with her arousal and giving herself completely over to him.

Waves of aftershocks jerked her hips off the couch. Sam laved her swollen sex with his tongue, kissing her most sensitive lips, before sliding his fingers back inside to bring her up to the verge of another intense release. Just as he felt her body shatter, he lowered his mouth to her again.

"Sam, Sam, Sam. *God, Sam.*" She grabbed his head, thrashing hers from left to right as her climax crested. He stayed right there with her, savoring every pulse, every sexy noise, her sweet taste, until she fell limply back and her fingers unfurled.

He gathered her in his arms and kissed her neck, her chest, her cheek, and finally her mouth. She returned the kiss with the energy of a sated lover, languid and tender.

"I want to thank every woman you've practiced on before this day."

He smiled because he understood she meant it as a compliment, but his heart hurt knowing the thought of him and anyone else was on her mind. But why wouldn't it be? Wasn't that exactly why she'd wanted to take things slow?

Her eyes came open, full of regret. "I can't believe I said that. I'm sorry. I hate thinking about you with other women." Her lips curved up in a sleepy smile despite the hurtful thoughts she must have had, and it made him fall even harder for her.

He kissed her softly. "I know you do. I hate thinking about

you with any other man. But we'll have no more of that. I'm yours and only yours."

A RELIEVED SIGH escaped Faith, but Sam's eyes shuttered, making her nervous again.

"I'm sorry my past is hurtful."

"You told me you don't apologize for your past," she reminded him, confused by his change of heart.

"No. I said I'm not ashamed of my past, and I'm not. Beauty in imperfection and evolution, remember? I'm evolving. We're evolving. But I am sorry if it makes you feel bad, or sad, or angry." He kissed her softly.

She wanted to start calling him Honest Sam, because he didn't even try to soften the blow of not feeling any shame about his past. Not that she thought he should be ashamed. As he said, and she had at first disbelieved, he wasn't a cheater because he hadn't ever committed. There could be no shame in exercising his freedom.

"It doesn't make me any of those things," she assured him. "Just a little jealous and maybe intimidated."

"If it makes you feel any better, I'm jealous of every man who's touched you before me. And I'd like to throttle whoever hurt you. But you shouldn't ever feel intimidated. No one could hold a candle to you."

She traced the line of his jaw with her finger, feeling safe enough in his arms to be just as honest as he was.

"I'm not as experienced as they are. I don't want to disappoint you." She gasped. "And *ohmygod*, Sam. You just did all those incredible things to me, and here I am, lying naked in post-orgasm bliss, and I didn't reciprocate. See? I'm not very good at this."

She crossed her arms over her chest as embarrassment claimed her. He lowered her arms and ran his hand from the center of her breasts down to her belly button.

"You're beautiful." He kissed her again. "And perfectly experienced. Just do what you feel, and if either one of us wants something more or different, we'll get there together." He kissed her again, searching her eyes with a tender smile on his lips. "Besides, tonight we're *behaving a little*."

He reached over her, grabbed his shirt, and helped her put it on. "There. Do you feel more comfortable now?"

She silently reached down and put on her panties. "Now I am."

He chuckled. "I love seeing you in my shirt, but I loved seeing you naked beneath me even more."

When their lips touched, she felt lighter, more at ease. Everything he said came straight from his heart. She wasn't used to hearing a man talk about needing to hear her sexy sounds, or lying naked beneath him, but she loved hearing those things coming from Sam.

They lay together for a long time, making plans for tomorrow evening and procrastinating the end to their date. When they reluctantly moved from the couch toward the door, Faith reached for her shirt and Sam caught her wrist.

"I want to think about you sleeping in my shirt tonight." He gathered her in his arms. "Besides, I need the cold air to cool me down on the way home." He pressed his hips forward, his arousal still rock-hard. "I hate leaving you."

"I hate it, too. I feel like we've been together for months. How can so much happen in so little time?"

"My mother once said that when soul mates find each other, from their very first kiss they feel like they've been together forever."

Her heart leaped at *soul mates*. Did he really believe that, or was he just throwing out his mother's wisdom? The way he was looking at her made her feel like he was wondering the same thing.

"Until tomorrow, sweet one." They kissed again, and Sam held her hand until he was out the door and their fingertips could no longer touch.

Faith watched him disappear down the steps before going inside. She stood at the window watching as he climbed onto his bike, shirtless, and drove away. Too amped up to sleep, she washed up, then grabbed her laptop and settled onto the couch to check in with the girls on WAC. She felt a little guilty for dating a guy who had the type of reputation that she warned the members to stay away from.

She typed in her password, thinking about Sam. He'd spent no time denying that reputation. Instead, he seemed to put all his energy into showing Faith who he really was. Or at least who he was *now*.

Several of the threads included comments about how hot and nice Sam was. One member said she'd gladly give up a night to be his *plaything*. Faith swallowed down the jealousy and discomfort that chased the comment. At least that alleviated her guilt.

She looked for Lira's posts and read one from this morning. The post began with her feelings of abandonment by her sister and how sad she was for Emmie to have lost her father and her aunt. Faith's heart ached for her. She was obviously struggling with wanting a clean break and wanting to do the right thing by her daughter.

She continued reading and was surprised to see that Lira was already working for Sam. *He's the most incredible boss, totally businesslike but friendly, too. After he gave me my assignments, which I'm super excited about, he asked how Emmie was taking the split. Faith, if you're reading this, if all goes well, I'll be at the Rough Riders barbecue to help out! I hope this works out, and I hope we can see each other if I am!*

Faith sat back in shock. Not only had Sam helped her with WAC, but he'd followed through with Lira. That made her feel even better than when he'd helped her connect with Brent. *Sam*

Braden, you really do surprise me.

They were meeting with Brent Thursday evening. Once she had that straightened out, she'd contact the women's organizations and resources she'd been tracking down and start building a network for the group. She typed a private message to Lira to let her know she was working on finding someone to talk with her and was surprised to see a message from her. Apparently Sam had emailed her a name and number he'd gotten from his sister Tempest, and she'd already made an appointment for a free consultation.

Faith sat back, jaw agape. A week ago she never would have imagined Sam would go this far for a woman he wasn't trying to hook up with. Now, knowing Sam better than she thought possible in such a short time, as shocked as she was, she had no trouble believing it.

A short while later her cell phone vibrated and she dug it out of her purse, smiling at Sam's name as she read the message. *My cold shower would have been more fun with you in it.*

She hugged herself, feeling his soft shirt against her skin. Thoughts of what they'd done came rushing back, making her hot all over. The poor guy. She really had left him blue balled. But he hadn't pushed or made her feel guilty. She wondered how many guys would have handled it that well, and then her mind reached further. Sam was used to sleeping with women the first time they went out—and more likely for many of them, the *only* time they went out.

That made her feel even more secure and special. With that in mind, she couldn't help teasing him. She texted, *If I'd known a shower was on the table I might have gone home with you.*

His response was immediate. *I can take another one. Come over.*

She laughed as she texted, *Can't. My boyfriend wore me out.*

She didn't bother to look away from the screen, knowing it would vibrate seconds later, as it did. *Better start working out to prepare yourself for next time. Your bf has a rep to maintain.*

She wondered about that reputation, and if people— *women*—in town would revolt when they found out Sam was off the market. She texted, *I won't ruin your rep and let people know you were a perfect gentleman if you don't ruin mine by saying I wasn't a lady.* Before sending it, she added, *It's your fault. That monster vibrator that you call a motorcycle is supreme foreplay!*

Her phone rang and Sam's name flashed on the screen. Her heart skidded to a halt.

"Hey," she said nervously.

"How's my girl?" His voice was low and husky, and her mouth watered like one of Pavlov's dogs.

Wishing you were here. She swallowed those words, because she knew he'd drive right over and she'd be worthless at work tomorrow if he did. Besides, she *should* wait to sleep with him, shouldn't she?

"Missing you," she offered.

"Me too. So you like my *bike?*"

She heard the sexy tease in his voice. "It gives an enticing ride. But I liked who I held on to better."

"I do like your answers. I had a really nice time tonight. I wasn't sure if you'd enjoy Whiskey's, but I wanted to share something special with you and I'm glad you went along with it."

She leaned back, fidgeting with the edge of his shirt and smiling at his thoughtfulness. "I loved being there with you."

He was quiet for a few seconds before saying, "Faith, that's not the only reason I called. I've been thinking about this since I was at your place, and after your text, I wanted to talk to you about my reputation. I wish it would just go away. I hate knowing that what I did in my past has such a big impact on you. I really respect you for giving me a shot."

"Sam." Her heart swelled to constriction. She didn't know how to respond. He was the most sought-after guy in town, and he was nothing like any of those other women thought he was. They may have gotten great sex—*she swallowed the bile rising in her throat*—but she had the best parts of him. His honesty and emotions.

"You don't have to say anything," he assured her. "I just wanted you to know. I never thought past what I was doing, and I never imagined I'd care so much about what anyone thought of my past. But I do. I care about the impact it has on you. I care about you, Faith."

Ohmygod. There was that blatant honesty again.

"Don't go reticent on me. Don't get scared off. I know I'm coming on strong—"

"I'm not scared off. I just"—she closed her eyes tightly— "never thought I'd like you so much, so fast, either." *Ohgodohgodohgod. Honesty is scary.* How the heck did he do it all the time?

"Faith?"

She heard relief in that one simple word. "Yeah?"

"Wish I could see the blush on your cheeks right now. Sleep well, sweet one."

Faith lay in bed that night thinking about Sam's reputation and wondering how she would feel when they eventually went out together to a restaurant or a bar in town. Wondering how *Sam* would feel. He said he didn't want to go out in town together until he was sure she wouldn't judge him based on the actions of others. That meant he expected it to be pretty uncomfortable. She closed her eyes and tried to imagine walking into Whispers on Sam's arm. Her heart immediately went into panic mode, and her eyes flew open. She didn't even want to try to picture it. Would she ever be ready for that?

Curling up on her side, she grabbed her phone and considered texting Vivian. She owed her a phone call, and she wanted to tell her she was seeing Sam, but Vivian would lecture her or remind her of all the things she'd said the night they were out.

She set the phone on the nightstand, putting off the call until she could give it her full attention. Closing her eyes again brought images of the night they'd taken a walk on the beach and the longing look in Sam's eyes when her friends had dragged her away. Chasing the memory were images of Sam, shirtless and perched above her, looking at her like she'd hung the moon. He made her feel cherished and safe despite his reputation. He made her feel *important*.

She clung to those feelings, counting down the hours until she'd see him again.

Chapter Fifteen

SAM STEPPED OFF the porch of his lakeside cabin Thursday morning and waved to Nate as he climbed from his truck.

"Look what the cat dragged in at two o'clock this morning." Nate hiked his thumb over his shoulder at Ty, getting out of the passenger side at a slug's pace.

"Jewel must have loved that." Sam shook his head. "Why didn't you crash here?"

Ty stretched his arms out to his sides and yawned. "Thought you might have company. I've been staying at Shannon's while she's out of town, but Nate's was closer."

Sam would have loved to have had company last night. He and Faith had planned on meeting around nine, but she had gotten called into the hospital to assist with an emergency surgery. Having to make it through Wednesday with nothing more than phone calls and texts had been far rougher than he'd expected. He'd woken up with a severe case of Faith Withdrawal, and couldn't wait to see her tonight.

"Where'd you go? The trails?" Sam asked. He and Nate both lived on the lake. Each had a couple acres of wooded property, and they kept it that way for privacy. Shannon lived in town, and Sam couldn't imagine where Ty had gone that he thought Nate's place was closer.

"Bonfire out on the ridge." Ty pulled the hood of his sweatshirt over his head and sank down to the porch step. *The ridge* was closer to Nate's than to Shannon's. It was a rocky landing at the edge of the mountain overlooking the river.

Nate and Sam exchanged a knowing glance. It wasn't unusual for Sam and Ty to stay out all night, catch a few winks in the morning, then work a full day at Rough Riders.

"I texted you about it." Ty squinted up at him.

"Yeah, I saw a text asking if I wanted to go out." Sam had shot back a quick *no, thanks*. "Are you running with us?"

"Yes, he's running with us." Nate's military side was coming out in more than just his tightly shorn sandy blond hair. "Come on, get your ass up. You can't wake my fiancée at two and expect me to let your lazy ass off that easy."

Ty shook off his hood and raked a hand through his long dark hair. He reached a hand toward Nate for help getting up. Nate shook his head.

Sam grabbed his hand and yanked him to his feet. "I'd let you crash while we run, but my little brother might go all army on my ass. Then I'd have to kill him, and none of us would get our run in."

They'd been running the trails together for years, that is, whenever they were all in town. Nate had spent several years in the military, and Ty's schedule was always erratic. Sam treasured whatever time he got with his brothers.

Ty shed his sweatshirt, and they took off down the road at a slow pace, giving Ty time to wake up. Within a few minutes they found their groove and fell into step along one of the four-mile trails.

"How long do I have to wait to get the scoop on Faith?" Nate asked. "Or are we pretending it's not happening?"

All it took was the mention of her name and Sam felt a goofy grin forming on his face. "Oh, it's happening all right."

"I knew you had big ones, Sam, but seriously?" The surprise in Nate's voice was palpable. "Cole warns you away from her, and the minute he's out of town you home in? What's up with that?"

"I think we know what's *up* with him," Ty teased.

"It's not like that." Sam ducked beneath the branch of a tree. "I didn't ask her out because Cole told me not to."

Nate scoffed. "No shit. We know that. You've had your eye on her for a long time. Hell, I remember a few months ago when you were at Tap It and she walked in with some dude. I thought you were going to strangle the guy if he made a move on her."

Sam clenched his jaw, remembering that night. Faith had looked hot in a little black dress with her hair clipped at the nape of her neck like a sexy schoolteacher. The guy she'd been with looked like a pocket-protector-wearing dork. *The antithesis of me.* He kicked up his pace to get that night out of his mind.

"But Cole's been warning him off for just as long," Ty added.

They ran in silence for a few minutes, winding up the trail, around a patch of overgrown bushes, and toward a clearing overlooking the river. One of Sam's favorite spots. He'd have to remember to take Faith up there sometime. Maybe to watch a sunrise or sunset.

"Dude, watch it!" Ty yanked Sam off the trail, and out of his reverie, as a snake slithered across the path.

"Thanks." Sam shook his head to clear thoughts of Faith, but she'd already seeped into the crevices and found a home.

Nate sidled up to Sam, running beside him as they wound around the clearing toward another trail. "You're really doing this, aren't you?"

"Yup."

"For how long?" Nate's tone wasn't accusatory; it was concerned.

He clenched his jaw, wondering if the concern was for him or for Faith. "For as long as she'll have me. Or as long as it takes to show her how right we are together."

"You son of a bitch." Nate laughed. "I never thought I'd see the day that Sammy Braden got bit. Happens fast, doesn't it?"

"I keep telling myself I'm not going over the falls. Self-preservation, I guess. But every time I think of her, which is all the damn time…" He paused, trying to collect his thoughts. "What was it like with you and Jewel? I know you loved her forever, but at some point you put aside thoughts of any other woman. Was it overnight? Because, man, looking back over the last year or two, it was like Faith was there all along. Lingering in the back of my mind like an itch I couldn't scratch. I was looking for her without realizing I was doing it; when we were out, every weekend at Rough Riders, I was just hoping to catch a glimpse of her."

"That's exactly how it happens," Nate answered. "One minute you're living your life, and the next you can't live it without her."

Ty blew by them and turned, jogging backward. "Do not breathe on me, share a drink with me, or come near me for that matter. I'm happy for you two, but whatever you've got, I don't want it." He laughed and fell into step beside them.

"I was right where you are two weeks ago," Sam told him. "This is so much better. You have no idea what you're missing."

Ty scoffed and changed the subject to his next climb, which was fine with Sam. He missed Faith so much that even talking about her was making him want to run over to her apartment just to see her smiling face.

The conversation turned to work, and Nate filled them in on the trials and tribulations of owning Tap It. "Can you believe I caught two of my waitstaff fooling around in the supply room?"

"I'm surprised it took this long." Sam chuckled. "Come on, Nate. Think about being twenty again."

"No shit," Nate said. "I swear I should hire all girls or all guys. The mix is like hormone overload."

"Do you have any admin staff you don't need?" Ty asked. "Sam needs an office manager before his desk disappears."

Sam filled them in on his trial run with Lira. "So far she's doing great. She got more done in one day than I would have in three. She's already got a Google calendar set up with the excursions that we have through next winter. I had it all on spreadsheets, but this is so much easier. With groups of ten or more per trip, I've got to have someone who can keep things organized, track insurance papers along with deposits and full payment, *and* someone who's not afraid to stand up to the creature-comfort seekers who want their money back because they decide Friday at seven that the twelve-person weekend outing they booked two months ago doesn't sound as fun as staying home and drinking in their living room."

"She'll definitely need a spine of steel. I can vouch for that," Ty said. "Corporate outings can be nightmares."

"You're not kidding. Anyway, I'll let you know how things go with Lira, and in the meantime, just in case she can't commit, or it doesn't work out, keep your eyes and ears open."

"Can't help you there," Nate said. "All I've got are hormone-infused kids looking to get laid. But I'll ask around."

After their run they tossed their shirts on the porch and paced the yard to cool down.

"Lake?" Ty arched a brow.

Nate slid a look to Sam, the challenge of their youth playing in his eyes.

"Aw, shit, really?" Ty's eyes bounced between them; then he took off running toward the lake with Nate and Sam on his heels.

Their laughter filled the air. Sam ran ahead, and Nate's heavy hand yanked him back and tackled him to the ground. Ty blew past, his deep laugh sending Sam and Nate to their feet. How many years had they raced to the water at their parents' house? Some things never changed, and as Sam jumped Ty from behind and took him to the ground, and Nate piled on top, he was glad for it. This competition, fed by years of loyalty and brotherly bullshit, was what life was about. They rolled around on the ground, tackling and challenging, and finally flopped onto their backs, panting between bursts of laughter.

Ty pushed himself up and raked a hand through his hair, reaching a hand out to Sam. "Come on, asshole. Let's go for a swim."

Sam reached for his hand, and Ty took off running, laughing like a fool.

Sam and Nate exchanged an eye roll, and a second later they pushed to their feet, sprinted down the dock, and pushed each other into the water. As Sam broke the surface, searching for his brothers, each one bobbed to the surface, and his mind shifted to new, startling territory. At almost thirty-one-years old, for the first time ever, he considered his interactions for more than the here and now. He wanted *this* one day. A family of his own, kids who played hard and loved harder.

Nate and Ty disappeared below the surface and Sam's mind reeled back to Faith. As his brothers dragged him under, his mind swamped with thoughts of Faith, he went down without a fight.

FAITH SPENT THE day running from patient to patient, handling follow-up calls and whatever else needed to be done, but nothing could sour her mood. When she'd finally fallen asleep last night, after a long unexpected surgery with Jon, she'd dreamed of Sam. One dream after another, each more sexual than the last, progressing from his transfixed gaze, to his hands and mouth all over her body. She'd awoken with a start, drenched in sweat and on the verge of orgasm. She'd had no choice but to close her eyes, delve into her mind for images of Sam, and surrender to the pleasures of her own hand—pretending it was Sam's.

It was nearing five forty-five, and Faith was back at her apartment waiting for Sam to pick her up for their appointment with Brent. She'd showered and changed and was sitting on the bed with her cell phone pressed to her ear, listening to Vivian breathe. She'd gone silent after Faith told her she was seeing Sam.

"Are you still there?"

"Yes," Vivian said with a serious tone. "I'm processing."

"Viv, I know what you're going to say. He's dangerous for me. He's everything I should stay away from. I know that's what we thought about him, but he's not at all like that when we're together."

"Of course he's not. What's he going to do? Pick up girls when he's with you? Faith," she said with a softer tone. "I just don't want you to get hurt. Promise me that you won't do what all of us do and rationalize his bad behavior because you *wish* he was a certain way."

Faith sighed, thankful that Vivian wasn't riding her as hard as she'd expected she might. "I promise. But he's really not like that. *He's* not even rationalizing it. And he thinks of me first, Viv. I know that's hard to believe, given his past, but he does. He doesn't even want to go out in town until he's sure I won't go back to seeing him as *that* guy when girls come up to him."

"Seriously? Call me jaded, but that sounds like he's thinking about himself, not you. He doesn't want to be in a position to have to shut them down, so he flips it to being about you."

Faith had thought about that, but she'd pushed those thoughts aside. Was she rationalizing?

"Hey? You still there?" Vivian snapped.

"Uh-huh. Just thinking."

"I'm not trying to cause trouble, but maybe you should test that out, see how he acts when you're in his stomping grounds. See how *you* feel about *him* in that situation. The last thing you need is to fool yourself into believing he's the man he shows you when he's not in taxing situations."

"That's what he said he's worried about. What *I'll* think of *him*." Her stomach fisted into a knot. Could he have bamboozled her with his good looks and sweet words? With his endless attention and thoughtfulness? With his honesty? No way. She didn't believe it.

But then again, maybe Vivian was right.

"It's the tough stuff that makes or breaks us." Faith's mother's words came without thought. She wasn't sure if she was saying them to herself or to Vivian.

"Right. Thanks, Mama Hayes."

They talked for a few more minutes about Sam, then moved on to WAC, the resource gathering Faith had been doing, and finally the impending meeting with the lawyer. By the time Sam arrived, Faith's thoughts were tangled and confused. She trusted him. *Really* trusted him. But she'd been hurt before, missed signs she probably should have seen.

"Hey." His lips tipped up at the edges, and in his gaze she read, *Finally, you're in my arms. I've missed you. Kiss me*, as his arm came around her waist and their mouths came together.

She stiffened for a second, thinking about what Vivian said, but she was no match for his panty-melting kisses or the feel of his heart beating strong and sure against her own. She couldn't hold on to more than a shred of the disbelief Vivian had stirred up. But that shred remained, niggling at her nerves, the whole way to Brent's office.

Sam opened the truck door, and when she turned to step out, he was right there, blocking her exit. An immovable force, searching her eyes, reading her worries like a billboard.

"What is it?"

"What?" She swallowed her willowy voice.

He stepped closer, heat rolling off him, consuming her, the concern in his eyes making her feel safe and important again. That feeling of safety battled with the devil whispering in her ear.

"You're a million miles away. Is it the meeting? Are you nervous?"

Yes clung to the tip of her tongue, but lying to Sam when he'd been nothing but honest with her wasn't happening. She closed her gaping mouth and shook her head.

"Faith, what is it? Did something happen at work?"

She shook her head again, feeling a little numb and guilty for doubting him. But what Vivian said made sense, too, and she needed to be cautious. Maybe she was rationalizing in order to see what she wanted to.

"Just a little overwhelmed." That much wasn't a lie.

He wrapped her in his arms and held her. "We can reschedule. Brent won't mind. Was it crazy at work? Do you want to chill instead?"

"God, you're so good to me." She silently chided herself for worrying, for not telling him why she was really sidetracked, and if she were being completely honest with herself, maybe also for not being one hundred percent sure if *this* was her rationalizing.

"I'm hoping that's a good thing and not a 'God, you're so good to me and now I have to break up with you.'" His smile told her he didn't believe she meant it the second way he'd suggested.

"It isn't. I'm okay. Let's go meet Brent."

"If you're sure." He held her hand as they crossed the parking lot and rode the elevator up to Brent's office.

She wrestled with her thoughts as they entered the empty office. She expected an attorney to have expensive furnishings, but Brent's office was fashionably minimalist. The lobby boasted four simple black chairs and a glass coffee table. Magazines were neatly stacked in a rack beside the glass-topped receptionist desk. It was obviously after hours, and the office was empty and dead silent.

"Let me text Brent and let him know we're here." Sam reached into his pocket for his phone.

Faith couldn't help but sneak a peek at it. It was the same phone he'd shown her. *Not a burner phone. See, Viv?* Guilt followed the thought. She shouldn't have let her mind run with the seeds of doubt Vivian had planted. Doubting him was asinine.

A door on the far wall burst open and a broad-shouldered blond-haired man with a gleaming white smile and open arms came into the lobby. "Sammy, how's it going?" He pulled Sam into a manly embrace.

"Awesome. Thanks for seeing us." Sam's arm circled Faith's waist again. "This is my girlfriend, Faith Hayes. Faith, Brent Holloway, the best attorney around."

"He's not kidding. I am," Brent said with a tease in his blue eyes. "Come on back." He led them through the door to his office.

Before taking a seat beside Sam, Faith caught a view of the ocean in the distance. She loved the water, and the sight helped ease her nerves. Sam reached for her hand and laced their fingers together, giving her another thoughtful smile, as if he knew she needed that, too. She was such a fool for worrying. She wouldn't even be here with Brent, taking care of the documents for her website, if it weren't for him.

"Faith." Brent splayed his hands on his desk. "Women Against Cheaters? I guess the name speaks for itself. Tell me what you're doing, what your goals are, and we'll see if we can figure this out and make it easy for you."

She explained how the site had come to be and the immense growth in membership over the past year. "I never expected to want to take it any further, but now I can see all sorts of ways to offer more resources for the members. I'm not sure of the best way to do that, but I'm working on at least trying to build a resource network that offers discounts and referrals for things like therapy, career consulting, maybe discounted legal fees." She couldn't miss the way Brent's eyes moved curiously between her and Sam.

She went on to explain the amount of donations she'd received prior to Sam's, which she still hadn't touched, and confided that she'd never sought out donations and didn't expect to get many.

"I think we can grow the donation network tremendously," Sam said.

Faith's head whipped around. Sam hadn't said anything to her about his thoughts on WAC since they'd made the appointment with Brent.

"Brent," Sam said, "you remember in school when we needed funds for team sports?"

"Door-to-door donations?" Brent arched a brow.

"Yeah, for a day or two, but after that I wrote a letter asking business owners to donate and gave my fundraising packet to my mother. She'd take it to her Peaceful Harbor Small Business Association meetings, and over the course of the next week donations rolled in hand over fist."

Brent laughed and pointed at Sam. "You cheated. I knew it! You used to get the highest donations of everyone."

"Hey, that wasn't cheating. It was smart business." Sam

turned to Faith. "The community would definitely get behind your efforts. You're helping women, single mothers. I know after talking with a few of the members for one afternoon I can't stop wondering how they're doing."

Faith's heart opened further with his confession, knocking the worries Vivian stirred out of sight. Her face must have given her emotions away, because Sam's gaze warmed.

"I do. I keep thinking about Brittany and how she must have felt when she walked in on her boyfriend cheating, and Lira," he said softly. "What her sister did to her? Doesn't it make you want to bring her into a better family?"

"Yeah," she said breathlessly. *And hearing you say that makes me want to be part of yours.*

Chapter Sixteen

SAM AND FAITH left Brent's office an hour and a half later with a solid business plan. The rules and regulations for nonprofits made that route too complicated to pursue, but Faith seemed pleased with the final decision. Brent was going to prepare the paperwork for WAC to become an official LLC, and he'd talk to Phil D'Amato about insurance. Once everything was in order, he'd forward it to Faith for signature. She was much more relaxed than when they'd arrived, which put Sam's mind at ease. Even though they were becoming closer, he worried about that sharp mind of hers and where it took her. Sometimes her eyes still clouded over with doubt. He looked forward to the day when that no longer happened.

He unlocked the truck door and pulled her in for a kiss. She went up on her toes, and that small move, trying to get closer to him, stroked every needy inch of him.

"Thank you for setting that up and for going with me. Brent's really terrific."

"Anything for you." He greedily took another kiss.

She held on to his shirt, gripping it as tight as she had the other night. She moaned into the kiss, and his body roared to life. He lifted her into his arms, her legs naturally winding around his waist as he backed her up against the truck and took the kiss deeper.

"Thought about you all day," he said, pressing kisses to the corners of her mouth. "You were so sexy in there, all business-like and professional."

She turned in to a kiss meant for her cheek. The kiss was hot and wet, urgent and eager. His hands slid beneath her ass, earning another heart-pumping moan.

"So sexy. I love hearing every sound." He sealed his lips over her neck.

"Sam—" Her head tipped back, giving him better access to all that sensitive, delicious skin.

His tongue played over the frantic pulse beating at the base of her neck, and her fingernails clawed at his skin, making him hard as steel. A car chirped, as if a remote locking button had been pressed, and he tore his mouth away, searching the darkness. He found Brent standing beside his car a few feet away, shaking his head.

"Christ," he mumbled. "I forget everything when we kiss. Including that we're standing in the middle of a parking lot."

"And that's bad?" Her tone was playful, tempting.

He pressed her harder against the truck, harder against his

arousal, and her eyes widened.

"I thought we were behaving." *Please tell me we don't have to behave anymore.*

Silence slithered between them like a serpent, and he wanted the forbidden fruit.

"We were." She brushed her lips over his in a series of near kisses, each one more scintillating than the last.

Were. Never before had one word scrambled his brain so fast. He couldn't even remember where they'd planned to go after seeing Brent. Sam was vaguely aware of Brent's car pulling out of the parking lot. With Faith in his arms, he opened the truck door and set her on the seat, allowing her to continue her relentless pursuit of near-kiss torture on his mouth. Every near kiss, every whisper of her warm breath over his skin, made his desire more intense. By the time she drew back, her eyelids at half-mast, his entire body throbbed with need. He shifted her in the seat and closed the door, stalked to the driver's side, and started the truck, futilely trying to regain control. The desire to take her, right there in the front seat of his truck, was overwhelming, but he had too much respect for her to take a chance of someone seeing them.

He pulled her against him and took her in another smoldering kiss, tempting himself to the point of madness. He fastened her seat belt beside him, wanting her near as he drove out of the parking lot. Her hand rested on his thigh, inching higher, squeezing. Faith slid her other hand up the far side of his face.

His eyes remained trained on the road as she began her assault, pressing kisses to his jaw, up his neck. She licked his earlobe and traced the outer shell of his ear.

"Faith," he said on a jagged breath. "I can only take so much teasing."

"I know," she whispered in his ear. "I can't help it."

He turned on to a side road, barely able to hold it together. Every muscle in his body was rigid, and if her thumb brushed any closer to his cock, he was going to lose his battle for control.

He rounded a bend and turned onto another side road, drove a mile or two, and pulled off onto the shoulder as Faith's tongue slid into his ear, obliterating his focus. He slammed the truck into park and in three seconds flat he had their seat belts off and Faith lying beneath him with a sexy smile on her face.

"You are trouble with a capital 'T.'" He nipped at her chin. "You taunt and tease." He traced her lips with his tongue. She tried to lean up and catch his mouth, but he pulled back. "Uh-uh-uh, sweet girl. Two can play at this game."

"Sam." She rocked her hips against his arousal.

"Tell me what you want, baby. You tell me to behave and then you drive me wild. I'm not sure where we stand."

She laughed softly, pulling his face closer. He fought the kiss, hovering a breath away as every inch of her fought to reach him. He ran his hand up her side, over her ribs, and cupped her breast. His thumb played over her nipple the way he knew she loved.

"Sam," she pleaded.

"Do you want me to behave, or do you want me to take you right here, hard and dirty? Slow and sensual? Or both, baby? Is that what you want?" He yanked her shirt up, lifting her bra along with it, freeing one beautiful breast, and licked her taut nipple.

"Ohmygod. Sam."

"I've heard my name enough to know what it is," he teased. "Tell me what you want." His mouth came down over her breast and he sucked—*hard*. Her entire body bowed off the seat. Still sucking her breast, his hand slid down her belly and into her jeans. His fingertips grazed her wetness. The pit of his stomach burned as he dipped a finger inside her. "God, baby, you're so ready for me."

She bit her lower lip.

"Oh no. None of that." Using his teeth, he tugged that lip free. "Talk to me, baby. I'm not going to give you what you need until you do."

She silently rocked her hips again, and he withdrew his hands from her pants and slipped those fingers into his mouth, sucking them clean. Her eyes widened, and their mouths crashed together in a messy, wet kiss. The ache between his legs pumped through his body, as he felt every lush curve, supple and eager. Her nails claimed his back, and when their lips parted, both of them barely breathing, the raw passion he saw in her eyes nearly did him in.

"You're the best kind of torture," he whispered between kisses. "But you're too important to me to get caught up in desire only to have you regret it later. I need to hear you tell me what you want, Faith."

Her eyes clouded over in that middle ground that worried him so much. *Fuck.*

"Faith?"

She shifted her eyes away, breaking his heart in two.

His foot hit the window of the truck. How had he misread her? He was sure she'd tell him she wanted him as much as he wanted her. And he wanted her more than he wanted his next breath, but not like this. Not when she couldn't look him in the eyes and tell him. And—*how could I have been such an asshole?*— not in the truck.

He closed his eyes for a second, trying to regain control.

"It's okay, baby." He kissed her lightly, tucking away his frustration and letting her know he understood her indecision. He backed out of the truck before he could give in to the heat blazing through him or the need throbbing in his pants— focusing instead on the emotions swelling in his spliced-open heart.

"Sam?" She sat up, eyes ablaze. "You're leaving me high and dry?"

"No, babe. I'm leaving you wet and hungry." He pulled her to the edge of the seat and pressed her hand to his zipper so she could feel the effect she had on him and that he was aching just as badly as she was. "And leaving myself hard as a rock."

She stepped from the truck and he reached for her hand. Her pouty lip cut him to his core. He bent down for a kiss, and she leaned out of his reach.

"Where's the guy with the rep for taking what he wants?" she asked, half teasing, half annoyed.

Frustration from holding back his emotions broke free. "The guy you wanted nothing to do with? That's the guy you want now? Because I can be any guy you want, as long as you make it *clear*."

She stared up at him with a perplexed look in her eyes that slayed him, but he was unable to stop the frustration from coming out.

"Tell me, Faith. Do you want the guy who takes what he wants, where he wants, regardless of the ramifications?"

"No. *Yes?* I don't know." She shifted her eyes away.

"Baby." His voice softened as he gathered her in his arms. "You're just as conflicted as I am. That's why you're sending mixed signals. I saw it in your eyes. One second you wanted me, but the next you weren't sure. That's why I stopped."

She trapped that damn lip again.

"It's okay," he assured her. "I'm right here, and I'm into you. *Long-term* into you. But, Faith, you've changed the way I think. I wanted to make love to you in the truck—with my hands, my mouth, my body. And I know the truck isn't the right place, but regardless of that, when we do make love, I need to know you're all in. The other night, you were right there with me. I felt it, saw it, *tasted* it. When you were teasing me on the drive over, you were knee deep into me, but when I was on top of you in the truck, beneath the passion, there was hesitation in your eyes."

The disappointment in her eyes was killing him. He was trying to do the right thing. Isn't that what she wanted? What she deserved? For a guy who thought he knew women, he suddenly felt like a bumbling idiot.

"Everything's different with you, baby. Looks are easy to misinterpret, but words are clear. I need clarity with you, just as you said you needed from me. *Complete transparency.* Once we get to that point, when I know you're not doubting me, I promise you, baby, I won't hold back another second."

FAITH STOOD WITH her heart lodged in her throat, watching Sam pace. Some men needed a suit and tie to look like they could take on the world. Not Sam. He exuded a staggering air of confidence regardless of what he wore or what he was doing, and she'd never seen that confidence waver, except when it came to her. He was known for taking what he wanted. *Except with me.* Everything really was different with her.

Isn't that what I wanted? What I demanded?

She'd unknowingly created this fissure between them, and

tonight what he'd seen in her eyes was Faith rifling through the things Vivian had said to her and trying to push them away, because in her heart she knew her friend was wrong. But Sam was *that* in tune with her. He'd read her emotions before she'd had time to process them. Where most guys would overlook the moment of hesitation she'd felt, Sam had clung to it. He was that worried about doing things right where she was concerned, and that endeared him to her even more and made her feel like a fool for doubting him at all.

She reached for him. His eyes were so full of regret, guilt seared into her heart.

"I'm sorry I overreacted," he said. "I shouldn't have said those things."

"You didn't. I overreacted. You were right, and I appreciate you caring enough to stop, even if I wasn't sure I wanted you to."

"So I *did* see hesitation? Thank God, because you were so upset, I thought I'd made it up in my head."

"You saw hesitation, Sam, but not because I wanted to stop. I was just working through my emotions. I talked to Vivian before we went to meet Brent, and she made me worry that you didn't want to be seen with me around town because…" She paused, knowing she didn't need to bring all that up. He knew why, and so did she.

"It doesn't matter why," she explained. "The truth is, I wanted you to make love to me, but I couldn't think fast enough, and it was embarrassing to admit that aloud. I want you, Sam. All of you. But sometimes a girl just needs to be *taken*."

"Christ, baby," he whispered, and touched his forehead to hers. "I know all about 'taking,' but when it comes to you, I won't ignore what I see. With anyone else—before you— maybe. But not with you, Faith. Never with you. It's taken all of my control *not* to take you these past few days, and I'll wait as long as you need, until you're sure."

"I know, and I appreciate that." She knew this must be torture for him, hearing that she was doubting him *and* that she'd led him on. She wasn't a tease—at least she didn't mean to be—but that's exactly what she must look like.

"Tell me what you were thinking or what Vivian brought up. That I want to be with other women? That I can't control myself if we go out to my usual hangouts?" The hurt in his voice cut her to her core. "And you still wanted to make love with me? No wonder you looked conflicted."

"No. I don't think you want to be with other women. I trust the things you tell me. But Vivian made me wonder if I was just seeing what I wanted to see." The confession felt like lead in her stomach. "But when we were with Brent I realized that my interpretation of you is totally different from anyone else's because I know the real you. Everyone else knows the guy you were or the guy they've heard about. So it makes sense that Vivian's view of you is skewed."

"But if you believe that, then what was the hesitation I saw in your eyes?"

"It's twofold. I was trying to push Vivian's words from my head because I know they aren't true. But also, it's easy to be confident and sexy when you're not paying attention."

"When I was driving," he said.

"Yes. Or texting," she admitted.

His eyes warmed. "You do send sexy texts."

"I'm better with you than I've ever been with anyone else. Sometimes it's all I can do to keep eye contact with you and not cover my face. You say things that make me blush, but I love hearing it."

"Baby, you don't have to be embarrassed with me. I want to honor your feelings, even when that means waiting to be closer. I want you to believe in *me*, no matter what anyone says. And people will say things, act certain ways. I haven't hidden that from you. *That's* why I wanted to wait to go out in town. Christ, your own best friend doesn't trust me."

"I don't care if she does or not," she said firmly, and even though it felt like a betrayal to her best friend, she meant it. She'd made a mistake letting Vivian's worries take over, even if Vivian was looking out for her.

"She's your best friend. Of course you care," he said. "Baby, you'll see that in action at the Rough Riders barbecue, and I'll handle it appropriately. Other women mean nothing to me. You mean everything to me, and I'm going to continue to do whatever I can to make sure you know I'll never hurt you, including backing off when I see something in your eyes that worries me."

The tenderness in his voice drew her closer, her throat thickening with emotions.

"But from now on," he said, "we need a 'go' signal. Something that tells me it's really okay, if it is."

"How about if it's not okay I say 'no' or 'stop'? That's something I can do."

"Yes," he said with a spark of heat in his eyes. "You're really good at that."

"I told you I'm not easy."

"I'll take real over easy any day. This is good, Faith. Getting all this out in the open is so much better than misinterpreting each other or worrying about things that aren't going to happen."

"Thank you for understanding. I can't believe we didn't have a bigger blowup about this. I'm sorry, Sam. I shouldn't have doubted you, but it's been a long time since I felt safe enough to put myself out there."

"Baby, you're always safe with me."

Chapter Seventeen

FAITH WAS SO relieved after they talked, but now, as they climbed out of the truck at Tap It, she was a nervous wreck. Sam said the last thing he wanted was for her to worry about what might happen someday, or to think he was avoiding being seen with her because *he* couldn't handle whatever might come their way. He'd insisted on taking her out in town. At least she'd talked him out of going to Whispers. That would have been too much.

"We really don't have to go here," she said for the hundredth time in the last fifteen minutes.

He folded her in his arms and smiled down at her.

"Hey, we're just a guy and his girlfriend enjoying a dinner date. I shouldn't have made a big deal about wanting to wait to go out in town. It was selfish. I wanted you to dig me so much that nothing anyone could do or say would change your mind." He tucked her hair behind her ear, calm as an afternoon breeze.

"But I *am* that into you. I had to move past Vivian putting doubts in my head, but I did move past it. You don't have to prove anything to me."

"That's good, baby. Then we should have a nice dinner together."

They headed up the steps, and Faith wondered what she expected to happen when they went inside. It wasn't like women were going to jump him in a restaurant. Maybe *she* was making too big of a deal out of his past, too. Maybe Sam was wrong and nobody would act weird once they saw them together.

Before pulling open the door Sam said, "There's only you and me in there. Just us. No one else matters."

They walked inside, the din of the crowded bar to their right mixing with the enchanting hum of the restaurant to their left. The tantalizing aroma of spices and grilled foods hung in the air.

The petite hostess smiled up at Sam. "Hey, Sam." She followed his arm around Faith's waist, offering Faith the same welcoming smile. "Hi. Two for dinner?"

"Yes, please. Natasha, this is my girlfriend, Faith." Sam's eyes honed in on Faith again. "Natasha went to school with Shannon."

"I sure did," Natasha said, giving Faith her attention rather than Sam. "Shannon's a hoot. Follow me. Let's find you a table."

Faith was acutely aware of the eyes of at least five woman

trailing Sam as they walked through the restaurant to a private table near the back. Her mind traveled to dark places she wished it wouldn't, but some of the women were blatantly staring. It made her self-conscious, and worse, she wondered if Sam had been with any of them.

After helping Faith with her chair, Sam sat across the table and reached for her hand. She noticed a couple nearby stealing a glance, probably because they knew Sam in some other context than a sexual conquest, but she couldn't help analyzing every glance.

"You look beautiful tonight." His voice brought her eyes to him. "Hey. There's only you and me here. Don't let anything ruin it. Are you in the mood for a drink?"

"Or three?" she answered, hating herself for being so insecure. This was silly. She shouldn't be this nervous. *We're just two people enjoying dinner.*

Their waitress sidled up to the table. She was a dead ringer for Scarlett Johansson. She gave Faith a cursory once-over. Then her overly made-up eyes shot to Sam, where they remained. "Sam, how are you? I haven't heard from you since the beach party."

He glanced up with a distant expression Faith had never seen. "Hi. Doing well, thanks." He turned a warm gaze back to Faith as he said, "Can we get a bottle of Arietta Cabernet Sauvignon please?"

The blonde narrowed her eyes. "Sure," she said curtly, then

stalked away.

"Did you…?" She held her breath, sure she didn't want to hear the answer.

"Sleep with her? No."

"Then why was she acting like that?"

A slow smile lifted his cheeks. "Because I *didn't* sleep with her."

She leaned forward and whispered, "But I thought you never told anyone no."

Sam rose to his feet, and Faith worried she'd offended him so badly they were going to leave. He moved his chair beside her, sat down, and took her hand in his again. His eyes bored into her. "I have turned women down. Women have turned me down. Not often, but it has happened. What else would you like to know?"

Embarrassment flushed her chest and spread straight up her neck. She wondered if skin could catch flames. How could she have asked him that? And he'd answered. *Honestly!* What was wrong with her? But, okay, now that they'd come this far, why not go for it? How much worse could it get?

She drew in a deep breath, prayed he wouldn't walk out, leaving her sitting there like the loser she must be for wanting to ask this, and said, "Can you just look around and tell me if you see anyone you have slept with so I can stop trying to figure it out?"

He turned and scanned the restaurant, then met her gaze as

calmly as he had before. "You sure you want to know? Or is this a chick trick, where you want to know, but when you find out, you lose your shit?"

She laughed, but inside she was dying. That had to mean he'd recognized at least one woman he'd slept with. "Don't tell me. Because it's probably a case of the latter."

He slid his hand to the nape of her neck and pressed his cheek to hers. How could one touch dissolve her tension so easily?

"There's only one woman in here I want to sleep with, and she's so busy trying to figure out who her competition is she doesn't realize she has none."

He brushed his lips over hers as the waitress brought the wine.

She set the bottle on the table, eyes locked on the back of Sam's head, and with a hand on her hip she said, "Looks like your appetite is as insatiable as ever. Are you ready to order?"

Without moving away from his near-kiss position, Sam said, "We need a few minutes, please."

Faith felt bad for her, regardless of the barb she'd tossed. Being turned down by Sam probably felt a hundred times worse than the jealousy the girl had stirred in her.

Sam kissed Faith softly, then relaxed into his seat, still holding her hand. "Can I ask you something?"

"Sure."

"Look around. Have *you* slept with anyone here?"

"Me?" She laughed as she glanced around the restaurant. Her heart nearly stopped at the sight of Roger Waylin, a guy she'd dated a few months ago. Her eyes snapped back to Sam. Thankfully, she'd turned down Roger's advances. "No. No one."

Sam turned, his eyes landing on Roger, sizing him up. Then those all-knowing eyes came back to her, and his mouth curved up in a satisfied smile. "Good to know."

He poured the wine and handed Faith a glass. "To us."

"The only people in the room." She touched her glass to his.

Sam stayed close throughout their meal, giving Faith his rapt attention, touching her thigh, her hand, her cheek. They fed each other from their own plates, and by the time they finished dinner, Faith couldn't remember why she'd been so nervous in the first place. They drank and flirted, and Sam kissed her so many times he kissed the embarrassment right out of her.

She leaned forward and brushed her mouth teasingly over his. "Want to get the check and go to my place to work on my *communication skills*?"

Heat flared in his gorgeous eyes.

Ten minutes later they were kissing their way through the parking lot, their bodies practically glued together as Sam fished out his keys.

"Sammy!" a woman yelled from across the parking lot.

Sam froze, his lips still on Faith's, his eyes serious.

"Sam! Hey, Sam! Let's have a drink!" another woman hollered.

Sam and Faith both looked in the direction of the sound of a group of women talking and giggling—and headed their way.

"Think we can ditch them?" he asked with a coy smile.

Yes! "Really?"

"Unless you want to stand around and watch me tell them to bug off."

She trapped her lip and immediately let it free. "Hurry!"

Chapter Eighteen

SAM AND FAITH stumbled into her dark apartment in a tangle of limbs and lips, laughter and pleas. Faith walked backward down the short hallway toward her bedroom, lifting Sam's shirt as they kissed, then leaning back just long enough for him to tug it over his head and drop it to the floor. She pulled her top off, and it puddled by their feet. He loved this confident side of her. With her eyes on Sam, she unhooked the front clasp of her bra, and the lace lingerie slipped to the floor. Her breasts were like incandescent moons against her tanned skin. She lowered her chin, looking up at him through her impossibly seductive lashes.

Sam drew her into his arms, his voice hoarse with desire. "Just the sight of you takes me to my knees."

He sealed his mouth over hers in a merciless kiss, his rigid length growing even harder with the press of her nipples against his bare chest. He took the kiss deeper, delirious from the emotions coursing through him. Beats of pleasure pulsed through him, limb by limb, up his torso, burning in his chest, unleashing his last tethers of restraint.

"Baby," he said urgently against her lips, before taking her in another rough kiss, much rougher than he'd intended. He didn't even know what he wanted to say. He just couldn't hold anything back—not a sound, not a look, not a pleasure-filled groan, like the one streaming from his lungs into hers.

He fisted his hands in her hair, deepening the kiss again, unwilling to relent before he got his fill. His hips jerked forward with the press of hers, shocking him back to the doorway where they stood. He gazed into her sultry, smoky eyes, hoping she was still with him.

"Yes, Sam," she said clear as day.

Thank fucking God. Their mouths slammed together in another brutal kiss, like explosives held back for too long. They stroked and groped and plundered each other's mouths, each struggling with the buttons on the other's jeans. Sam grabbed his wallet from his back pocket as they stripped off their clothes, leaving a trail to the bed. He took out a few condoms and tossed them on the nightstand, still kissing Faith. Their mouths parted long enough for Sam to drink in every lush curve. When his gaze rose to hers, her eyes were locked on his eager cock and her tongue slicked across her lower lip.

"Holy Christ you're beautiful," he said, bringing her eyes up to his.

"So...so are you."

"Faith, you have no idea what you do to me. Every word." He brushed his thumb along her lips. "The way you look at me." As he took her in a languid kiss, his insides went soft with emotion, while the rest of him grew harder. The clashing sensations sparked a surge of desire.

He swept her into his arms and laid her on the bed. "The answer was no," he said as he followed her down. Her brows knitted in confusion and her knees fell open as he settled between them. "In the restaurant. I didn't see anyone I had slept with. I wanted you to know, but thank you for liking me enough not to pursue it."

She reached for him. "It's behind me now. Even if you had, I would still be here."

It was all he could do to resist plunging deep inside her, to feel her heat swallow every inch of him and truly make her his. He kissed the corners of her mouth, her chin, and sucked on her luscious lower lip, relishing the eager noises coming from her as she writhed beneath him.

She lifted her head and her eyes—God, her eyes said it all— *I want you. I need you. Make love to me.*

"Tell me," he coaxed.

"I want you, Sam. Make love to me."

He knew how hard it was for her to say the words and had to take her in another mind-numbing kiss to keep from blurting out, *Thank you for trusting me*, which would only embarrass her more. Instead he cradled her face in his hands and said, "All night long, sweet girl."

She gripped his waist, lifting her hips against his hard length. Her wetness teased his sac, sending spikes of heat down his spine. He trailed kisses down her body, loving her breasts, grazing the sensitive nipples with his teeth, then sucking the way she loved, as his hands played over her hips. He kissed every rib, every inch of her belly, until she was panting. Moving lower, he dragged his tongue around her damp curls. The scent of her arousal drew him in. He spread his hands on her inner thighs, lowered his mouth, and feasted on her wet flesh. There was no holding back the urgency and longing that had been trapped inside him. He stroked and sucked and thrust his tongue deep inside her. She clutched at the sheet, arching against his mouth, groaning through clenched teeth, and he knew she was holding back. He plunged his fingers into her, crooking them to reach her pleasure point.

"Come for me, baby. Let go," he urged. "You taste so good, look so beautiful. Show me how much you want me."

Bringing his mouth to her again, he sucked that sensitive bundle of nerves until it was stiff and swollen, and her entire body arched as she shattered against his hand and mouth. Her inner muscles tightened and pulsed. His name left her lips like a prayer, followed by a string of indiscernible sounds of pleasure as she dissolved against him.

LUST COILED TIGHT and hot in Faith's core as Sam claimed her oversensitive flesh again, expertly stroking and licking her toward oblivion. Orgasms had never felt like this before. They simmered and sparked with each slick of his tongue, mounting to near bursting with each stroke of his fingers. Her skin was wet with perspiration, electrically charged, sizzling, rocking, arching, reaching for release.

When Sam's mouth left her, she gasped, lifting her head with the shock of cold air washing between her legs. The look in his eyes as he hovered over her sex, still loving her with his fingers, was raw passion. Good Lord, the man was sex personified. He must have known that seeing him like that—so greedy for her, his mouth wet with her juices, his fingers stroking the secret spot inside her, would take her right up to the edge. His big, hot hand slid over her belly and trapped her nipple between his fingers. He squeezed, and she felt it right between her legs— lightning hot. His lips curved up seconds before his mouth covered her sex again, and he plundered with his tongue *and* his fingers, squeezing her nipple and sending waves of pleasure radiating from her core, down her legs, her arms, all the way to the tips of her fingers and toes. His teeth grazed her flesh just rough and hard enough to spark the orgasm free. Violent pleasure tore through her body, crashing and convulsing with searing heat, peaking with the intensity of a tsunami. Then she was falling again, *down, down, down,* as Sam licked and kissed, staying there until the world came back into focus.

Sam didn't rush, didn't plunge his eager cock into her. He went up on his knees, stroking his formidable erection, squeezing the base as a bead formed at the tip. She loved seeing him touch himself and knew he was trying not to come. The way he was looking at her, like she was the most exquisite creature on earth, made her feel bold—and greedy. On shaky arms she pushed up to a sitting position, hesitating as reality came crashing in.

"Sam, have you…?" She had to ask. Needed to. For her safety.

He cupped her cheek, his eyes warm and loving. "I don't have unprotected sex, baby, and I've been tested twice a year. I didn't commit, but I wasn't stupid."

She breathed a sigh of relief and laved her tongue over his swollen glans, getting her first taste of him. His hand remained at the base as she toyed with his balls, licking them, feeling them tighten against her tongue. She felt his eyes burning into her as she dragged her tongue over the back of his hand to ride up his hard length. He pushed his shaft out toward her, and she took him in, pulling a delicious groan from somewhere deep inside him. She moved his hand, replacing it with her own, stroking his length as she sucked him to the back of her throat. Her cheeks hollowed as she withdrew, then took him in deep again. She didn't want him to come, not yet. But she wanted to give him the same pleasure he'd given her. She wanted this intimacy for both of them.

Palming his length, she lowered herself back down to the bed, forcing herself to maintain eye contact with Sam.

"Condom," he said.

She guided his cock over her pubis and pulled him down. "I want to feel you against me first."

"God, baby," he whispered as he wrapped his strong arms beneath her shoulders and cradled her head. "You're testing every shred of my control."

His mouth stole over hers, invading it with his tongue, pumping air from his lungs into hers. Her hands moved over his back, to his bare ass. She grabbed on to the firm globes, causing his hips to piston. He growled—*growled!*—into the kiss, and whatever resistance she'd had snapped.

"Condom," she said, reaching to the side.

His lips tipped up at the edges as he laced his fingers with her searching hand and held her down, devouring her mouth again and driving her out of her mind.

"Sam!" she said between kisses. "Can't take it."

He deepened the kiss, then tore himself away, making her entire body shudder. His penetrating gaze bordered on predatory, but she saw right through all that thick desire to what he was really looking for, and it opened her heart to him even more.

"Make love to me, Sam. *Now.*"

He snagged a condom, tore it open with his teeth, and was sheathed and perched above her in seconds flat. Her knees fell open wider as he lowered himself down, chest to chest. He felt so good, so warm, so strong. She thought he'd slam into her, unable to hold back a second longer, but Sam never failed to surprise her.

He took her in a slow, scintillating kiss, sparking fire behind her knees, in the crook of her arms, places she never knew could spark. He entered her slowly, kissing her as her body stretched to accommodate his girth until he was buried inside her. Their eyes connected, the urgency quelled to a decadent, sensual hum as they began to move and found their rhythm. Sam moved with potent mastery, gripping her hips and angling her body just so, then driving in impossibly deeper, striking pleasure points inside her she'd never known existed. All that controlled strength bunched beneath her hands as he took her right up to the peak of another climax, holding her there, panting and desperate. Just when she thought she might explode, he quickened his efforts and spirals of ecstasy burst inside her.

"Sam," she cried.

He lifted his face, a mask of tension and potent masculinity. "Again," he said through gritted teeth.

He lifted her legs beneath her knees and wound them around his waist as he found that secret spot again and again. She couldn't hold back the noises streaming from her as heat scorched through her, and every breath-sucking pulse made her body jerk and thrust. Sam reared up, his body stiff and tight, and with the next thrust he surrendered to his own intense release. His hot breath stroked over her slick skin as he gathered her in his arms.

"I'm so into you," he said in a gravelly, sated voice. "You own me."

"You're not a man to be owned," she told him, even though it, like everything he did and said, made her feel safe. "You're a man to be experienced."

"Rationalize it any way you want, but know in your heart that you own me." He pressed a kiss to her forehead. "I am a happily branded man."

Faith's breath caught in her throat. Dare she let herself believe him?

They lay together for a long time. After a while Sam strode to the bathroom in all his bold, naked glory to ditch the condom. Faith had a fleeting thought that he might take one look in the mirror and remember the Sam everyone else knew him to be—and maybe even want to be that man again. Her heart ached at the thought, especially after everything he'd said, but she was trying to be real. She readied herself for the blow, sitting up and gathering the sheet over her chest.

Sam came out of the bathroom, and in one sweep of the gratified look on his face, the curve at the edges of his mouth, and the emotions playing in his eyes, she knew the only blow she needed to prepare for was what it *really* felt like to be Sam Braden's girl.

Chapter Nineteen

LEAVING FAITH LAST night had been near impossible. Sam hadn't been prepared for the emotions that had consumed him when they were making love. He'd not only wanted to stay, but he'd wanted to claim a drawer and set his toothbrush beside hers on the sink. For a guy who, as a rule before going out with Faith, rarely exchanged phone numbers, much less spent the night with a woman, this was bordering on ridiculous. It was crazy. *Insane.* And what was worse was that he'd wanted it so badly, he worried he'd smother her, take too much of her time, invade her space, and push her away. He scoffed at that thought now. Women loved attention, didn't they? But she hadn't asked him to stay, so maybe he was right to worry. The truth was, he hadn't thought this much about a woman...*ever.* Whoever said *absence makes the heart grow fonder* had been spot-on. Here he was more than fifteen hours later, after a long day of work, driving over to pick up Faith for their date and *still* kicking himself in the ass for not staying over.

Instead of sleeping with her in his arms, he'd gone home and texted Cole *again*, asking him to call him the minute he got back in town next Saturday morning. Sam didn't want to take a chance of his brother hearing about him and Faith from anyone else. He knew Cole had turned off his phone, and he'd given their family the number at the resort in case of an emergency. Sam debated using that number now, but easing Faith's mind wasn't an emergency to Cole.

Taking the steps to her apartment two at a time, Sam's heart raced with anticipation. They'd texted a few times during the day, but that was nothing compared to holding Faith in his arms. How could a few hours apart feel like a lifetime?

He knocked and barely had time to blink before Faith answered the door wearing a pair of barely there shorts and a bikini top that showed off every lush curve beneath her open Rough Riders sweatshirt. He couldn't resist drinking her in, from her gorgeous face all the way down to her long legs, which he could still feel wrapped around his waist, squeezing him as she came.

She smiled up at him with more than a hint of wickedness in her eyes. "I guess this is okay, then?"

"You look positively sinful." He'd asked her to dress in a bathing suit, but now he was questioning the date he'd planned. How would he make it through the evening without devouring her? He stepped inside and slid his hands around her waist, beneath the sweatshirt, to her incredibly soft skin. The door clicked shut behind him.

Her arms circled his neck, and she went up on her toes. "I think you need to kiss me now."

"I do like it when you communicate."

His mouth covered hers hungrily, arousing all of his best places. She pressed her soft curves against him, and he couldn't resist taking hold of her perfect ass. She moaned at the intimate touch.

"Missed you, baby." He kissed her again, her body melting against him as he trailed kisses along her neck to the sensitive flesh just beneath her ear.

"I thought about you all day." She went up on her toes again, her hands clutching the back of his neck. "You know that drives me crazy."

"Yeah. I do."

She tipped her head back, giving him better access and writhing against him, making those sweet, seductive sounds in her throat. An invitation too hard to resist. He slid one hand along the edge of her bikini bottom and slipped a finger beneath, dipping into her wetness.

"Mm. Knowing you're wet for me drives me crazy."

"God, Sam." Her voice was barely a whisper.

He drew back and kissed her, searching her heavily lidded eyes, and swore she was right there with him, but he needed reassurance. "Can we play, baby?"

"From now on you have a blanket 'yes' to touch me unless I

specifically tell you to stop." She crashed her mouth over his, her tongue sweeping, searching, *taking*.

Sam hooked his hands in the waistband of her shorts and tore them down, bathing suit and all, and backed her up against the wall. Her cheeks flamed as he nudged her legs open wide before taking her in another urgent kiss.

"Close your eyes," he coaxed, running his hands up and down her thighs. When she closed her eyes, he slid one palm down the center of her body, loving the flush of her skin, her heated, anticipatory breaths. He kissed her neck, light, whispery kisses, trailing his fingers just below her belly button.

"I love the way your breathing changes when I touch you." He reached lower, sliding one finger between her legs and dragging it up over her clit. She sucked in a breath, and he repeated the rhythm again and again. She rocked her hips forward, but he didn't take the bait. He settled his mouth over the curve of her neck, teasing her swollen sex with one slow stroke after another. With his other hand he tugged her top down on one side, freeing her beautiful breast.

"When I tease your nipple, you feel it here"—he pressed his fingers between her legs—"don't you, baby?"

"Yes," she said in a trembling whisper.

"Let's see if I can make you come without entering your sweet body."

A mewling sound escaped her, spurring him on.

She'd told him last night she wanted to be taken, and that

played in his mind like a melody. He licked around her nipple, bringing it to a taut, needy peak, and pressed his thumb to the sensitive bundle of nerves between her legs. She gripped his biceps, urging his hand lower, but he resisted dipping inside her.

"No, baby. Trust me. Let yourself go."

Her head tipped back, breathing hard. He took her nipple between his fingers and squeezed. She went up on her toes, bringing his fingers lower, between her wet folds again. He stroked and rubbed and sucked and squeezed until she was a panting, wet, trembling bundle of nerves on the verge of climax. Her nails cut into the backs of his arms, and he claimed her in a punishingly intense kiss that spiraled through his very core. His desire built, pounding for release as she cried out his name. Her sex pulsed against his hand, begging for him to delve inside, but he continued his relentless pursuit of her pleasure.

"That's it, baby." He sank down to his knees, held her trembling hips against the wall, and brought his mouth to her quivering sex.

She fisted her hands in his hair, going up on her toes as she came again, hard and loud. As she came down from the crest, she panted out his name.

"Sam. I need you inside me," she begged, trying to push his board shorts down with shaking hands.

He laced his fingers with hers, kissed her again, nearly coming at the thought of her tasting herself on his tongue, his lips, his breath. It took all his willpower not to bury himself deep inside her, but he wanted so much more with Faith. He wanted her to know that what he felt for her went so far beyond the physical she'd never question it again.

"We have a date."

She kissed him again, then tore her mouth away. "Wait, what?"

The sound of her voice chipped away at his resolve. "Our date?"

Her eyes filled with determination. "You are *not* leaving me like this. Take me Sam. *Now.*"

The world spun away as he pulled a condom from his wallet, pushed down his shorts, and sheathed himself. In one hard thrust he was buried deep. They both stilled at the intensity of their joining. She felt so good, so tight, so eager. Passion raged through them with every thrust, every animalistic noise, as he pounded into her. They ate at each other's mouths, shoulders, arms, chests, everywhere they could grasp. The sounds of their frantic lovemaking filled the small apartment. His thoughts fragmented until only one thought held firm. *Faith. Faith. Faith.* Heat pooled at the base of his spine as he neared release. He lifted her into his arms, taking her deeper.

Her head tipped back. "Oh God. I'm gonna come."

He cupped the back of her head in a raw act of possession and brought her mouth back to his again, wanting to feel the surge of emotions as her climax hit. Her sex tightened around his cock, milking the come right out of him. Every hot jet took him higher, brought them closer together.

As they came down from their high, he was lost in her. Faith gazed into his eyes and ran her fingers along his cheek. "You're everything I never thought you were."

Still caught up in her and his all-consuming emotions, his answer took no thought. "You're everything I always knew you were."

AFTER WASHING UP, kissing and teasing as they dressed, and finally making it down to Sam's truck, they were on their way to their clandestine destination. As they drove down tree-lined roads, with Faith tucked possessively against Sam's side, his arm lazily draped over her shoulder, she felt more relaxed than she had in ages. Maybe sex should always come before a date. *Maybe I should come before each date.* She laughed softly at the thought.

"What's funny?" he asked.

"Nothing. Just thinking about things."

He kissed her temple and his eyes went serious. "Things as in *us*?"

Did his mind ever relax? Would it ever? Or would he always want to be right there with her, emotionally and physically? That, she realized, was the most wonderful worry of all.

"Nosy tonight, aren't you?" She couldn't tell him what she was thinking about. It was bad enough that she'd demanded that he *take* her. She'd turned into a vamp. A vixen. *A monogamous slut.* She laughed again. *Oh crap!*

He looked at her out of the corner of his eyes. "You're having a party and I'm not invited?"

"Believe me, you *don't* want to know what I was thinking." She knew that was a fib. He would love knowing she was thinking about how much she loved what they'd done, but that would also lead to more playtime, and she was curious about the date he'd planned.

He turned onto a dirt road. The sun hung low in the sky, casting a romantic glow over the river. Sam parked between two tall trees and turned toward Faith. His eyes were so warm, so loving her thoughts stumbled. He brushed his thumb over her lips.

"You couldn't be more wrong. When you smile, it makes my whole world brighter. I want to know what makes you laugh as much as I want to know what sparks that minx inside you." He took her in a sensual kiss.

"How do you do this to me?" She trapped her lip between her teeth and immediately released it. *Sheesh.* He affected her so strongly, in the very best of ways.

"What's that exactly?"

"Make me feel like I can tell you anything? Like I want to tell you everything?"

He held her gaze, the *pull* she'd come to expect between them stronger than ever.

"The same way you make me want to be a better man."

"Sam." She didn't care how dreamy her voice sounded. She felt dreamy. He was dreamy. "Were you always this honest with other women? It's disarming."

"I told you my filter was set to *honest*. Come on." He led her out of the truck and grabbed two inner tubes from the back.

How did I miss those? She knew the answer. She'd been captivated by a certain tall, dark, enticingly honest and hot man. He handed her a cooler, then tossed a blanket over his shoulder and carried two towels under his arm.

"We're going tubing?" she asked with an excited smile. She hadn't been tubing since she'd first moved to Peaceful Harbor.

"Is that okay?"

"More than okay. But where are we? I've never seen this part of the lake."

"Because it's on my private property." He nodded across the water, where the tip of a roof was visible over the trees.

"You live here? On the water? I had no idea." It made sense, with how much he loved his business. She could see him living out here in the woods with the lake at his back. It was a very Sam setting.

"I own a couple of acres. Nate and Jewel live around the bend, not far from my place. But you're sworn to secrecy about Paradise Cove." He led her through the trees toward the water's edge.

She smiled at the name. "Paradise Cove?"

"Don't poke fun. My cove, my name."

Sam dropped the inner tubes by the edge of the water and spread the blanket out on the sandy shore. He set their things down, placed his hands on his hips, and raked his eyes down Faith's body, leaving a trail of heat in their wake. "Time to strip." He raised his brows in quick succession.

"You're such a man." She teasingly rolled her eyes. "We just did it back at my apartment."

"I didn't mean so we can fool around, but…" He took off his shirt and tossed it onto the blanket. "Baby, that was an appetizer. Quick and dirty." His eyes turned sinful as he closed the gap between them and embraced her. "You haven't been loved properly today, and we have years to make up for." He kissed her neck, her ear, her cheeks, her nose.

She laughed at his playfulness. "Years, huh?"

"Ages," he said, coming in for a full-on assault of her mouth.

Good Lord, he could kiss. His mouth was hypnotizing, hard and fast, then soft and sensual, without ever breaking their connection. And the way he held her, like he never wanted to let her go, made her insides tight and hot. She went up on her toes and realized she was practically humping him, gyrating her hips, clawing at his back. Holy moly, she was already damp again. He was, without a doubt, the very best kind of addiction, and she wanted no part of a twelve-step anti-Sam program.

She pushed away, smiling at their intense connection. "You're turning me into a sex maniac."

"There's nothing wrong with wanting your man." He reached for her again and sank his teeth into her neck.

"Ohmygod. Sam!" Laughing *and* panting, she wrenched free from his grip. "There is when every kiss makes me want to do dirty things no matter where we are." She grabbed an inner tube and strutted off to the water.

Suddenly his arm swooped around her waist. She shrieked and kicked as he carried her into the water under one arm, his tube in the other.

"Sam!" She wrapped one arm around his neck and her legs around his waist, struggling to keep hold of her inner tube. "This was your plan, wasn't it? To get me hot and bothered and then get me to cling to you like a monkey?"

"I wish I was that creative, but the truth is, you looked hot strutting into the water, and I just couldn't resist picking you up."

Wow, she loved hearing that.

He kissed her quickly and she dropped her inner tube, then lifted her under her arms and set her on it. "Now stop trying to get into my bathing suit and let's enjoy the water before it's pitch-dark."

"You're a pain."

He hopped onto his inner tube and reached for her hand.

"Never said I was easy."

She laid her head back and closed her eyes as they drifted around the cove. "Everyone knows Sam Braden is easy." She opened one eye, peering at his suddenly clenched jaw, and chided herself for the comment. "But I know the *real* Sam, and he's more complicated than a Rubik's Cube."

Chapter Twenty

SAM AND FAITH floated around the cove, warmed by what was left of the retreating sun. Their voices were joined by the peaceful sounds of leaves rustling as the evening breeze swept over them and the water lapping at their inner tubes. Sam's eyes were closed, and he looked more at home on the water than he did on land.

Faith squeezed his hand, bringing his eyes to hers. "How did you end up with Rough Riders? Did you always know you wanted to do that kind of work?"

"I've always loved the water, rock climbing, skydiving. Just about any high-adventure sports. In college I studied geology and environmental engineering, trying to figure out what I wanted to do, and appeasing my parents with a degree, of course."

"Your parents seem really nice, though I don't know them that well."

"You will," he said easily, warming her from head to toe.

"My dad's ex-military, and, well, my mom is anything but. Dad was steadfast about each of us earning degrees, and he really wanted us to follow in his military-career steps, but I knew that wasn't for me. I'm too rebellious, too restless. Nate"—his tone turned thoughtful and slightly pained—"was the only one who was wired for that type of life."

She knew about Jewel's brother being killed overseas, and she'd heard that Nate blamed himself, though she didn't know the whole story.

"Anyway, I tried internships in both geology and engineering, but I wanted more. As childish as it sounds, I didn't want someone else directing my days."

"That's not childish. It sounds like you knew yourself well enough even then to know what would make you happy."

"I wasn't as focused as I could have been. I spent a year after college going on as many treks as I could, backpacking, staying at hostels, camping out. I was hiking the Colorado Mountains with my cousin Wes, who lives out that way, and he was the one who suggested I look into adventure companies. At that time Rough Riders was just a boat rental business with five kayaks. Not much to it."

He pulled her inner tube against his. "You felt too far away." Smiling as he held their inner tubes together, he said, "I met with the guy who owned the place, and he was looking to retire. He didn't want much for the business, because it barely earned anything."

"Weren't you afraid of failing? Of risking your money?"

He shook his head. "Fear never entered the picture. I was ecstatic. I couldn't wait to dive in and make it my own. Ty was nineteen or so at that point, but he'd been climbing for years, and he and I had spent summers together going on excursions from the time he was a teenager. He helped me tremendously when I first started, outlining what type of adventures to offer, where to go, what to accept, where to draw my lines. Even back then he was like an encyclopedia of knowledge. He's so freaking smart he blows my mind."

She knew he and Ty were close, but she'd had no idea how deep their friendship went. "So you just dove in? Your parents didn't try to talk you out of it?"

"Pretty much. I don't think my dad was thrilled with my choice, but he knew me well enough to realize if he tried to talk me out of it, it would only make me want it more. He told me what to expect as a business owner. Who knows? Maybe that was his way of trying to talk me out of doing it, or maybe he was just laying the truth out for me. I expect it was the latter. He gave me all sorts of resources and networks to learn about seasonal businesses and the impact of recessions on companies like mine. It was all very valuable information, and it helped me circumvent many of the pitfalls."

"And your mom?" Maisy Braden had stolen Faith's heart when she'd lain her own on the line. *Please don't break my boy's heart. He's tough as nails, but he's also sweet as sugar.*

Sam turned his face up toward the sky with a sigh. "My mom has always told us that no matter what we do, we have to love it. As focused as my dad is on career stability, my mom's focus is on personal happiness. They complement each other well."

When he turned his warm eyes back to Faith, they were filled with emotion. She didn't want to go a day without seeing that look in his eyes.

"Tell me about the adventure side of the business," she said, realizing she knew almost nothing about what his business entailed beyond boating.

"I host all sorts of expeditions, mostly on the off-season. Mountain treks, climbs, camping trips, rafting excursions."

"So, you travel a lot?"

"Some months more than others."

She nodded, feeling her heart crack open at the thought of missing him while he was away.

"Hey." His voice turned thoughtful. "We'll figure this out. It's not like I'm gone all the time. Sometimes just two or three nights. I've got a buddy, Cal, who helps me with the trips out West, and now that Tex is on board, I don't have to go on every trip."

"I don't want to change your business, Sam. I can deal with you being away. I'll stock up on ice cream and try not to think about you out on some mountain, or river, with damsels in distress vying for your attention." She shifted her eyes away, her stomach clenching at the thought.

"Hey, Braden's Girl," he said with such a loving tone, it drew her attention.

The look in his eyes filled the crack in her heart. Every time she doubted him, one look into his honest eyes told her it was a wasted emotion.

"This shouldn't be a deal breaker, Faith. I want this to work between us, and I'll do whatever it takes. And as far as girls go, I don't mix that type of pleasure with those trips. I never have, and you can thank Cole for that. He pounded that into my head when I first bought Rough Riders."

She imagined her boss—smart, professional, caring Dr. Braden—giving Sam life lessons on business and sex. It was a strange thing to imagine, but what was even odder was the thought that Sam would have listened to anyone where women and his very active sex life were concerned. That told her how much Sam respected Cole and that he'd never put his business at risk, and there was no way she'd ever ask him to.

He sat up, expertly balancing on the inner tube as he leaned in so close she could kiss him if she tried. It was the intense look in his eyes that stopped her from trying.

"I've never had a reason to think outside of my original business plans, but that doesn't mean I can't or won't do it. I told you I'd never let you down, and I meant it. There's never been anything tying me to this area in the off-seasons." He reached for her hand. "Until now."

Chapter Twenty-One

SETTLED ON THE blanket as the sun dipped from the sky, Sam poured them each a glass of wine and began unpacking the dinner he'd prepared. He couldn't stop thinking about his off-season adventure trips and how to make it work now that he and Faith were together. He didn't want to be away from her for long spans of time, but he didn't have the answers. Not yet, at least.

"Let's see. We've got summer orzo with shrimp, mixed with vegetables, because food needs color to taste good." He winked. "Watermelon-cucumber salad, snap peas, radish salad, grown from Tempest's garden, and French bread. It's not much, but it's light and should taste pretty good. And for dessert—" He tossed a pack of Skittles onto the blanket.

"You really do like them?"

He took great pride in saying, "Filter set to honest, as I said."

"Sam, this looks delicious. You *made* it? When did you have time?"

"I can't tell you all my secrets. Besides, I'll always make time for us."

She was looking at him like she was seeing him for the very first time, wide-eyed and full of wonder. "You put me to shame. My dinner usually consists of a PowerBar and ice cream."

"Hey, a guy's got to learn to fend for himself. Well, that and after spending enough nights living in the woods, you find new pleasures in the little things you took for granted when you had a roof over your head."

"I bet that year off did wonders for your survival skills. Thank you for going to all of this trouble." She speared a shrimp and put it in her mouth. "Mm. This is really good."

They ate and chatted about Sam's year off after college, and the conversation circled back to Rough Riders. Sam told her about Lira working for him, which she said she'd seen on the Women Against Cheaters website.

"Lira said you found a therapist for her to speak with, too," Faith said.

"Actually, Tempe found her. She found a few therapists who are willing to talk about helping your members. I'm not sure if they'll offer free sessions or discounts, but I've got their information in the truck."

"You talked to Tempe about my site?"

"The morning after the car wash I had breakfast with my family. Tempe is a music therapist, and she knows so many people. I asked if she knew of anyone. No big deal."

"Sam, that's a huge deal. Thank you." She hugged him. "You've done so much, between helping Lira, the donation, connecting me with Brent, and now this. Thank you."

"I told you at the car wash that I wanted to help."

She nibbled on her lip. "I'm sorry I didn't believe you."

"It's okay. I might not have believed me either." That earned him a genuine smile that warmed him to his core. He set their dishes aside and took her hand as he rose to his feet. "Walk with me?"

"I love that you like taking walks."

"I like them more when you're with me." He grabbed her sweatshirt and helped her put it on. "It'll get chilly since your bathing suit is wet."

They walked along the shore, listening to the water lap gently against the rocks.

"How did you end up in Peaceful Harbor working for Cole? Did you always want to work in the medical field?"

She nodded. "I love helping people, and I love medicine."

"But why Peaceful Harbor? It's not exactly a booming metropolis."

"I went to college near home, and I always thought I'd graduate, work in my hometown, get married…" She gazed out over the water with a pensive look on her face. "Things changed, and it was too hard to stay in Oak Falls, so I started looking for a job online and saw Cole's ad. It's close enough to drive home whenever I want, and Cole and Jon are so nice."

"So, a few interviews with them and you were sold?"

"Pretty much."

Sam could see there was more to this story, and he wished she trusted him enough to share it with him. But he wouldn't push the subject. She was here, and that was enough for him until she was ready to talk about it.

They walked to the other side of the cove, where they climbed to the top of a big boulder and sat with their feet hanging over the edge, looking out at the moon's reflection dancing off the inky water. When Faith leaned her head against his shoulder, he lifted her hand and pressed a kiss to it. The affection he felt for her grew insurmountably every time they were together. His father's words sailed through his mind: *Your first real taste of adult love. The type of love that consumes your every thought. Once you get a taste of that, you'll do anything and everything for more. You'll want to drown in it.*

"I left Oak Falls because my boyfriend cheated on me."

Faith's voice pulled him from his thoughts, and the high that he was riding deflated with her confession. He bit back the immediate reaction of wanting to slaughter the guy who hurt her, and focused on the trust she was placing in him. He wrapped her in his arms.

"I'm sorry. That must have been very painful."

"It wasn't fun, that's for sure. He said I didn't give him enough attention, that I didn't really want him, or have room in my life to make him happy. It was unexpected, to say the least, but staying in my hometown wasn't an option. We'd dated for so long. I thought I'd graduate and marry JJ." She shrugged, but the hurt in her eyes, in her voice, was thick as tar.

"It was humiliating, and it hurt for a long time. It was like we were on this path, and then we weren't. Or he wasn't. Same thing." She paused and drew in a deep breath. "It took me months to shake off the idea that he'd cheated because I'd somehow done something wrong, or hadn't been enough for him. Now I know he did me a favor, but then? I guess I was so busy with school and work that I never gave it much thought. Or maybe I never gave him much thought, which is worse, actually."

"Baby, cheating is never the answer." It took effort to soften the anger he felt toward this JJ asshole. "Even if you two were having trouble, that's not the way to handle it. The guy didn't deserve you."

She gazed up at him. "It's so weird that you, of all people, would get that. You said you'd never had a girlfriend."

"I said I hadn't had a girlfriend since high school. Since I was sixteen, to be exact."

"First love?" she asked with a curious smile.

"I don't know. First everything, I guess," he admitted. "But I was a kid. I didn't even know what love was. First infatuation is probably more accurate."

"First heartbreak?"

"First and last." He gazed into her eyes, wanting to share what he'd never shared with anyone before. "We only went out for two months, but at sixteen our hormones were on fire, so every minute felt like a lifetime. Her name was Keira Jacobson, and she lived twenty minutes outside of town. Man, I haven't thought about her for so many years, it seems like a lifetime ago. But she was all I thought about back then. I met her at a football game and saw her a few times each week after that. And one day I showed up early. I can't remember why. Maybe I cut my last class or something. I went to her school and saw her kissing some other guy." He shrugged.

"So you broke up?"

He shook his head. "Not right away. Not until later that night, after she told me he meant nothing to her, he was just a friend, and they got carried away—a few times."

"Oh, Sam." She climbed onto his lap and wrapped her arms around his neck. "I'm sorry. I hate that you know what that feels like."

The empathy in her eyes was real, and it touched him deeply, especially since she knew he'd never committed to anyone since then. "I was a kid. I blocked her out of my mind and carried on."

"And decided nothing lasts forever," she said, clearly remembering what he'd said about wabi-sabi. "And that's when you began your no-commitment lifestyle."

"You remembered."

MELISSA FOSTER

"I remember everything you ever say. It's bordering on obsession." She grabbed his cheeks and kissed him. "Don't judge me."

The teasing glint in her eyes made him want to tell her he loved that she remembered his words. That he wanted to be her obsession. It sure as hell wouldn't be teasing if he did.

"My only judgment is to say you're incredibly brave. You moved away from your family, friends, the future you had planned, and you started over in an unfamiliar place."

"Look who's talking. You go on all sorts of adventures that I've never even thought about trying. Skydiving?" She rolled her eyes. "So scary."

"You'll try them with me." He wrapped his arms around her waist. "We'll try everything together. But there's a world of difference between bravery with physical things and the courage to leave everything you know. I still live in my hometown, surrounded by the people who love me unconditionally, and I'll probably never move away from them."

She searched his eyes with a serious gaze. "That's different. I never would have left my family and friends if I'd thought I could deal with seeing my ex all the time, but I couldn't. But you? After you got hurt, you were brave enough to stick around and lock away that huge heart of yours that I lo—like so much."

Sam couldn't stop the greedy grin from spreading across his face. "You love my huge heart."

"I *like* your huge heart." She pressed her forehead to his

chest. "Like, like, like."

He didn't need to hear her say it. He'd seen her emotions in her eyes, and that would hold him over until they were both ready to admit that what was happening between them was above and beyond anything they'd ever felt before. But he couldn't resist teasing her. "What other *huge* things of mine do you love?"

"Sam!" Her cheeks flamed red.

He pulled her into a chaste kiss. "I love your huge boobs—I mean *heart.*"

She smacked his chest and they both laughed.

"Stop thinking about my boobs. Tell me what happened with Keira."

"She didn't have huge boobs."

She smacked him again. "You're such a guy! I meant have you stalked her on social media or anything like that?"

"You know me better than that. I don't stalk, although I'd stalk you." He leaned in for another kiss. He loved that Faith wasn't jealous of what he'd felt for Keira as much as he loved that she didn't judge him for the way he'd lived his life.

"I heard her father took a new job and they moved away a few weeks later. What about you? Did you love that guy's *huge heart,* too?"

"I thought I loved him, but…"

She bit her lip, and he brushed his thumb over it.

"I like when you touch me like that," she admitted quietly.

"And I like hearing what you like."

"Sam, this is going to sound like a line, but it's not. I promise. In those two years, I never felt for him what I feel for you, and we've only been together for a few days."

"Ditto," he whispered, kissing her again. "But I was infatuated with you for way longer. The whole time I've known you."

"Ditto."

Sam had known she was into him from the way she became flustered and shy around him when he visited Cole at work, but hearing her say it gave him immense pleasure. "You were my forbidden fruit."

"Forbidden?"

"Cole warned me away from you from the very first time I saw you."

Her eyes widened.

"Don't get upset with him. He's a smart man. He didn't want me to ruin your life. He values and respects you as an employee, and he cares about you as a person. And unfortunately, he, like everyone else in town, knows what I was like. Too risky for your protected heart."

He remembered the afternoon in her office when she'd said that to him and how conflicted she'd looked despite her confident and earnest tone.

Her cheeks pinked up at her words coming back at her, and in the space of a breath she harnessed that embarrassment and it morphed into a tease. "You're not bad without your book cover."

"Not bad, huh? I'll have to try harder."

She rested her head on his shoulder again. "Just keep being who you are. I really like *my* version of Sam."

He knew he'd never stop being the best man he could be for her. Not in a week, a month...*a lifetime*?

Chapter Twenty-Two

SAM AND FAITH stayed at the lake until after ten, talking and kissing and doing what they did when the end of each of their dates neared. *Procrastinating.* Faith watched Sam stow the towels and blanket behind the seats, anxiety burgeoning in her chest. She began making up excuses to stay out later. *We could go out for ice cream. Take a walk on the beach. Go dancing.* But she was wearing a bathing suit, and she didn't want any of those distractions. She wanted more time with Sam. To learn more about him, spend more time in his arms. The degree with which that desire consumed her knocked her off-kilter.

They walked around the truck to the passenger door, and as he reached for it, she said, "Sam—" at the exact second he said, "Faith—"

His lips curved up. "You first."

She fought the urge to bite her lip, fought the anxiety tingling in her chest, and borrowed courage from the loving look in his eyes.

"I don't want the night to end."

"I was trying to figure out how to get you up to my place without sounding like a letch."

"Okay." The word came fast, and as she said it, her anxiety fell away. Being with Sam was the rightest thing she'd felt in as long as she could remember. Probably since the day she walked into her first physician assistant class, that's how clear her mind had become. She knew then she was making the right choice, and as Sam's eyes gleamed with happiness, she knew she'd found the right path again.

He lived down a long, heavily wooded road. Butterflies took flight in Faith's stomach as they pulled down a gravel driveway and parked beside his motorcycle, a four-wheeler, and a Jeep.

"Do you have company? You can take me home if you do."

Without a word he kissed her, taking it deeper in answer to her offer. "Still want me to take you home?"

"Only if you're coming, too." Her eyes widened. "I mean…"

"You meant exactly what you said, I hope." He kissed her again.

It was a kiss so different from the urgency they'd shared before their date. Everything felt different, less frantic, more *real*. Their relationship had somehow shifted through the course of the evening. Or maybe it had been shifting since they'd first come together.

Sam stepped from the truck and helped her out. "I don't

have company. They're my toys."

"Ah, I should have known," she teased.

Sam's cabin was built atop a grassy knoll with several large windows, nearly all of them open, overlooking the water. There were no gardens or pristine landscaping in sight. Wild shrubs and trees of varying heights and types sprang up like sentinels on the lawn, reminding her of what he'd said about finding beauty in imperfection. Two brightly colored kayaks were nestled on the grass by the woods, and a circle of chairs surrounded what looked like a fire pit. A long dock jutted out over the dark water. It was so peaceful, so different from the concrete streets below her balcony; it felt a world away, not mere minutes.

"It's really pretty out here," she said as they climbed the steps to the porch.

He kissed her again. "You're really pretty out here."

He was so openly affectionate, greedily kissing her so often, she came to expect it as much as she reveled in it. She still couldn't imagine how such a loving man could go without a real relationship for so long, but she counted herself lucky. There were plenty of women who'd probably tried to catch Sam, and if they had, she never would have had the pleasure of being with him.

He opened the front door, revealing a masculine living room–kitchen combination, with dark furnishings, a wood-burning stove, and dark wide-planked wood floors. The walls were littered with pictures of Sam and his family and, she assumed, his friends.

He turned on the stereo, filling the room with a soft melody. "Make yourself comfortable. I'll be right back." He disappeared through a door to the left of the kitchen.

Faith checked out the pictures. Sam's eyes were alight with joy as he hung from a rope on the side of a rocky cliff. In another he sat in an enormous raft with Ty and a few other guys, water spraying over their backs. She moved from one picture to the next, drinking in the rugged, sexy man she was falling for harder by the second. She came to a picture of Sam and Cole, both dressed in waders, standing in knee-high water and holding fishing poles. Sam's hair was windblown, standing on end, his cheeks pink, probably also from the wind. She imagined a younger Sam, listening to Cole's advice when he started his business, and she prayed her and Sam's relationship wouldn't hinder his and Cole's. Knowing Cole had warned him away from her worried her a little, but she wouldn't let that drag her down. Not when everything Sam did lifted her up.

She walked around the cozy room and came to a picture of Sam and his parents. He looked like a surly teenager, with lanky arms and legs, his hair in need of a trim. She lingered there, wondering what it must have been like to be his girlfriend at sixteen. She wished she'd known him then. Was he as loving then? Did he treat Keira as special as he treated her?

"That was taken out at my uncle Hal's ranch in Weston,

Colorado. See the horses in the back?" Sam wrapped his arms around her from behind. His breath smelled minty.

"I wish I knew you then," he said, turning her in his arms. "I could have kept you from ever dating the guy who hurt you."

Her heart squeezed. "And maybe I could have kept you from getting hurt, too."

"I wish I hadn't wasted all that time fighting my attraction to you. I wish I had asked you out the first day I saw you."

"I wouldn't have gone," she said honestly. "I was too broken back then. I wasn't ready, and you probably weren't ready for me, either."

"Then I hope we can make up for that time, because I'm not sure I'll ever get enough time with you. Even if we spent every day of the rest of our lives together, I think I'd still feel like it wasn't enough."

Could they do this? Build a world of wishes and hopes so fast? Is this what love was? Did it hit you out of the blue, when you weren't looking for it? With the least likely person?

He rubbed his nose against hers, swaying to the music. "What's that look? What are you thinking?"

Their bodies were so in sync, like they'd been dancing together for years, just as they'd been the night on the roof of Mr. B's. Could it be that their hearts were, too?

"That *this*, *us*, is so big," she admitted. "I feel so much."

"Me too. Let's not fight it."

His mouth brushed over hers, and she breathed him in. His

scent had become familiar, too. One whiff sparked feelings of safety and desire. They danced in a slow circle, feet barely moving, hearts tripping over each other. She pressed a kiss to the center of his chest, conscious of every point their bodies touched and the feel of his hands spread possessively across her lower back. If she could stay right there in his arms forever, she'd die a happy woman.

His mouth came coaxingly down to her in a kiss that was passionate without being rough and made her feel like she was going *up, up, up* on an invisible cloud. When their lips parted, she missed his taste. *Missed* it, didn't *burn* for it. This was bigger, a pronounced longing from secret places deep inside her. Hidden places she didn't know could want, places that made her feel on the verge of tumbling over an edge. Sam gazed into her eyes, and the raw emotions she saw drew her right in. She was utterly lost in him. In them.

"Stay with me tonight," he whispered against her cheek, and then those satiny dark eyes found hers again. "Let me love you until the stars fade and hold you until the sun rises."

Her throat thickened with emotions. Her voice came as a threadbare whisper. "Love me, Sam."

Sam laced his fingers with hers, and as he led her into the bedroom, she knew she'd remember this moment, the look in his eyes, and the tremulous, aching love blooming inside her forever.

STANDING BESIDE HIS bed, the bed Sam had never shared with a woman, in the cabin that had been his sacred space until Faith, Sam realized his life had split into two distinct times. Before Faith and after Faith. He hadn't thought twice about bringing her to his favorite cove or bringing her home. He stripped away her clothing, kissing each area as it was revealed, before moving on to strip himself bare. Feeling the heat of Faith's hungry, loving gaze move down his body, he was consumed with emotions bigger than he could name.

He held her gaze as he sheathed his eager length and lowered her down to the bed, whispering, "I want to share everything with you."

"Yes, Sam. Everything," she said, reaching for him.

He cradled her face in his hands, pouring all of his emotions into this moment, this embrace, this kiss, as he sank into her tight heat. She raised her hips, taking him deeper. His head spun, bowled over with the intense emotions consuming him. He laced their hands together and shifted his hips, stroking over her pleasure points. Her body quivered and bowed beneath him as they found their rhythm.

"I'm falling so hard for you, baby. So hard."

He claimed her mouth, thrusting faster, harder. Her fingers curled around his, and her eyes slammed closed.

"Open your eyes, baby. Let me see what you're feeling."

Her eyes fluttered open, fire, lust, and need battling for domination. He lifted her legs around his waist and slowed their pace, wanting that look and the sensations mounting, building, pounding inside him to last forever. Her nails dug into his skin, bringing exquisite pain with pleasure so intense he couldn't hang on to a single thought.

Her thighs tightened around him and he captured her mouth again.

She clung to him again, gasping and pleading. "Sam. *Sam—*"

She arched up, burying her face in his neck and surrendering to the forceful climax. A stream of pleasure-filled cries filled the room, echoed in his mind, driving him further into her. Desire coiled at the base of his spine, drawing his balls up tight against her slick heat. She clawed at his back and bit down on his shoulder—shattering his last shred of control. He held her so tight he feared she'd bruise, but he was powerless to loosen his grip as he came, and came, and came.

A sheen of sweat covered them both as they clung together in the aftermath of their lovemaking. Sam's thoughts whirred and staggered, defying every effort to trap them in place. He rolled onto his side as he slipped from her body, and she moved with him, lying on her side so they were nose to nose.

Their lips reached for each other, sneaking kisses with the last of their energy. They lay there so long, Sam lost all sense of time. At some point he got up and took care of the condom. They went in and out of sleep, making love in the waking hours and catching naps in between. Each time they came together was more intense and more intimate than the last, and by the time dawn snuck in through the windows, Sam was so full of Faith, he could barely think of anything else.

As she slept, he brushed her hair from her forehead, pressed a kiss to her soft skin, and whispered, "I'm drowning in you, sweet girl."

Chapter Twenty-Three

FEW THINGS COMPARED to waking up in Sam's arms. Unfortunately, Faith's plants wouldn't care if she slept better enveloped by Sam's incredibly hot bod, or if the mind-blowing sex was worth the lack of sleep. She needed to remember to water them when she got home. It had been an incredible, blissful week since she and Sam began spending nights at his cabin, and every time she went home she was rushing, checking the WAC site, gathering clothes for the next day, or giving in to Sam's kisses. Like the food that was probably spoiling in her refrigerator, the plants were undoubtedly dying a horrible, drought-laden death.

Sam stood beneath the shower spray, rinsing shampoo from his hair. She loved watching the soapy water drip over his hard body. Yeah, those plants could wait. Nothing compared to being with Sam. He pulled her beneath the shower spray and kissed her neck. They'd just made love, and her body still flamed with renewed desire.

"What are you thinking about?" he asked between kisses.

"You. Sex. And my plants, but mostly sex. With you." *Ramble much?* Two weeks into their relationship and he still scrambled her brain.

He turned off the water and stepped from the shower to retrieve a towel.

"Lucky me," he said as he wrapped it around Faith and drew her against his glistening frame.

"Are you nervous about me talking to Cole?" he asked, placing lazy openmouthed kisses against her shoulder.

They were both having difficult conversations today. Sam insisted on being at Cole's when he and Leesa returned from their honeymoon, so Cole would hear about their relationship from him first, and after the conference call she had scheduled with a women's group, Faith needed to have a heart-to-heart with Vivian. She'd been avoiding her calls since their last conversation. She knew Vivian was trying to keep her from getting hurt, but her doubts about Sam made Faith stumble over her own beliefs. She didn't want to undermine their relationship, especially when Sam was trying so hard. She believed in him, and somehow she needed to convince Vivian of that. Never again would she allow anyone else's opinion of Sam to sway her. There probably wasn't a woman on earth who knew him like she did.

She closed her eyes, pushing away those thoughts and enjoying the feel of his lips brushing over her skin.

"Faith?"

Eyes still closed, she said, "Yeah?"

He stopped kissing her shoulder, and she opened her eyes. "Cole. Your *boss*. You remember him, right? Big, serious guy? Told me to stay away from you?"

"What about him? Oh! Sorry." She'd been so lost in her own thoughts she had forgotten he'd asked a question. "No, I'm not worried about whether he'll accept our relationship." She was much less nervous about Cole finding out they were dating than she had been when they'd first started going out, but she had a fleeting worry that she didn't want to talk about.

"But?" Sam was looking at her with a serious, expectant gaze, and he deserved the truth, even if she didn't give it much weight.

"But I wonder just a little tiny bit. A sliver of a worry, really. Probably not even worth talking about."

"We don't have those, remember? Every worry is worth talking about."

He was good at making her communicate. It was one of the things she loved most about him, but that didn't mean it was easy to bring this up.

"But it's not a big worry."

He cocked a brow and wrapped his arms around her waist. "Baby, you're killing me here."

"You know…" She ran her finger down the center of his chest, thinking she could distract him. "Your willingness to hear the good with the bad and deal with it head-on is one of the things I like most about you."

"Because there's nothing we can't handle."

That made her smile, and she had a feeling he was right.

"And?" he pushed.

Damn. Even if they could handle it, it felt like a betrayal to say it, but he deserved the truth. "Okay, fine. But I'm not *really* worried about it. I was thinking about my job. What if something happens between us?"

"Something like we break up?"

She lifted a shoulder. She didn't even want to think about the possibility, but she wasn't naive. She of all people knew that things went wrong in relationships, and she was trying to be realistic, even if the idea of breaking up felt very remote.

He kissed her softly. The confident smile she loved so much rose all the way to his eyes. "Then you *really* have nothing to worry about."

She loved his arrogance toward their relationship, and just like always, she believed him. "Your brother is going to think I've slipped you drugs or something."

He toweled off without answering, and she had a feeling he was thinking the same thing as she followed him into the bedroom.

She slipped on her panties, watching him watch her. She swore he had a little remote control that sent electric currents through her every time he got that wanton look in his eyes. It didn't help that he was buck naked and fully aroused.

He stepped toward her, his eyes darkening, her heart melting.

"Sam." She shook her head, taking a step backward.

He stepped closer. "What?"

She flattened her palm against his chest, keeping distance between them, despite her needy body begging for his touch.

"You said you wanted to be at Cole's when he arrived, and I have a phone conference with a women's group in half an hour." She'd also planned on setting up the resource page on the website. A few of the companies she'd emailed had sent links to their intake forms, and she wanted to make them available to the members as soon as possible. If she and Sam fooled around, she'd not only miss the call and probably spend another day avoiding Vivian, but she'd also be worthless while she recovered. Sam made love like he did everything, to his best ability every single time, which meant sucking her dry of every ounce of energy she had. She loved it. Craved it. But today she needed her energy. And yeah, maybe she was a little worried about that little convo with Cole he was going to have after all.

He gripped her wrist and lifted her palm, pressing a kiss to the center of it. "And that's a problem because...?"

Jesus, he stole her breath, her brains, and if he came any closer, her bones would liquefy and slither between the cracks in the floor. He dropped his gaze to her mouth, lingering there, making her lips tingle with anticipation.

"Sam," she whispered.

He held his hands up in surrender. "No hands."

"Like that helps?" Her nipples ached for his touch. She was an inch from giving in. "All it does it make me want you more."

"One kiss." He stepped closer, his hard shaft pressing against her panties as he lowered his mouth to hers.

"You're insatiable."

"Only for you." He nipped at her lower lip. "What are you thinking about now?"

"Huh?" Her mind was nowhere to be found.

He chuckled. "What's on your mind?"

"What do you think?"

"I love when I'm on your mind, but you were a million miles away. Thinking about the work you have to get done for the site?" He kissed her neck, pressing his body tightly against hers.

Good Lord did he feel good. "Mm-hm."

"And are you nervous about talking with Vivian?"

"A little." *But it's not my nerves causing my body to quiver right now.*

"Are you inviting her to the barbecue? It's only two weeks away."

Thinking about the barbecue shook her out of her hor-mone-induced trance.

His brows knitted. "Are you *nervous* about the barbecue?"

"No." She rolled her eyes at his intense stare. "Maybe a

little, which is really stupid." She turned to grab her shorts, and Sam pulled her against him.

"It's not stupid. We're honoring your feelings, remember?"

"You make it really hard to honor my feelings because they make no sense. I have no reason to be nervous about it. You are nothing short of the most wonderful boyfriend on earth. But your whole family, and practically the whole town, will be there, so yeah, I'm a little nervous. Stupid. Stupid. Stupid."

"You're right. There will be tons of people. Most of the groups I've taken out on trips will be there, too. It's a marketing event, community building, a time for me to firmly make my mark with my sponsors. But that's not what you're worried about."

She dropped her eyes, embarrassed to admit her jealousy. He lifted her chin. He always lifted her chin, made her face what she'd rather not. There was no judgment in his eyes, no tension at all. Nothing short of adoration, which amped up her embarrassment for the green-eyed monster clawing at her. They'd come to that point in their relationship where words weren't necessary. Understanding that could only come from mutual respect, and their intense connection, silently passed between them.

"Just know here"—he laid his palm over her heart—"that I've got this. I won't let you down."

She drew in a deep breath and nodded. "I know. Sadly, because it makes me a total loser, this isn't about you. It's about my own stupid jealousy."

That cocky grin showed up again. "My girl's jealous?"

She rolled her eyes. "A tiny smidgen. And don't even think for a minute that it's because I'm worried about how you'll act. I only wish it was, but you've squashed that excuse to bits. Nope. This is all me."

"You know I love that, right?" He laughed, kissing her cheeks until she pushed him away, laughing. "You should invite Vivian."

"Why?"

"Because not only will I prove to you that you have nothing to worry about, but she'll see it firsthand. You'll feel better knowing she's on your side. And maybe then you won't dodge her calls." He kissed her again and grabbed a pair of briefs from his drawer.

You knew I was dodging her calls? Of course you did. You've infiltrated my brain. "You don't have to prove anything to me, but I'm not sure it's a good idea to invite her."

He stopped with his briefs midway up his thighs, and his gaze turned sinful. "You want to play naked games?"

With you? Always. Ugh! How did he get her so off topic? "No. I mean inviting Vivian. She's more jaded than I was when I met you. And she doesn't know you like I do. She'll scrutinize everything."

"That means you don't have faith in *me*. No naked games for you, sweet girl." He finished pulling up his briefs and patted her ass. "It's a good thing one of us does."

Chapter Twenty-Four

FAITH WATERED HER sickly plants, begging them not to die. She finished her call with the women's center and read and answered posts on the WAC website. Hilary had been offered a promotion at work, and Brittany had met a new guy. They both sounded excited but wary. The forums were buzzing about the work Lira was doing for Sam. She and the girls were weighing the pros and cons of moving away from her hometown, even though she didn't have an offer for a full-time job yet. They listed all the important things to consider, like finding a babysitter and pediatrician for Emmie and the cost of living, which shouldn't change much from where she lived now. Apparently her ex wouldn't fight her moving away with Emmie, which spoke volumes about how little he cared. But by far the biggest pro was also the biggest con—moving away from her family.

Faith was careful not to weigh in too heavily on Lira's decision, even though they weren't talking specifically about moving for a job with Sam. Partially because her opinion of Sam was biased and partially because she had no idea how moving Emmie away from her no-good father would affect her in the long run. She assumed it would be for the best, given his lack of desire to see her, but that wasn't something she had any experience with. No wonder Lira needed to talk to a professional.

She left a comment telling Lira she hoped it worked out well and then got busy designing the resource page. But now she was thinking of Sam, and her mind drifted to the barbecue. She thought she'd be more worried about Sam talking with Cole, but that didn't make her stomach go crazy the way thoughts of the barbecue did. Sam's comment about her not having faith in him was circling her mind, too.

She had *complete* faith in him. It was herself she didn't trust. Jealousy was an evil, nasty competitor, one she hadn't dealt with very often. She'd had a hard time at first when they'd gone to Tap It, but Sam had sent that green-eyed-monster running for the hills with his confident, honest ways.

"Have faith," she whispered to herself as she reached for her phone and called Vivian.

"Hello. You've reached Faith's former BFF," Vivian said in a nasally tone. "I'm out searching for a new friend. Please leave a message."

Faith cringed, feeling more than a little guilty. "Sorry I haven't returned your calls."

"Just tell me one thing. Do you have a new BFF or are you smothered in Sam?"

"No one could ever replace you, so it's the latter." She closed her eyes, waiting for Vivian's warning.

"Smothered in Sam? Hm. How is the playboy?"

"Vivian."

"Sorry. How is lover boy?"

Sarcasm practically dripped through the phone.

"He's absolutely wonderful, but I want you to see that for yourself. Are you free the weekend after next?"

"For you? Maybe. Is he really wonderful?" Her tone softened. "He treats you well? As well as I think you deserve?"

"He really is and he truly does, but I want you to witness it for your own peace of mind. He's hosting a barbecue at Rough Riders and, well, I could use your support." Faith didn't realize how nervous she was until the words left her lips.

"You're worried. I hear it in your voice."

"I'm not worried about Sam. I just don't know how jealous I'll feel if a bunch of girls he's partied with show up. I could use a friend with me." She paced her living room.

"How do you know who he's partied with?"

"I don't. And honestly, it doesn't matter who he's partied with. I know it must seem unbelievable given what you know about Sam, but I feel like he and I could take on the world. Like nothing could come between us." She told Vivian about dinner at Tap It and the few times this past week they'd run into other girls he'd either partied with or hooked up with—she didn't know and didn't want to know—when they were out. Sam had handled each interaction with the same confidence and appropriateness as he had the first.

"Wow," Vivian said. "Seriously, Faith. He really did turn himself around for you."

"Right? And I promise, Viv, I'm not just seeing what I want to see. He's the real deal. He's romantic and thoughtful, and I'm an idiot for being nervous like this. It's so embarrassing to know I might get jealous. But it's normal, right? To be nervous about this? His family will be there, too, which is also nerve-racking and probably making me more worried than I should be."

"It's totally normal, and of course I'll come up."

Faith sighed with relief. "Thank you."

"I've got to run in a sec. Mom and I are getting mani-pedis and going shopping."

"She broke up with her boyfriend?" Vivian's mother took her on the same mother-daughter date every time she broke up with a man.

"Yup. That's okay. The guy was a bore, and I like our breakup dates. Speaking of breaking up, I read on WAC that Lira is working with Sam. Is that true?"

She filled her in on the boom in Sam's business and the legal documents Brent had drawn up for WAC, and when she told her about how instrumental Sam had been in getting that done, Vivian was clearly impressed.

"Faith, he really wasn't just trying to get in your pants with that donation."

"I told you. He wants me to get involved with the small businesses here to solicit donations. I'm not sure about all that yet, but he has good ideas. I told you, Viv. He's wonderful. It's so strange to think we've come this far. It's…"

"Fate," Vivian said. "You have finally found a man who deserves you. Don't quote me on that, though. I'm withholding judgment until I see it for myself. We all know that orgasm goggles can be worse than beer goggles."

"You're so crazy! First you make me doubt him, then you pull for him, and now you're taking that back?"

"I said I'm 'withholding judgment.' But he's kind of giving me a girl hard-on for helping Lira and for helping you with the legal stuff. Now you're officially a business owner. I can say I knew you when…"

"Whatever." Faith laughed. "Maybe you'll meet a guy at the barbecue and eventually move here, too. How fun would that be?"

"I'm still on my hiatus from all things male, sorry."

They talked for a few more minutes, and by the time they hung up, the bees in Faith's stomach had calmed. Vivian would never let her act like a jealous girlfriend at the barbecue. She'd help her laugh it off, which was *so* much better.

She went back to working on the resource page and her

mind drifted to Lira. She was contemplating moving away from everything she knew, the town where she'd grown up, and starting over completely *with* a baby. She was running from humiliation and her broken heart the same way Faith had. But Faith had only had to care for herself during that time, and she had Vivian and her family's support. And now her biggest worry was whether she would feel jealous over some girls who didn't even matter.

Her problems weren't problems at all. They were annoyances. Lira had real issues: a family that not only didn't support her, but made her life harder, and a baby to raise, hopefully with better morals than her own sister and mother had. Breaking that cycle wasn't going to be easy.

But anything was doable, if a person wanted it bad enough. Breaking cycles, habits, *impressions.*

Wasn't Sam proof of that?

What Lira was hoping to do would take a Herculean effort, and she needed support. The hell with her crazy family. Lira had Faith, Vivian, and all of the other members of WAC emotionally supporting her day and night.

She navigated to the WAC forums and found Lira's latest post. There were fifty-seven responses by thirty-one unique users. Thirty-one friends pulling for her, offering advice, building her up.

And, Faith realized, Lira had Sam giving her a path toward a new job and, possibly, a new life.

Her Sam. *Have faith in me.* She had faith in him, all right.

Thinking about how lucky they both were for having Sam in their lives and of what Vivian had said about *fate*, she posted a comment.

Lira, it's the tough stuff that makes or breaks us. I'm so proud of you for not letting your ex break you! I think fate might be on your side, and I think everyone in our group would agree that the families we create through friendship are often stronger, and more helpful, than those we're born into. I have faith in you, Lira. If you want to make a change bad enough, you'll make it happen. Good luck with the job. I'm here to help you in any way I can.

IT WAS AN ambush, and probably unfair, given that Cole and Leesa had just returned from their honeymoon. It was selfish of Sam to wait for Cole on his front porch, but word traveled fast in the Braden family, and Cole deserved the respect of hearing about Sam going against his word directly from him.

He paced Cole's front porch, his stomach knotted up as a black sedan pulled into the driveway. Sam and Ty had both offered to pick them up from the airport, but Cole had wanted to extend their lavish honeymoon to the very last second. *Giving Leesa the best trip of her life.* Sam hadn't understood why Cole would go to such efforts when the honeymoon was over, but now that he was with Faith, the motivation behind his brother's efforts became crystal clear. Sam loved Faith's smile so much he'd go to the ends of the earth just to see it. He loved all of her smiles. Her embarrassed touch-me smile, her flirtatious I-know-you-want-me smile, and her confident I'm-a-career-woman smile. But the one he loved most was the smile that played on her lips in the first seconds after she awoke. The smile that told him there was nowhere else she'd rather be, no one she'd rather wake up next to than him. The smile that told him she was his girl.

Cole helped Leesa from the car, both smiling, tanned, and beautiful. Sam had never seen Cole look so relaxed as he draped an arm over Leesa's shoulder and looked at her like she was his world. Leesa tucked her blond hair behind her ear, returning that smile tenfold. Sam got that, too, because he felt it every time he was with Faith. He felt like a voyeur and second-guessed his intrusion.

"Hey, Sam." Cole's voice jerked him from his thoughts.

"I thought I'd welcome you back." Sam sprang into action to settle his nerves and grabbed their bags from the driver.

"I can get those," Cole said, eyeing the luggage.

"You've got your hands full." Sam leaned in and kissed Leesa's cheek. "You guys look great."

Leesa sighed. "It was unbelievably lovely. Your cousin really knows how to make a person feel special."

"Treat arranged for massages, nightly champagne, exclusive

use of a beachfront restaurant on our last night there." Cole unlocked the door, and Sam followed them in. "He went all out."

"I wouldn't expect anything less," Sam said. Everything Treat did was elaborate. He'd arranged for their distant cousin Blake Carter's double wedding on an island, and when a storm ruined not only the wedding, but everyone's attire, he'd had new duds brought in within twenty-four hours. The wedding took place just as beautifully as they'd hoped, in another of Treat's exclusive resorts.

"I promised Tempe I'd call her as soon as I got in, so I'll leave you two alone." Leesa kissed Cole, and Cole held her against him, taking the kiss deeper.

Sam turned away, but Leesa's giggles couldn't be missed, and Sam couldn't be happier for them.

"Love you," Cole said in the soft tone of a gratified lover. Then his hand landed on Sam's shoulder, and his tone went serious. "Welcoming committee?"

"You're not buying it?"

"Hardly. Come on." Cole led him out to the back deck.

A breeze swept off the ocean, bringing with it memories of their youth. They'd spent too many nights to count hanging out by the water, talking about whatever floated their boats at the moment.

"Good to be home?" Sam asked, trying to calm his nerves.

Cole pointed to the chairs, and they settled into them.

"Good to be anywhere as long as I'm with Leesa." He leaned forward, elbows on knees. "I got your texts and thought about calling, but I knew if it was a problem with Mom or Dad you would have called. So what's up, Sam?"

Sam had mentally practiced this speech for days, and now he couldn't remember a word of it.

"I wanted to tell you in person, before you heard from anyone else." He held Cole's gaze, seeing so much of his father's calm, even demeanor, so different from his own. It was oddly comforting. "I'm seeing Faith."

Cole's eyes narrowed. "Faith, as in my employee? The only person in Peaceful Harbor I asked you not to toy with?"

"Yes, and I'm not 'toying.'"

Cole laughed under his breath. "Sam, that's all you do. You take, you play, you mess around, and you move on." He rose to his feet and paced. "You promised me you'd stay away."

"No. I promised you I wouldn't fuck up her life, and I'm not."

Cole stared at him in silence for long enough to make Sam's gut ache. When he finally spoke, his tone was even, calm, not accusatory. "Why Faith, of all people, Sam? She's a nice, smart girl, and she has no family here to pick her up when you toss her aside. And"—his eyes turned stern—"she's my employee."

Sam bit back his visceral reaction and tried to answer calmly, which was what Cole reacted best to. "Because I've wanted to go out with her since I first met her. You know that, Cole. You know my trips to your office were more often than not because I wanted to see her."

"Right, the whole challenge thing. I forget about that with you."

Sam closed the distance between them, anger storming inside him as he met Cole's opposing stare. He had an insurmountable amount of respect for his brother, and it was that respect that kept him from blowing up.

"You've never steered me wrong," Sam said in a heated tone. "Not in business and not in other aspects of my life. And yeah, I was the guy who took and played and messed around. You're right about all of that. And you're right that Faith is good and smart. She's also sweet, and sexy, and funny, and all of those things drew me to her."

"You were drawn to her looks. She gets so flustered around you she can barely see straight."

Sam nodded, fuming inside. "Isn't everyone attracted to looks first? Weren't you with Leesa?" He didn't wait for Cole to respond. "And yeah, she got flustered around me. Sometimes she still does, and that makes me fall harder for her every time. And maybe you're right about the challenge thing."

He broke away from Cole, too restless to stand still as he verbalized what he'd known all along. "Maybe it started out as me wanting to win her attention." He drew his shoulders back and met his brother's gaze again. "But it sure as hell didn't stay that way. Everything changed the night of your wedding."

"Jesus, Sam. You slept with her the night of my wedding?"

Sam scoffed. "*That's* what you think of me?"

Cole lowered himself to the chair again with a heavy sigh. "Isn't that what everyone knows of you?"

Sam crossed his arms, his chest deflating with the piercing truth. He sat across from Cole, wondering why he'd thought this conversation would go any differently.

"Yeah. That's what everyone knows of me." Sam scrubbed a hand down his face. "But it's not who I am anymore. Not with Faith. And I thought of all people, you'd understand that."

Cole searched Sam's face, and Sam wondered what he saw. A disappointed brother? A man standing on the precipice of emotions so enormous he had no idea which way was up? Or the guy he used to be?

"Sam, I want to believe you. You're my brother and I love you. And you're a Braden, which means somewhere beneath the rough, playboy exterior is a man who knows how to be loyal to more than just his family. Hell, I *want* you to fall in love and be as happy as Leesa and I are, and you know I think the world of Faith. I'm just skeptical. What happens when you get bored?"

"Christ, Cole. Do you even know her? She's incredible. I won't get bored."

"You don't know that," Cole said in a kinder tone.

"I do know it, Cole." He smacked his hand over his heart. "In here, where it matters. I never thought I'd have to prove myself to you, of all people."

Sam rose to his feet and Cole followed. When he stepped away, Cole grabbed him by the arm and spun him around.

"Sam—"

"What?" His anger couldn't be disguised, though he wasn't sure if he was angrier at Cole for not believing him, or himself, for having boxed himself in with his reputation. He shrugged out of Cole's grip. "I respect your honesty, and I'm glad you had a good time on your honeymoon. I didn't mean to fuck up your homecoming. I just wanted you to hear it from me before you heard it from Jon or Ty, or anyone else." He took a step away, then looked over his shoulder, meeting Cole's tormented gaze. "Just do me a favor. Don't let any of this effect Faith's job."

"Come on, Sam. You know me better than that."

With a curt nod, Sam walked away, swallowing the jagged pill of knowing he'd have to prove himself to every goddamn person in town—and he had no one to blame but himself.

Chapter Twenty-Five

MONDAY MORNING SAM went for a run before the sun came up. He hated leaving Faith, but he'd been stewing over his reckless past since his conversation with Cole, and if he was honest with himself, he was disappointed in Cole's reaction. All of those emotions had him tied in knots, and if he didn't run off some of the restlessness, he'd explode.

He pushed himself hard, running farther than normal. The familiar pounding on the forest floor usually helped him clear his mind. He crossed the road and entered a trailhead by Nate's place, catching sight of his brothers heading toward him. He kept up his pace, knowing Nate and Ty would catch up. A few heavy footfalls later, they fell into step beside him.

"Thought you weren't running today," Nate said.

"Needed it."

"Trouble with Faith?" Ty asked.

Sam slid him a *get real* look. "If there were, I'd be with her, not trying to run the fucking frustration out of my body." He couldn't believe they hadn't heard what was going on. He was sure Cole would have confided in one of them.

"What's the issue?" Nate asked.

"Nothing I can't handle."

"No doubt," Nate said. "But why go it alone?"

Sam chewed on that question as they ran up a hill, then fell into a single-file line to navigate the narrow trail between a patch of pine trees. They'd always leaned on one another, but he'd gotten his reputation fair and square. He'd earned it, even encouraged it, *on his own*. He could deal with the reputation, but the trouble was, he wasn't dealing with it on his own. Faith was right there with him, willing to face those who knew him *when* and hold her head up high, despite how uncomfortable it might be. *Goddamn Cole.* He'd shaken up Sam's rock-hard confidence. If his own brother didn't immediately believe he was serious about Faith, what would the people he used to party with think? And how much bullshit would he have to deal with at the barbecue?

The trail widened and leveled out, and they ran side by side again.

"I'm not going it alone," Sam finally said. "Faith's right there with me. And I hate knowing people might not believe I'm serious about her. I hate knowing she might see all the bullshit that went along with my past."

"Ah," Ty said. "Now I get it. It's one thing to know it, but another to see it. That's easy. You can handle blowing off anyone who comes onto you, and I'll play interference." He flashed a devilish grin. "Not like I mind."

"I can handle anything, but I worry about Faith. I told Cole we're dating, and he gave me shit. That didn't help."

"Of course he did," Ty snapped. "That's Cole. He's the steady hand, the straight-and-narrow road walker. He can't handle the trails like we can, or the shit that comes with them. He's worried about his employee, and he knows you can handle anything. But Faith? Shit, Sam. She's worked for him for a long time. He's going to worry about her as if she were his sister."

"Maybe that's the trouble. I thought he'd see how serious I am about her and accept that I've changed, regardless of how fast it happened, but instead he made me feel like I was playing Russian roulette with her life." At first he hadn't told Faith what Cole had said, partially because he didn't want to upset her and partially because Sam knew he'd prove his brother wrong and it would soon be water under the bridge. He'd simply told her that Cole wanted to be sure he wasn't going to hurt her, which was true. While it wasn't a lie, he'd omitted part of the truth, and that had gnawed at his gut. He'd come clean last night, and Faith had seemed as pissed at Cole as Sam was with himself for having the reputation in the first place.

"You know Cole has to look at things from all angles to put the pieces together," Nate said.

"Not with Leesa."

"Don't fool yourself," Nate said. "You think he didn't approach his relationship the same way he does everything? He might not have shared it with us, but you can guarantee he dissected the hell out of his emotions."

"Even so, he opened my eyes. Every goddamn person in this town sees me as *that* guy, and I don't give a rat's ass about having to prove them all wrong. But I do care about how it'll affect Faith."

"So what's the plan?" Ty asked.

Sam shrugged, heading for another trail, not yet ready to stop torturing himself. "To be myself. That's the only person I know how to be, and the fact that it's a different guy from the one everyone expects doesn't mean shit. All that matters is that Faith comes out of this unscathed at the end of the day."

"Nah, you've got that wrong," Nate said. "What matters is that she comes out feeling even more confident about your relationship, which she will. Because you've never set your sights on a damn thing and half-assed it."

They ran together a few miles and spent the last twenty minutes giving one another shit about everything and nothing, which helped Sam get out of his own head. As the sun crept over the horizon, he broke away and headed home.

He looked out over the water, thinking about how much he'd always loved living there, on the water and in Peaceful Harbor. Sam knew he was as imperfect as the rocky riverbed, but in his heart, regardless of how many times he'd gone over the falls, despite the dents and scars he'd accumulated along the way, he also knew he was perfect for Faith. She needed a man who was loyal, a man who adored her, a man who cared about the things she was passionate about. Sam was that man.

His thoughts returned to his brothers. Ty was his adventure buddy, always willing to dive into risky situations headfirst. Nate was serious, never afraid to challenge him. He had a soft spot for the underdog and never put up with bullshit. Where Sam and Ty were quick to make decisions, Nate was more like Cole than he'd ever admit, often needing to see things from all sides before coming to a decision. And Cole? Cole had always been the *good one*. Never one to get into trouble or buck the system, he always looked out for the rest of them, sometimes even taking the heat for things his younger siblings had done.

That's what Sam tried to remember now as he mentally rehashed their conversation. Cole was careful, meticulous, but above all, he was caring, which was probably why he made such a good doctor—and, Sam had to admit, such an insightful brother. The more he thought about Cole giving him hell despite how it might make him feel, the more he appreciated his brother's stance—and the more he realized they weren't so far apart after all.

Whether Cole realized it or not, his concern for Faith's well-being mirrored Sam's, which meant they were still on the same team.

FAITH DIDN'T USUALLY wish for days so busy she didn't have time to take a lunch break, but today she was glad for a jam-packed schedule. Cole was back from his honeymoon, tanned and more relaxed than she'd ever seen him, which didn't say much. Cole didn't relax at work. *Ever.* He was always thinking, as evident in the serious slant of his brows and the intense look in his dark eyes. She could practically see the gears churning, retrieving medical data he'd probably learned ten years ago and still remembered every detail of. He was incredibly smart, but never arrogant, which said a lot, considering he was at the top of his field.

Today that serious slant was almost nonexistent, and his gaze was easy, not taxed, which told her his honeymoon had done him a world of good. She was happy for him, but that didn't mean she wanted downtime where conversations could turn personal. Sam had reluctantly told her how Cole had reacted to their discussion, and it pissed her off. She worried she might say something she'd regret.

She imagined the awkward conversation they might have. He'd say something like, *So, you're dating my brother?* Into which she'd read, *So, you're fucking Sam, the player?* Her hands fisted just thinking of how that would feel.

After this last patient, she was done for the day. Maybe she'd gotten lucky and Cole wanted to have that conversation even less than she did.

She set her patient's foot down on the exam table after checking her range of motion. Jackie Geiger was eighteen, had just begun running, and had come in with bilateral knee pain.

"You said you just started running two weeks ago?"

"Yes. Three miles a day." Jackie was also an avid swimmer, biker, and had been on the basketball team throughout high school.

"And you're stretching before and after?"

"Well, no, not really. I basically climb out of bed, put on my running clothes, and take off." She shrugged, but the apologetic look in her blue eyes told Faith she already knew how bad that was for her joints.

"Based on the exam, and since your pain is bilateral, I think we're looking at an overuse injury. Let's give your knees two weeks to rest, without running, biking, swimming, or other sports that could exacerbate the pain."

Jackie sighed. "Not even swimming?"

Faith smiled. "Not unless you like pain."

"Okay," she relented.

"Great. You can take ibuprofen for the pain. Two weeks of pampering your joints should take care of it, but schedule a follow-up in two weeks and we'll reassess and do more tests if necessary."

"Then I can run again?" she asked hopefully.

"If your pain is gone, but I'll want you to ease into it *and* stretch before and after. You only have one set of knees. Let's keep them healthy." Faith reached for the door. "Go ahead and get dressed, and stop by the front desk to schedule the follow-up appointment on your way out."

Outside the exam room she filled out Jackie's chart and pulled her cell phone from her pocket to check her texts as Cole came around the corner.

The easy look in his eyes turned a tad serious. "Was that your last patient?"

Her nerves prickled to life. "Yes." It used to be so easy to talk with him, but now it felt like the air between them thickened with tension. Maybe it was just her nerves getting the best of her.

"Great. Do you have a minute to talk? In my office?"

No. Definitely not. I don't want to talk about sleeping with your incredibly hot brother. "Sure."

A smile lifted his lips, but she was too nervous to determine if it was a casual smile or something else as she followed him into his office. He closed the door behind her, and her stomach pitched.

This isn't good. Act natural. Sit down. Good. Smile. She couldn't quite pull that one off and decided to play dumb. Act like there was no chance this was about Sam.

Cole sat in the chair beside her. He'd never done that before, and it made her even more nervous. He always sat behind his desk. Angling his body toward her, he crossed his legs and breathed deep and loud.

"Well," he said, his smile lifting his cheeks. "Are you as nervous about this as I am?"

"Um? Nervous? About what?"

He arched a brow.

You're totally not buying this act. "Yes. A little terrified. Please know that I love my job. I hope dating Sam won't hurt my career here, because I love the patients, and you and Jon are so wonderful. I promise I won't allow my relationship to impact my work." *Except when your brother shows up unannounced and strips down to his skivvies. Oh God, now I'm thinking about Sam in his underwear!*

"I wouldn't expect your personal life to interfere with work. You're too professional to let that happen."

"Yes. Right. I am." *Whew.*

His brows knitted, and that *whew* went out the window.

"I figured we should get this out in the open. I'm sure Sam told you I asked him not to ask you out." He spoke calmly and confidently, like the professional he was.

"Yes, and I wanted to talk to you about that." *I did? Holy crap, shut up!* She had no idea where her confidence was coming from, but she felt protective of her relationship with Sam, and of her independence. "I appreciate you worrying about me, but I can handle those types of decisions on my own."

He nodded in silence, his assessing gaze rolling over her face.

I'm fired. Totally fired.

He drew in another loud breath, taking all of the air in the room with it. "I'm sorry I overstepped my bounds." He paused, and she finally breathed. "You're a hard worker, Faith, and an excellent physician assistant, and Sam doesn't exactly have a history of stable relationships. I just didn't want to take a chance of you two..." He shifted his eyes away, and when they came back to her, he let that thought hang in the air for a moment. "Of you two getting together and, well, of you getting hurt. You're a nice girl, Faith, and the idea of Sam hurting you worries me."

She bit back the fury vying for release and gripped the edge of the chair, willing herself to speak professionally.

"While I understand where you're coming from, given Sam's reputation, he is nothing short of the most thoughtful, caring, and insightful man I have ever met." As her heart poured out, her tone softened. "Everything about him has been unexpected, and I didn't make the decision to go out with him lightly." She smiled with the memory of him whipping off his shirt at the car wash after she'd blown him off. "The poor guy has worked really hard to gain my trust."

"Sam?" Cole's brows lifted with surprise.

"Yes, Sam. Your brother, the guy everyone knows has never committed to a woman in his life, has committed to me. And I trust him, Cole. That's really all you need to know." Boy did that feel good. And scary. Definitely scary.

Cole nodded, and a smile formed on his lips. "*That* was unexpected."

She laughed softly. "Yes. For me, too. I'm sorry. I shouldn't have been so vehement, but...I am." She stopped short of saying, *falling hard for Sam.* That was private.

"You really believe Sam can change?"

"No. I believe he *has* changed," she said, and couldn't hold back what followed. "But it's disappointing to see you don't."

"It's not that I don't believe he can change. Sam's incredibly intense, focused, and smart. He'll do anything he puts his mind to." Cole rubbed his chin, as if he was thinking. "But this is a side of Sam I thought was long gone."

His shoulders dropped, and his tone softened. "I thought I needed to see you guys together to believe this was real, but that makes me an ass, doesn't it?"

A laugh slipped out before she could remember Cole was her boss, and she shouldn't agree with *or* laugh at that comment.

"It does," he said with a laugh. "I'm an ass. I'm sorry for butting into your business."

"It's okay," she said, even though it wasn't. He was still her boss.

"No, it's not. You're my employee, not my sister. I had no business trying to keep him away from you in the first place."

"I appreciate that your heart was sort of in the right place. But I have faith in Sam." And then, despite her faith in Sam, she had to ask, "You're not going to fire me if something goes wrong between us, are you?"

He stared at her in silence for so long she feared his answer would be, *What other choice will I have?*

He rose to his feet and she stood, too, pulling her shoulders back, preparing for the thing she feared most.

"This *Sam.* The thoughtful, caring, insightful man you described, that's the *real* Sam. That's the brother I thought he'd buried too deep to find. I don't think we have to worry about that particular scenario. Unless, of course, you decide to ditch Sam, in which case…" He shrugged with a tease in his eyes as they walked out of his office.

"Seriously? You're going to turn this on me?" she said jokingly.

She was so relieved she wanted to hug him, but she didn't because he was still her boss. *Thank God.*

Chapter Twenty-Six

SAM PULLED UP to the cabin Monday evening, surprised to see Tempe's car in his driveway and a bonfire down by the water. He'd worked later than he'd expected, taking extra time to talk with Tex about upcoming trips they were hosting and his availability. Tex had proven to be a reliable hard worker, and Sam was pleased to hear that Tex had no plans of taking off anytime soon. He'd checked in with Lira about her progress and had ended up taking an hour to review the new charting systems she'd put into place. She was doing a spectacular job, and she seemed to enjoy the work. Things at Rough Riders were falling into place nicely, and from the text he'd received from Faith, it sounded like her talk with Cole had gone well, too, which had made his day.

He probably owed Cole an apology for storming off, but he needed another day or two to nurse his wounded ego. He'd had no idea he was such a pansy ass, but apparently his brother's view of him mattered a lot more than he cared to admit.

Pushing that thought from his mind, he stepped from the truck. The sound of Tempe's guitar greeted him. On his way down to the bonfire Faith's beautiful face came into focus, illuminated by the flames of the fire. She was laughing at something Tempe must have said. Seeing her with his sister touched him in a deep, unexpected way.

"Hi," she said as he leaned in for a kiss.

"Hey, baby. Missed you." He turned to Tempe, giving her a warm hug. "I wasn't expecting you, sis. It's nice to see you."

"Sorry I didn't call first, but I was so excited about finishing my song, I wanted to come play it for you." Tempe's blond hair was pulled back in a ponytail. She smoothed her summery skirt and rested her guitar on her knee.

Sam sat in a chair beside Faith and reached for her hand. "Great. I can't wait to hear it."

"I was just thanking her for the referrals for Lira and the other members," Faith said.

"Hey, when it comes to emotional health, I'm always willing to help," Tempe said. "Besides, you never know. One day I might need that website of yours."

"Like hell," Sam said. "I'll kill anyone who cheats on you."

Faith squeezed his hand. "Brotherly love at its best."

"He's totally not kidding," Tempe said. "With my dating life, I don't think we're in jeopardy of him having to kill anyone."

They all turned at the sounds of tires on gravel.

"Did I miss the invitation to the party?" Sam said, wondering why Nate was there. And Jewel. They both stepped from the truck and waved.

"I told him I was coming over," Tempe said. "I didn't invite him, but when has Nate ever needed an invitation?"

None of them needed invitations, but Sam had gotten spoiled, having Faith all to himself these past few weeks. His disappointment at losing a few hours alone with her surprised him.

"He doesn't." Sam turned to Faith. "Sorry, baby. So much for our night alone."

"We get plenty of time alone. I'm glad they're here."

He knew from her tone she was, even if she was a bit nervous. Sam rose to greet Nate and Jewel.

"So I guess you got lucky?" Jewel waggled her brows.

Sam hugged her. "Luckiest guy on earth."

"Shit," Nate said, pulling Sam away from Jewel. "That would be me, thank you very much." He squeezed Tempe's shoulder on his way past. "Sis. Good to see you."

Nate stood in front of Faith's chair and opened his arms. "Get on up here."

Faith turned beet-red as she rose to her feet, and Nate pulled her into a hug.

"How can I not hug the woman who tamed Sammy?"

"Sam will never be tamed," she said as Sam pulled her onto his lap. "And I wouldn't want him to be. Monogamous is enough for me."

Nate laughed. "That's why you're the perfect woman for Sam."

"Get used to it," Jewel said to Faith. "This family tends to say whatever they want." She kissed Nate. "Especially my man."

Another car pulled down the driveway, and they all turned. Sam's muscles corded tight at the sight of Cole's car—followed by his parents' car and Shannon's, which he knew Ty was driving.

"Oh yeah, I might have told everyone we were coming over." Nate flashed a Cheshire-cat grin. "Nothing better than slowly easing in to the family."

Sam shook his head as his family took over the lawn. The next hour was spent roasting marshmallows and listening to *Remember When* stories about Sam.

Faith soaked up every story, teasing him every so often. If he'd thought seeing Faith with Tempe had given him unexpected pleasure, seeing his family bring Faith into their inner circle filled parts of him he hadn't known were empty. The only niggling to the spontaneous get-together was the way he and Cole were eyeing each other up, both obviously biding their time, waiting for the right moment to talk.

"Remember when Sam learned to horseback ride at Uncle Hal's?" his mother said, her blue eyes filled with amusement, obviously excited to share one of his most embarrassing moments. "He was eight and a total show-off..."

Cole chose that moment to come to Sam's side. "Can we talk?" he asked discreetly.

Sam felt Faith's eyes on them and held up a finger, indicating he'd be right back. "Sure." They walked away from the group, and Sam didn't even try to pretend that the entire family wasn't holding their breath just as he was.

"Listen, Cole. I owe you an apology."

"What?" Cole shook his head. "Sam. I owe you an apology for the way I reacted to you. It was unfair and uncalled for. You're an honest guy, and I had no right to disbelieve you. I'm sorry."

A lump lodged in Sam's throat, and from the emotions washing over Cole's face, he thought he might be suffering from the same.

"Thanks," Sam said. "But you were right to worry, and you were watching out for my girl, so how upset can I really be? I shouldn't have stormed off. The truth was tough to hear, but hey, that's what it takes to change, right? Isn't that the first step? Admitting you have a problem?"

"You didn't have a problem, Sam. You got hurt as a kid and never gave yourself a chance to deal with it. You buried it."

Sam thought about that and knew it was at least partially true.

"You just had a different lifestyle than I did," Cole said. "But not that different. You were more active, but hell, I didn't commit for years either. I was an ass, Sammy, and it wasn't fair of me not to take you at your word. I'm sorry."

"Next time you don't believe me about something this important, I'll kick your ass," Sam teased.

"Actually, your girlfriend sort of already did. I was wrong. You guys are perfect for each other. I had no idea she was so tough."

Cole draped an arm over his shoulder, and a little piece of Sam's world shifted back into place.

"Tough doesn't even begin to describe her. You know I don't believe in reliving the past, and thankfully"—his eyes found Faith—"neither does Faith. We both focus on the now, and the future. And from where I'm standing, my future looks pretty damn perfect."

Chapter Twenty-Seven

IF BLISS WERE a place on earth, Faith had found it in Sam's arms with his hard, hot body wrapped around her and his face nestled against her neck. Saturday mornings had become her most favorite day of the week. She took advantage of his slumber and visually explored her man's bedroom. She was used to sleeping in it by now, but in the three weeks they'd been staying there, she had been so consumed with Sam, she hadn't paid much attention to what the bedroom actually looked like.

It felt potently masculine, like Sam. The sheets, blankets, and throw rug were shades of brown, burnt orange, and gold. Dark wood trim surrounded three enormous windows and French doors that led out to a deck overlooking the lake, where they'd taken to having breakfast. Her WAC folder sat beside her laptop on the intricately designed wooden table built from driftwood that sat between two distressed leather chairs in front of the windows, where they'd sat and talked for hours last night.

She marveled at the sturdy iron chandelier with faux flame–

colored candles hanging by chains from the vaulted ceiling above the foot of the bed. Every element looked sturdy and well thought out, putting her plain white walls to shame. But that was one thing she loved about Sam. He made her slow down and see things differently. Where her living room had been a place to get things done, every room in Sam's house was a room to enjoy. Like every part of Sam, they were all unique and interesting.

They'd moved her plants to his living room, and with a little love and a lot of water, they'd miraculously come back to life. Her hairbrush, lotions, and perfume bottle sat atop his dresser, beside his cologne. Her toothbrush hung beside his in the bathroom. *This is how it happens. One day I was single, and the next I woke up in Sam's arms with my heart so full it's staggering to think about. I'm definitely the luckiest girl on earth.*

She turned in Sam's arms, and he tightened his grip around her waist.

"Don't get up," he said in a sleepy, sexy voice.

"I'm in no hurry."

"Mm." He kissed her shoulder.

"I'm admiring your room. I never realized how private it felt. Your whole cabin does."

"I like it that way." He opened his eyes and stretched his legs. His arousal pressed against her thigh, bringing awareness to all her girly parts.

She ran her fingers through his hair, and he closed his eyes again. "Mm. I love it when you touch me like that."

She waited for a sexual innuendo to follow, and when he said, "You're the first woman I've brought here," she was shocked. Knowing he hadn't brought women here confirmed what she'd been feeling and made her feel even more special.

His eyes came open, and he pressed his lips to hers. "Don't look so surprised. I told you everything was different with you."

"Everything you do surprises me, Sam. How can I not be surprised? All this time you haven't said a word about that, but it makes sense now. I was just thinking about how you seem private to me, too, just like your cabin. You sneak off to Whiskey Bro's when you want to chill without the pressure of being *on* all the time. You live out here without neighbors."

"Nate's my neighbor."

"Yes, but he's not that close. And you don't keep girls' numbers or do social media, except for Rough Riders."

Amusement filled his eyes. "You stalked me?"

"No." She laughed. "I was curious when I was posting the pictures for WAC the day of the car wash. You weren't on there, but Rough Riders was. It's all very interesting."

He sat up against the pillows, and she settled in against his chest. "How is that interesting?"

"Because before we started dating, I'd seen you a few times at Whispers and around town, and you were always surrounded by people—guys and girls. I thought you were the kind of guy who had an entourage every minute of the day and liked it that way. The only time I saw you alone was when you'd come to the office to see Cole."

"To see you," he corrected.

"Right." She rolled her eyes. She loved knowing that he had come in to get a glimpse of her even though he'd resisted her for so long. "Now that I know you better, I can see your cabin is another escape, where you don't have to be *on*, like Whiskey's."

"You think you've got me all figured out." He pressed his lips to hers and ran his hand down her arm, sending shivers along her entire body.

"Not even close, but I love getting to know so many sides of you. You're even more complex than I imagined, in a good way."

"Then I hope you never figure me out completely so you're always intrigued. I've been thinking about our talk the other day and the trips I host. Have you ever gone camping or rafting? Or rock climbing?"

"My sister and I used to go rafting, but not in big rapids like you ride. And JJ, my cheating ex, liked doing all those other things, but the furthest I got was climbing a rock wall."

His eyes flashed cold for a second. "I hate knowing that he was anything like me."

"He wasn't anything like you in the ways that matter. He just liked doing some of the same things." She touched his cheek, and his eyes warmed again.

"Thanks, baby." He kissed her again. "Back to us. So you're

not afraid of adventure-type sports. That's a plus."

"Even if I were, I'd try them with you, because you enjoy them. I want to share those things with you, if that's what you're wondering."

"It is, sort of. You get time off from work, right?"

"Sure, two weeks. Three after next year, I think."

"We may have to modify that a little," he said with an air of confidence that made her curious about what was percolating in that handsome head of his. "Then there's no reason you can't come on some of the trips with me."

Her heart skipped a beat. "You're talking like we're a given."

"Aren't we?" He lifted her chin and gazed into her eyes. "When I think of tomorrow, I see you there with me. I want to think about us and where we're headed."

She was falling hard for him, too, but hearing Sam say it made her throat too thick with emotion to respond.

"Let's go someplace for the night and try it out," he said excitedly. "See how we like going away together. We can go for a hike, fish, and sleep under the stars, or take a raft down the river and pick a spot."

"I've never slept beneath the stars. That sounds amazing, but you have your big event coming up. How can you afford the time off?"

"I love that you worry about me, but the event is set. Now that Lira is handling the coordination and contacting clients, we're in good shape. She's amazing, by the way. When she comes down for the barbecue I'm going to talk with her about coming on board permanently."

"You can't imagine how happy that makes me. She needs this so badly, Sam. You'll change her whole world." She touched his cheek and added, "Just like you've changed mine."

He pressed a tantalizing kiss to the hollow of her neck. "Ditto, baby. I need to take care of a few things in the office, but then we can take off. All you have to do is pack and decide what you're up for. A river ride to an undetermined destination, an afternoon of skydiving, a hike, or whatever your little heart desires."

"Like you don't already have the entire trip planned," she teased. Little did he know that everything her heart desired was right there in that room.

AFTER SAM WENT to work, Faith went home to pack. He had given her a very male response about what to pack. *Bring comfortable clothes, extra shoes, and only the necessities you can't live without.* What did that mean? Only the necessities she couldn't live without? She consulted her good friend Google and was overwhelmed with lists of gear and clothing, special shoes and lotions, but she stopped cold at the mention of going to the bathroom in the woods. *Holy crap!* How had she not thought about that? That was going to be embarrassment overload. Not for him, of course, because all guys loved talking about their bathroom habits, while women pretended they never went.

She either needed a good excuse to back out of going on the trip, or she needed expert help. She grabbed her cell and called Charley, the only female she knew who had wilderness experience *and* knew her well enough to tell her if she should just back out. She didn't want to back out of the trip. She loved spending time in Sam's world, seeing him surrounded by elements that had been his steady calling forever.

"Hey." Charley sounded out of breath.

"Hi. Do you have a sec?"

"Oh my God!" Charley yelled. "How big? Yay!"

Faith listened to Charley hooting and hollering, probably forgetting she even had Faith on the phone. Her voice went in and out, as if she were flailing her arms. Faith leaned back, smiling at Charley's footloose behavior. When Charley came back on the phone, she was panting.

"Sorry. Dane got a shark. It looks like an eight footer, but we'll know soon. They've been trying for hours, and they're tagging it now. You should see it. It's gorgeous."

Faith cringed at the thought of being anywhere near a shark. But she was more curious about who Dane was. Charley almost never dated. She was too busy with school, her internship, and her part-time job at the bar. Faith didn't think there was a man on earth who could keep up with her.

"Who's Dane?"

"He owns the Brave Foundation. I've told you this before, haven't I? Dane Braden? The guy I'm interning for?"

"No, all you've ever said was…Wait. Dane *Braden?*"

"Yeah. I'm *sure* you've heard of him. He's only the best shark tagger around."

"I'm not exactly in the shark-tagging field, remember? Is he related to Sam Braden?" She heard Charley yell, "Hey, Lacy! Is Dane related to a Sam Braden?"

"If he's in Maryland, his wife said yeah, he is. Why? Do you know him?"

"He's *my* Sam." For some reason the connection made her smile. She liked knowing that the man Charley worked for was related to Sam. It made her feel a little closer to Charley.

"Wait. Is he the guy who sleeps with everyone under the sun?"

Faith rolled her eyes. "Who told you that?"

"Vivian, of course."

She was going to kill her! "God. When?"

"I don't know. A few weeks ago? The weekend she was at your place, I think."

"Well, he doesn't anymore, thank you very much."

"Huh."

She pictured Charley's hand on her chin, her index finger tapping her cheek, the way she did when she was contemplating marine biological things Faith couldn't begin to understand.

"Before you overscrutinize my boyfriend, I need your help."

"With the boyfriend? Yeah, not really my field of expertise."

"No kidding. We're going on an overnight rafting trip, and I was searching online for ideas about what to pack. I hadn't even thought about going to the bathroom in the woods. Char, what am I going to do?"

"People do shit in the woods, Faith."

"What about toilet paper? Will it attract bears? Not only that, but how about—"

"Hold on," Charley said in her *shut up now* tone. "Before you get into a panic, it's not nearly as bad as you're building it up to be."

"So I shouldn't cancel the trip?"

"Ohmygod. Really? Because you might have to pee in the woods?" Charley laughed. "I love you, sis, but only you would consider such a thing."

Charley filled her in on biodegradable toilet paper, digging holes and covering the waste, and other not-so-pleasant things she really needed to but would rather not know about.

"But I thought Sam owned a rafting company?"

"He does."

"Then he's got this shit down pat. Ha! Didn't mean that pun. You have nothing to worry about. Pack comfortable clothes, shoes, sunscreen, and little else."

"Are you sure you're not part guy? That's pretty much what Sam told me to bring."

"I like him already." Someone hollered, and Charley said, "Gotta go. Good luck and don't stress over this. You can hide, he won't see you, and no bears will eat you. Love ya."

Faith stared at her cell phone, shaking her head. She loved her whirlwind sister to death, but *don't stress over this?* Like going to the bathroom in the woods with Sam around wasn't going to be the only thing she thought of until she actually did it? Maybe she could hold it...*for two days.*

THE RAFT MEANDERED down the channel like a snake in the grass, smooth and easy for the first half hour or so into their trip, flowing faster the farther away from civilization they went. Sam paddled from his seat in the rear, keeping an eye on Faith, who was paddling like a pro. Sam had given Faith a quick safety course before they left Rough Riders, and he was sure she'd listened to exactly none of it, because she'd been too excited to get on the water. They'd been rafting for well over an hour, and by the position of the sun, he'd guess closer to two.

Faith looked over her shoulder, flashing a bright smile that reached her eyes. He couldn't remember ever seeing her look so beautiful, or so happy, as she tipped her face up toward the sun, then turned her attention back to the river.

"Are you related to a guy named Dane Braden?" she asked.

"He's my cousin. You know of him?"

She glanced back again, and he leaned forward and kissed her. They lingered there, their mouths barely touching. Sam felt their almost kisses in every ounce of his body, as enticing as a full-on, mind-blowing French kiss.

"Mm," she said, turning back to the river. "Charley interns for his foundation."

"Cool. I forgot Dane was out in Harborside. I think he and his wife are due to have a baby soon."

"Well, apparently that didn't slow him down, because they were tagging a shark this morning."

"Nothing will ever slow Dane down. He's one of those guys who has a vision and makes it happen. He's relentless."

"Kind of like someone else I know." She glanced over her shoulder. "This is so beautiful. I'm glad you suggested it."

"There aren't many things more life affirming than a river. Isn't it hard to believe that a little trickle of water can become a stream and eventually a river?" His eyes skated over the rocky riverbanks, dense trees, and greenery sprouting up from the dusky water. "Think of how many plants and animals this river feeds. She gives and gives and gives—food, water, transportation."

"You talk as if it's a person."

"She is. Like a lover, she kisses the shore, captures your attention, and requires a great deal of respect."

"As your lover, I hope I don't ever smell like the river."

"Ah, but you do. Earthy, alluring, and unspoiled, with an

underlying scent of 'I want Sam.'"

She laughed. "How do you make everything sound so wonderful?"

"Just telling it like it is."

"Then tell me what all that white is up ahead of us." She glanced back with wide eyes and whipped her head around.

They were nearing an area of small rapids, nothing to write home about.

"Speed bumps. They cause a bit of a splash but pose no threat."

"Says the man who's afraid of nothing."

He heard the worry in her tone and reassured her. "Remember how I taught you to paddle through rapids?"

"Uh-huh."

"Good. The raft will tip up a little, and you'll get wet, but we'll just keep maneuvering down the river. It's a wide, clear channel, babe. I promise you'll be fine."

As the river picked up speed, the raft lifted and dropped, spraying their gear, which was secured to the front of the raft, and soaking Faith.

She shrieked, then laughed. "I'm soaked!"

"It's my evil plan to get you out of your clothes."

They rode the rougher water, laughing and teasing. Faith shrieked when water splashed over her face, but it was a shriek of delight, which made Sam even happier. Faith had been so cautious with him that her confident approach to rafting and camping had surprised him. He'd thought she'd be just as wary about the new experience. The difference, he knew, was that now she trusted him completely.

Faith turned her wet, happy face toward him. "That was so fun! I want to do it again."

He leaned forward and planted a hard kiss on her cheek. "Don't ever doubt that we were made for each other. You kicked ass, baby."

Experiencing one of his greatest joys in life with Faith, feeling her excitement, watching her handle the raft without ever missing a beat, and knowing that sharing these adventures could be theirs, too, made Sam feel full to near bursting.

Chapter Twenty-Eight

WATCHING SAM DO anything was an effort in drool prevention, something Faith hadn't quite mastered yet. But as Sam unloaded the gear, marking a site for the tent, stacking pots for cooking where he would later build a fire, and pulled out his guitar, much more than saliva pooled inside her. Her rough and rugged boyfriend had a romantic heart, and that made hers tumble in her chest.

"You brought your guitar?" She took it from him as he retrieved a smaller bag from the pile of gear resting on the rocky shore.

An easy smile lifted his lips. "Figured I'd play for my favorite girl, but I think you'll like something else I brought even more."

She rolled her eyes. "Condoms?"

"Well, there is that." He held up a box of condoms. "But I thought you might like this even better." He held open the bag and she peeked inside. "Biodegradable toilet paper, biodegradable baby wipes, and…" He withdrew a bottle of hand sanitizer.

She placed the guitar on top of the tent roll and hugged him. "I think you might be the best boyfriend in the history of the universe."

"Who knew toilet paper had so much power?" He dropped the bag and kissed her longingly.

The sun began its slow descent, casting an ethereal hue over the site where they'd chosen to spend the night, and a gentle breeze rustled the trees. After a few more toe-curling kisses, they reluctantly parted and began setting up camp. Faith did more watching than helping, because her highly capable man whipped through the process of erecting the tent and digging a fire pit with lightning speed. They gathered firewood together, and Faith's mind began to wander.

"We don't have to worry about bears, do we?" She picked up branches to use as kindling.

"Nah. I'm pretty sure bears can take care of themselves." He patted her butt as she bent to retrieve another branch.

"Seriously, are there bears around here?"

"Sure, bears live in the woods, but the chance of you seeing any is slim." He stepped over a rock and picked up a thick branch. "You're more likely to see snakes, spiders—"

She spun around. "Sam!"

He tugged her against him with his free hand. "Stop worrying. I'm not going to let anything happen to you." He sealed his promise with a kiss.

When their arms were full, they carried the wood out of the forest and set it beside the fire pit.

Sam brushed the slivers of wood and bark from her shirt. "We need to get you out of these wet clothes."

"Are you being thoughtful, or is that another ploy to get me naked?"

He answered her with a devilish grin as he crouched and began steepling the wood into a teepee in the center of the fire pit. She didn't know why she'd worried about what to pack, or even where to go to the bathroom. Like always, Sam had everything under control. And to him, having everything under control meant paying attention to what she needed first. She smiled with the thought, her mind drifting to their earlier conversation. *When I think of tomorrow, I see you there with me, and I want to think about these things and where we're headed.* Sam was everything she could ever hope for in a man, even if he was the last man she'd ever expect to fall for. *Unexpected Sam,* she mused. *My unexpected future?* Her heart swelled with the thought.

When he glanced up at her, his wet shirt and shorts clung to his chest and legs and his eyes clung to *her.* He blew her a kiss, and she lifted her hand and caught it, pressing her palm to her cheek. She disappeared into the tent to change before her heart spilled out in words. Sam had set their things beside the sleeping bags. She picked up a clean, fluffy towel he'd laid out for her and hugged it to her chest, reveling in his thoughtfulness.

After changing, she stepped from the tent in the clothes Sam had bought her from Chelsea's Boutique. The fire crackled and sparked in the dim evening light, and the reflection danced in Sam's dark eyes. He turned, drinking her in as he rose to his feet and stripped off his shirt. He held it in his fist and gathered her in his arms.

"There's my sexy girl."

"Thanks for the towel."

"I'll always take care of you." He kissed her tenderly. "I love seeing you in this outfit. It reminds me of the night you *chose* me."

"How could I resist? It wasn't like you'd back down, so I figured I might as well go with the flow."

"Is that what you're doing? Going with the flow?"

"I'm way past going with the flow." *I'm falling over a cliff.* The words hung on her tongue. She changed the subject before they could fall out. "I half expected you to maul me when I was naked."

"I thought about it. 'Fantasized' might be a better word. But I knew you were nervous about big bad bears and thought I'd give you privacy." He kissed her neck, sending a shiver down her spine. "The only wild animal you need to fear is the one inside me, begging to come out and play."

"That animal doesn't scare me at all."

He leaned back and searched her eyes. She recognized the look in his eyes. He was looking for the clarity they'd spoken of earlier on in their relationship. He'd given her complete transparency from the very first moment he'd asked her out, and finally she was able to give him the same. She trusted him wholly and completely. How could he see anything else?

She wrapped her arms around his neck and kissed his scruffy chin. "Crystal clear?"

"You have no idea how much it means to me."

Fighting the lump in her throat, she said, "I do. It's big to me, too."

"I'll never let you down, baby."

"I know." She pressed a kiss to the center of his chest. "Your skin is cold."

"I took my shirt off so I wouldn't get you wet. Sit by the fire and warm up. I'll change and make dinner in a few minutes. Oh, and see those bushes over there?" He pointed off to the right, just past the edge of the forest. "I put all the bathroom stuff back there. Dug a few holes, too, so if you had to go you wouldn't have to dig." He said it like only a man would, as if it were no big deal.

She covered her face with her hand. "I'm blushing, aren't I?"

"Like a Christmas light." He moved her hand and kissed the tip of her nose. "I won't say anything more about bathroom stuff. We'll pretend you never go."

She playfully pushed him toward the tent, planning to take advantage of the privacy and take care of her bathroom needs while he changed—and silently thanking the camping lords for making him so wise.

SAM GRILLED SAUSAGES and vegetables and served them over rice, earning bonus points from Faith with his campfire-cooking skills. The sun set in the distance as they ate, streaming ribbons of blues and purples through the darkening sky. Sam had always loved camping, but having this time alone with Faith, away from the demands of work and the confusion of family members and outside influences, made him cherish it even more.

The river licked at the shore, and a cacophony of tree frogs, crickets, and other wilderness sounds joined the melody of Sam's guitar as he strummed out James Otto's "Groovy Little Summer Song." Faith swayed next to him on the blanket beside the fire as he sang about a song they could dance to, one they could romance to, and fall in love to. His chest was full of emotions, playing out in his deep voice, and he realized he wasn't just singing one of his favorite country tunes. He was singing it to Faith. Her gaze was also full of emotions—and clarity. The clarity he'd longed for was there all the time now, and it brought him to his feet. He felt the need to move, but not with the same restlessness he'd always felt. This was different. It was a deep-seated, unstoppable urge to move *with* Faith, to bring her further into his world. He reached for her hand, bringing her up beside him. His fingers fell back to the strings like they were coming home, and he picked up where he'd left off, dancing with Faith as he sang the words that were meant for her.

She moved gracefully, with a hint of embarrassment in her beautiful eyes. He blew her a kiss and brushed his shoulders to hers, and her momentary shyness disappeared. Faith picked up on the chorus, singing softly with a voice so sweet Sam wanted to climb inside it and bed down for the night. He continued strumming long after he'd finished the song, just to see her move with the moonlight kissing her cheeks.

"I've never heard that song before."

"No?" He set the guitar on the blanket and took her in his arms, lacing their fingers together, and continued dancing slowly to the beat still thrumming inside him.

She tipped her face up to him, smiling. "I could listen to you sing all night long. Your voice is so soothing."

He touched his cheek to hers and closed his eyes, enjoying the feel of their bodies moving as one. "It sounds that way to you because of how you feel about me."

"Does it, oh wise one?"

They danced in silence for a few wonderful minutes without the need for more.

"You calm the restlessness in me." His words came unbidden, and once they started, they flowed like the river. "You center me in a way I don't fully understand. When I'm not with you, I'm thinking about you." He took her hand and they sat on the blanket. The warmth of the fire illuminated her beautiful face. He brushed her hair from her shoulder, unable to think any solid thoughts as words continued to come out. "When we're together, I don't want the time to end, which sounds cliché. But I've never felt these things before."

"Sure you have," she said with a playful smile. "When you were sixteen."

He laughed under his breath. "Not even close." He thought about that for a moment. "This is bigger, more real. What I feel for you isn't hormone driven. Maybe it was at first. At sixteen I felt invincible. I never thought anyone would choose someone else over me. At almost thirty-one I know how wrong that is. People come along every day. Doctors, lawyers. People who are more a part of your world than I am."

"But I don't want a doctor or lawyer—"

He pressed a kiss to her lips. "I know that. I'm just saying that I'm no longer invincible. I have faults and weaknesses, and our relationship has brought home the reality of them. Faith, I'm falling in love with you."

Her eyes dampened as he let those words sink in, not just for her, but for him, too. He hadn't expected the confession, but he wouldn't have stopped it if he had.

"Sam," she whispered breathlessly.

"You don't have to say anything, but I couldn't hold it back. You're my weakness, my hidden fault line. I'm nowhere near perfect, and I know I'll make mistakes."

Her brows knitted, and he knew she thought he meant the kind of mistakes she never wanted to be hurt by again.

"I don't mean cheating. I told you, those aren't mistakes at all. Cheating takes a cognitive decision to hurt someone, and I'll never do that to you. *Ever*. I mean mistakes people make every day. Telling you I'll be home at a certain time and getting caught up at work. Or beating the daylights out of someone who says something disrespectful to you."

He'd added that last part to earn the smile she shared, but he also knew it was the truth. He'd do anything for her.

"When you turned me down at the wedding and you asked if I'd already run through all the women there, it was like something inside me clicked. I didn't want any of those women, Faith. I wanted you, and you made me question everything I knew about myself to earn your trust."

She dropped her eyes, and he lifted her chin and kissed her again.

"I'm glad you did. You were right. I wasn't worthy of you when I was running around. I didn't know it then, but I needed you to turn me down, because in here"—he covered his heart with his hand—"I knew you deserved a better man than I had been up to that point. You deserve to know without a shadow of a doubt that you can count on your partner for anything—a shoulder to cry on, a hand to hold. A friend to discuss your career and hobbies with, to laugh and tease and make love with under the stars. A man who will love you whether you gain fifty pounds or fall prey to terrible illness. A man you'll never have to worry about lying, or cheating, or breaking your heart."

He took her face in his hands and gazed into her eyes. "I am that man, Faith. I am your man."

Serenaded by the sounds of nature and the sure and steady beat of their hearts, she reached for him. Love played in her soulful eyes, in the tenderness of her touch, as their mouths and their bodies came together, sealing his vow with their passion.

Chapter Twenty-Nine

FAITH AWOKE TO the mattress sinking beside her. *Sam.* It had been a week since the night of their camping trip, when Sam had given his heart over to her completely, and she'd been floating on a cloud ever since. She'd been too overwhelmed with emotions to tell him she was falling in love with him that night, and ever since she'd been waiting for the right moment. She wanted to give him as wonderful of a romantic memory as he'd given her. And over the past blissful week of evening walks, watching movies—and missing the endings because they were too lost in each other—and talking about their hopes and dreams, she tripped over the edge. She loved Sam, wholly and completely, and tonight was *the* night she was finally going to tell him, after his event was over, when he was still riding the high. She had every romantic second of it planned.

She reached for him without opening her eyes.

"Morning, beautiful." He pressed his warm lips to hers as her eyes came open.

He smelled like soap, and sunshine, and *Sam*. She blinked the sleep from her eyes, and his handsome face came into focus.

"Hi. You showered without me?"

"I went for a run and didn't think you'd appreciate six miles' worth of sweat."

"I love when we earn that sweat together," she teased. Sitting up, she caught sight of her name above the Rough Riders logo in the center of his black tank top. Her heart kicked in her chest. She tugged at his shirt so she could read it more clearly.

"'Faith's Man?'"

"I got you one, too." He held up a matching tank top that read, SAM'S GIRL.

"Ohmygod, Sam." She snagged it from his hands, grinning so hard her cheeks hurt. "I thought I was 'Braden's Girl.'"

He gathered her against him. "There are going to be quite a few Bradens at the barbecue. I want it to be perfectly clear which one of us is lucky enough to be your man."

Her heart was so full of Sam she must be smiling like a lovesick fool. She didn't care that Vivian would have a field day teasing her about their shirts or that every woman there would probably think she'd *forced* Sam to wear one. The fact that Sam would not only think of something like that, but proudly wear one himself, made her tumble head over heels for him anew.

"You're not going to be embarrassed to wear it at the barbecue with all your clients, friends, and family there?"

"Baby, I'd wear *you* if I could." He kissed her again, and she clung to his shirt, keeping him close.

"Thank you for being so patient with me from the very first time you asked me out and for putting yourself out there in so many ways."

"We've both put ourselves out there."

"Not in the same way."

"Don't minimize my girl's efforts. You took a chance on the riskiest guy in town. That's putting yourself out there. All I had to do was be the man I was born to be—only I never realized it until you came along." He tugged her up to her feet and hugged her.

"I need to get down to Rough Riders and you need to get home to meet Vivian or she'll cut my balls off for monopolizing you. The barbecue starts at six. You sure you guys won't be too busy gallivanting around town and forget?"

"Not on your life, Mr. Braden." She snagged the tank top from the bed. "Especially now that I have a swanky new shirt to wear." She went up on her toes and kissed him. He latched on to her waist and took the kiss deeper.

"I'll miss you," he said.

"I'll miss you, too. You sure you don't want me to come earlier? I can have Vivian meet me there."

"It's going to be complete mayhem during the day. Teenagers and young families, with no room to breathe on shore or in the water. Eight of Patrick's friends are helping for the afternoon. Between them, Lira, Tex, and me, we'll be fine, but we won't have time for anything other than keeping kids from getting into trouble. Enjoy your time with Vivian. But I would like you by my side when the real event starts." He looked down at his shirt. "You won't leave your man hanging, will you?"

My man. "With you is the only place I want to be."

"THERE MUST BE two hundred people here." Vivian flipped her blond hair over one shoulder and scanned the crowded beach. They'd arrived at Rough Riders half an hour early and the beach was already packed.

Faith scanned the crowd. She'd seen a number of motorcycles in the parking lot and wasn't surprised to see Bullet and Dixie standing with a group of people by the boathouse. As they moved through the crowd, she saw Bones talking with Cole and Leesa. The polo shirt Bones wore covered his tattoos. Without his ink on display, or the rugged jeans and leather boots, he looked more like a doctor than a guy who hung out in—and owned—a biker bar. It was nice to see that side of Sam's life mingling with the more public side.

"How will you find Sam?" Vivian asked. "Maybe he should have had blinking lights sewn into those shirts."

"Shut up." Vivian had been teasing her about her SAM'S GIRL shirt all afternoon. "I'll find him. Come on."

They wound through the crowd surrounded by the aroma

of grilled hot dogs and hamburgers, sounds of laughter, and the hum of excited conversations. Faith listened for Sam's voice. If only she were taller, she could look over the crowd, but as it was, she was staring at chests and backs and tops of children's heads.

"Faith! Vivian!"

Faith whipped her head around. Lira waved and pushed through the crowd. She wore a Rough Riders T-shirt and a wide, beaming smile that made her look like a whole different person than she had at the car wash. Her skin was radiant, and she no longer looked broken. Faith hugged her, trying to keep threatening tears from falling. Sam really had given Lira a new lease on life.

"Isn't this amazing?" Lira said. "I can't believe how many people turned out. Sam said it's the biggest event yet by at least eighty or more people, and he attributed it to my efforts." She squealed and hugged Faith and Vivian again. "Thank you so much for having that car wash! That day changed my whole life. Sam offered me a full-time job this morning."

"Congratulations!" Faith hugged her again. "I'm so happy for you. So you're really going to move here?"

"Well, we're not sure yet. I have so much to get organized. I have to find a place to live, babysitting, you know. So much to consider. But he's letting me work remotely until I figure it out. Oh, and Sam introduced me to his friend Brent, who's hooking me up with his law partner who handles divorce cases." She leaned in close and said, "He said his partner would help me pro bono. I couldn't believe it."

Brent moved through the crowd and joined them. "Hey, Faith. Great to see you again." He leaned in and hugged her. "Nice shirt."

She looked down, having forgotten her shirt said SAM'S GIRL, and laughed. "Sam's idea. Brent, this is my friend Vivian."

"How's it going?" Brent gave her a hug, too.

"Better now," Vivian said flirtatiously.

Faith rolled her eyes and noticed that Brent claimed the spot beside Lira. Apparently Vivian noticed it, too, because she elbowed Faith and raised her brows.

"Your boyfriend really outdid himself." Brent's eye skimmed over the crowd.

Faith followed his gaze and spotted Sam standing by the water with Ty and a group of girls. She expected a spear of jealousy to pierce her chest, but it never came. There was no longer any room in their relationship for such an ugly emotion. Sam lifted his eyes and searched the crowd. She loved him so much she ached with it. His eyes landed on her, and her heart swelled. He blew her a kiss, said something to the group he was with without breaking his visual connection with Faith, and headed in her direction.

Vivian tugged on her arm, bringing her back to the moment. Brent and Lira had moved on to a private conversation.

"Remember how adamant I was about you *not* taking that walk with him?" Vivian said quickly.

"How could I forget?"

"He's turned out to be really good for you. Not only do you seem happier than I've seen you in a long time, but when you told me you gave your boss hell for not believing in Sam? That's new, Faith. You've changed, too."

Yeah, she'd changed all right. For the better. She wasn't skittish about their relationship, or untrusting. Sam made her feel loved, and special, and confident in all aspects of her life. They made a good team in every way possible. He moved with deft confidence and a seductive gaze locked on her, despite the many female eyes watching his every move.

She was unable to take her eyes off of the man who'd renewed her faith in relationships. And maybe even in herself.

His arm circled her waist as he lowered his cheek to hers and said, "God, I've missed you, baby." He pressed a kiss to her cheek, making her heart go all sorts of crazy.

"I'm glad you made it," he said to Vivian, before pulling her into a hug.

Vivian made a dreamy face, eyes to heaven, mouth agape. "I take back everything bad I ever said about you," she said to him.

Sam reached for Faith, bringing her to her favorite place, tight against his side. "Do I even want to know?"

"No," Vivian and Faith said in unison.

"I'm going to get a drink," Vivian said. "I see a super-sexy guy over there who needs ogling."

Faith and Sam followed her gaze—to Tex.

"I have a thing for tats," Vivian said before making a beeline for Sam's employee.

"She's also on a hiatus from men, so Tex is safe."

"Tex is a big boy. I'm not worried."

Faith wrapped her arms around Sam's neck and went up on her toes for another kiss. "This is incredible. Are you happy with the turnout?"

He flattened his palm against her back, holding her close with a devilish look in his eyes. "I'm pleased with the turnout, but even happier that you're here now."

"We got here at five thirty, but it was already packed."

"People showed up early. No biggie. Did you have fun with Vivian this afternoon?"

"Yes, and you know what the best thing is?" Before he could answer, she said, "I was worried about being jealous, but I'm not. Not even a little."

"That's good, because you never have a reason to be." His eyes shifted to Cole heading their way. Sam draped his arm around her waist again, a smile forming as his brother joined them.

"Hi," Cole said, leaning in to hug Faith, then embracing Sam.

Since the joint apologies the night of the impromptu bon-fire at Sam's house, things had been easy between Faith and

Cole at work again, and tension had eased between the two brothers.

"Hi. Where's Leesa?" Faith asked.

"She's with our mom, Tempe, and Jewel. I swear they'll be talking about our honeymoon forever." Cole's eyes skimmed over Faith's shirt and then landed on Sam's with amusement.

"Got something to say?" Sam challenged.

"Never thought I'd see the day," Cole admitted.

"They were Sam's idea," Faith said quickly, as if she needed to explain.

Cole held his hands up in surrender. "You don't have to worry about me saying anything. I know better than to make a smart remark about your boyfriend."

"You're never going to let me live that down, are you?" He'd teased her a few times about Sam unleashing her confidence to superhuman levels, but she knew it was all in fun, because the only people Cole teased that way were those closest to him.

"I'll take care of that." Sam fake punched Cole, who feigned a block and threw his own fake jab.

Standing up to Cole hadn't been easy, but she was glad she'd done it. And seeing them horsing around like only family could, she knew their brotherly bond could withstand anything.

Just like us.

Chapter Thirty

SAM MADE THE rounds with sponsors and guests, ensuring everyone got his attention. Lira had done an incredible job of rallying previous sponsors and clients. Groups of climbers and rafters he hadn't seen in more than four years had shown up, and several signed up for future trips. Sam solidified a handful of new sponsors, and Lira took care of gathering their information. She'd organized online sponsorship forms and set up a table with four laptops where sponsors and guests could sign up. She'd also prepared business cards with the site information to hand out as people left. Sam knew he'd made the right decision by hiring her, and he felt good knowing she and her daughter would have proper insurance and job security.

As the evening wore on and the crowd thinned, he followed the sound of Faith's laughter to a blanket by the water, where she was sitting with Vivian, Jewel, Tempe, and Leesa. He made his way over and sat beside her. The girls silenced almost immediately.

"Did I interrupt?" he asked, chuckling to himself at the furtive glances they were trading.

"We were talking about you," Tempe said.

Jewel smacked her hand. "Really, Tempe? You're not supposed to tell him."

He looked at Faith, who pressed her lips together like she was trying not to laugh. "What did you tell them?"

"Nothing. Well, not much," she admitted.

"She didn't have to tell us anything. Sam, those shirts? Shannon will get such a kick out of them." Tempe lifted her phone and clicked off a few pictures.

He shook his head and laughed, but nothing could dampen this day. He had his girl by his side, a new employee, and the event was a great success.

"You took her to your cove!" Tempe said as she put her phone away. "That's *huge!*"

"Christ," he mumbled. It wasn't a secret, but Tempe was a little too overjoyed with this news. He'd probably hear about it for weeks.

"I think it's sweet," Jewel said.

"And meaningful," Leesa added.

"And romantic," Vivian said, bumping Faith's shoulder.

He felt oddly proud of all those things, each of which he'd teased Nate and Cole about when they'd fallen in love with Jewel and Leesa.

"If you don't mind, I'm going to leave you girls to discuss

how incredibly awesome I am as a boyfriend." He pulled Faith up to her feet to hug her and her drink spilled down the front of his shirt.

"Oh! I'm sorry!" She swatted at the mess.

He reached behind him and pulled it over his head. "Not a big deal. I'll get a shirt from the office."

Faith stared hungrily at his bare chest.

"Why don't you come with me?" He looked over his shoulder and said, "I'll bring her right back."

"Yeah, right," Tempe called after them.

"I'm so sorry." Her hand brushed over his damp chest, his abs, and when she looked up at him, he couldn't help but lean in for a kiss.

"No, you're not."

They hurried into the office, kissing every few steps. Once inside, their mouths crashed together. Faith's hands moved over his back, and his moved under her shirt, earning a sexy moan.

"We can't do this," she said as he devoured her neck. "Oh God, that feels so good." She panted out a few breaths. "We can't..." He rocked his arousal against her. "Maybe we can."

He leaned back and gazed into her lust-filled eyes. She'd become his world. The very air he breathed. Seeing her so torn between satisfying the fire burning between them and doing the right thing reminded him of the million reasons he'd fallen in love with her. She was as careful as she was naughty, and she was *his*.

"You're right."

"I am?" Her forehead wrinkled. She hooked her finger into the waistband of his jeans. "You sure?"

"Not in the least. But you're *probably* right."

The office door opened and Nate stuck his head in. "Dude—" He closed his eyes. "Sorry, man. I should have knocked."

Faith turned beet-red. Sam groaned, gave her a quick kiss, and grabbed a shirt from a shelf in the closet where he kept extras. "It's cool. We weren't doing anything."

Nate opened his eyes. "I'm really sorry."

"I'm going to find Vivian." She hurried out of the office.

"I didn't mean to embarrass her." Nate cleared his throat. "Or cock block you. Pull your shirt down, will ya?"

Sam looked down at his erection and tugged his shirt on. "Jealous?"

"Of that worm?" He scoffed.

"Is that what you're calling pythons these days?"

Nate laughed. "A group of guys just showed up. One of 'em's asking for you."

Sam followed Nate out, scanned the area for Faith, and spotted her by the refreshments with Vivian. His mood brightened, as it did every time he saw her.

"Sammy!" Jacob Warner, a thick-bodied, blond-haired guy who had gone on a few trips with Sam a couple of years ago, shook his hand and pulled Sam closer, smacking him soundly on the back.

"Warner, how've you been? Still climbing?"

"Hell, yes. When I got the call about the barbecue, I had to come. Man, you changed my life." His smile reached his dark eyes. "What you said to me after that climbing trip set me free."

"HOLY SHIT, FAITH." Vivian bumped Faith with her elbow, interrupting her conversation with Lira, and pointed up the beach.

Faith's eyes locked on Sam. "I know. My man's hot, isn't h—" She clutched Vivian's arm as the man Sam was talking to came into focus, bringing with it a surge of anger and hurt that nearly brought her to her knees. *JJ.*

"What is that asshole doing here?" Vivian seethed, already on the move with Faith clutching her arm.

Faith hadn't seen JJ since she'd moved, and even though cognitively she knew it was him—the man who'd broken her heart and forced her away from the life she'd spent years building—seeing him *there*, talking with Sam, didn't make sense.

JJ laughed at something Sam said.

Her brain stumbled. She stumbled. *Oh shit.* He knew Sam? How? What the hell was going on?

"I've got this," Faith said to Vivian. She was sure smoke was pluming from her ears, and she didn't care. He didn't deserve to be there, with *her* boyfriend, in *her* happy place. Anger obliterated hurt, propelling her fast and determined to reclaim her space beside Sam.

"Man, Sam, that trip changed my life," JJ said.

"We had a killer climb," Sam said.

"No, man. Not that." JJ abruptly silenced as Vivian pulled her forward. His eyes filled with confusion. "Faith?" JJ shook his head, as if he, too, was trying to piece together this fucked-up reunion.

"Hey, baby." Sam reached an arm around her waist, where he inevitably felt her muscles tighten like concrete. His eyes turned serious. "You okay?"

JJ's eyes dropped to Faith's shirt. "Wait. SAM'S GIRL? You two?" He waved a finger at the two of them. "You're together?"

"Warner, this is my girlfriend, Faith," Sam said with the same pride and confidence he always had.

"You know JJ?" She couldn't keep the disbelief from her voice.

Tightening his grip on her, he said, "JJ? As in your ex?"

"Yes." They both turned to look at JJ, who had a big-ass grin on his face.

Anger clenched Sam's jaw, tightening each of his features as it made its way into his narrowing eyes. "Goddamn," he muttered. He crossed his arms over his chest, lowered his chin, and stepped toward JJ, planting his legs like columns of strength and creating a barrier between him and Faith.

"This is freaking ironic," JJ scoffed. He took a step back and scrubbed a hand over his face. "This can't be happening."

Faith's mind spun. Why was he here? How did he know Sam? Why didn't *she* know he knew Sam?

JJ locked amused eyes on Faith. "You're *dating* this guy? The guy who *told* me to cheat on you?"

The air left Faith's lungs. She stumbled backward, reaching for Vivian.

"I said a lot of shit back then," Sam said adamantly. "But I never would have told you—or anyone else—to cheat on a girlfriend."

"Don't *pretend* you don't remember hanging out in that bar with one chick under each arm," JJ spat. "Going on about how monogamy wasn't natural, and..."

His words blurred together. *Sam told him to cheat? Monogamy's not natural?* She turned away, feeling a fissure make its way down the center of her heart as Vivian guided her away.

"Faith, wait."

Vivian turned to say something, but she must have seen something in Sam, because she let him gather Faith in his arms. *God. In your arms. My favorite place. I have so many. All with you.* Faith looked into his loving eyes, and for the first time ever, fear looked back at her.

Seeing Sam's fear frightened her. Was she making a mistake with him?

"Did you say those things?" Her voice sounded frail and foreign.

"Baby, I said all types of things back then, but I never would have told him to cheat. That's never been a part of who I am. You know that. But could I have said that monogamy wasn't natural or being tied down sucked?" He searched her eyes as they filled with tears, and the pain in his nearly took her to her knees. "Yes, I could have. I probably did. But that's not who I am now."

Honest Sam. Her Sam. She closed her eyes and pressed her lips to the center of his chest. "I need time to process this. You should go back. This is an important event, and people are still here."

Chapter Thirty-One

FAITH PACED BY the water's edge after finally convincing Sam to return to his guests. She wasn't about to let JJ "the Asshole" Warner ruin Sam's event, even if she felt like someone had torn her guts out and spread them over the sand, then put them back inside her, gritty and ill fitting. At least she'd kept it together enough to control herself from telling JJ what he could do with that snarky-ass amusement she'd seen in his eyes.

"Tell me what I can do," Vivian said for the tenth time in the past half hour.

Faith sat on the sand, staring out at the water. "Nothing."

"You sound so calm. I wanted to haul off and hit JJ for being such a smarmy bastard."

"That's why I love you." Faith pulled her down beside her. "I'm not calm. I'm terrified. And I'm trying to figure out what the hell just happened."

She turned toward her best friend, who had been with her when JJ had accidentally texted her an invitation meant for someone else. Vivian had helped her get ready for their clandestine date, which she'd stupidly been elated about. Who wouldn't be excited to meet their boyfriend at a hotel room? *Someone who would have clued in to the fact that he'd told her he was going out of town with his buddies for the weekend.* She'd knocked on the hotel room door with a swarm of butterflies in her belly, mentally wondering if this was *it.* The night he was going to propose. She hadn't been prepared for the lingerie-clad woman coming out of the bathroom when he'd answered the door in nothing but a pair of boxers, or the feeling of devastation and humiliation when she'd run through the lobby crying, feeling like she'd fallen through a wormhole to a place where nothing made sense.

Vivian had been her savior, her sounding board, and she'd given Faith the tough love she hadn't realized she'd needed to pull her shit together and move on.

"Viv, you've seen me and Sam together. Am I looking at us through orgasm-colored glasses?" As she choked out the words, their acidic taste burned all the way to her gut, and she knew her answer. This was nothing like what happened with JJ. And as much as she'd needed Vivian during that awful time, this was different. Vivian was no longer the person she needed to get through this. She could do that. She and Sam. "Wait. Don't answer that."

"How can I not answer? Of course you're not looking at him through orgasm-colored glasses. I think you found a diamond in the rough with that man. Although"—Vivian bumped shoulders with Faith and pointed to Sam walking up the beach toward them—"I don't think it would matter what glasses you wore. You can only see him as who he is. He's been brutally honest with you from the very first time he asked you out, remember? You asked him if he'd already gone through all the women, and he told you there were still a few left."

At the sight of Sam closing in on them, Faith's mind scrambled. Luckily, she didn't need to think. She remembered every word they'd spoken that night.

"He said he wanted *me*."

Sam crouched beside her. "Hey, baby."

"Your guests…?"

"Ty and Tex are wrapping things up. You've been down here a long time." Every word was laced with worry. "I can't take being away from you for another second. This is where I want to be. With you, dealing with all the shit that went down. Please don't send me away."

Tears filled her eyes. "The last thing I want is to send you away."

Vivian touched Faith's arm, a silent message of support passing between them—*I'll leave you guys alone, okay?*

"I'll help Ty and Tex clean up, and then Tex can take me back to pick up my car." Vivian hugged Faith and whispered, "Don't judge. His tats are hot and I've been on a *long* hiatus."

Faith needed the smile Vivian's words gave her, but when

she turned back to Sam, he was reaching for her hand, and her heart tumbled anew.

"Want to walk and talk or sit?" he asked.

She silently pulled him down to the sand and drew in a deep breath. Gazing out over the river brought memories of their rafting trip and the night Sam told her he was falling in love with her. She'd had such big plans for tonight, none of which included the uncomfortable tension hovering around them.

"I'm sorry, Sam. I hope I didn't make a scene up there and embarrass you."

"You didn't make a scene, but it would take a lot more than that to embarrass me." He reached for her hand, and she was glad he did, because it meant he needed the connection as much as she did. "Baby, I'm sorry for whatever I said to Warner—*JJ*—that might have led him to hurt you."

"I know you are. I've been thinking about everything we've gone through. Everything I've gone through since he and I broke up. I thought he'd broken me back then. He devastated me completely. Shattered my safe little life into a million pieces, but he didn't *break* me. He kicked me in the gut and woke me up. I think I needed it. No man is that unhappy in a relationship unless there's a reason. *I* was the reason. He was right about that."

"Faith—"

"Hear me out. I'm not saying he should have cheated. He was a supreme asshole for doing that. But that doesn't change the fact that the things he said back then were true. I was wrapped up in work and school and friends and family. But I wasn't wrapped up in *him*. His cheating forced me to take a look at myself and to figure out who *I* was. And it was a long, hard road, Sam. I cried a lot, doubted myself and my ability to love and be loved, but I also found my pride and discovered that I *am* a person who goes all out for work and who makes a website because she's hurt. That's me. That's never going to change."

SAM'S HEART HAD lodged in his throat the moment he'd made the connection between Warner and Faith and *himself*. He hated that today had unearthed so much hurt from Faith's past. Hurt he'd give anything to obliterate.

"Faith, you don't have to tell me who you are. I know who you are. I love who you are, how hard you work, and that you go out of your way to help others. I love that you call me on my shit and that you blush when I turn you on. I'm not Warner. I respect you and want you to have a full life—with me and on your own."

"I believe you," she said, eyes trained on the ground. "But self-doubt slid in somewhere between knowing who I was and what happened up there, and it made me wonder if I had regressed. Did I fall back into my old patterns of being too wrapped up in work or my website to see what was right under my nose? Did I go from one man who would cheat to another?"

His chest compressed with the weight of her confession. Had his past finally come back to slaughter him?

"I can't deny that voice in my head appeared in all this, because if I did, then I'd *know* I had reverted to the person I used to be, and I'm not that person. So I'm going to tell you the rest of what went through my head over all of this, because that's who *we* are. You and I honor our crazy feelings, right?"

We. We still have we. Thank Christ. "Absofuckinglutely. The good, the bad, the crazy, and anything in between. If you feel it, I want to feel it, too."

"Good." She looked into his eyes and with a trembling voice said, "It was really hard to hear him say you told him to cheat on me."

He bit back the urge to once again define what he would or wouldn't have said, because he'd said his piece, and he knew she needed him to hear her out.

"Then I remembered what you've said to me since before we started going out," she said in a softer tone. "Cheating is a cognitive, willful act, a decision someone makes knowing the pain they'll cause to their partner. Sam, it wouldn't have mattered what you said to him back then. If he was going to cheat, he was going to cheat. He took what you said as, I don't know, some kind of warped blessing to act on what he wanted to do or something."

He let out a breath he hadn't realized was trapped. "Thank God you see that."

She smiled, giving him another lifeline to cling to. "The other thing I figured out during this terrifying time of introspection that I wish I never had is that who he was, or is, doesn't change who I am now. Or who you are. I'm stronger than I was, more aware of who I am and what I want. And more importantly, I didn't jump into this relationship—our relationship—with my eyes closed. I know who you are, and I trust you, Sam. Explicitly."

She shifted onto Sam's lap and wrapped her arms around his neck. Emotions bloomed in his chest.

"When I agreed to go out with you," she said in the same sweet tone she usually used with him, making his chest constrict for a whole new, wonderful, reason, "I accepted your past as part of the package. What happened with that jerk was part of that package, the same way he's part of my baggage, which you so graciously accepted."

"Baby, do you have any idea how incredible you are? Or how proud I am to be your boyfriend?"

"Right." She laughed. "The crazy girl who talks in circles?"

"No. The intelligent, stubborn woman who won't back down from her principles. I couldn't love you more." He pressed his lips to hers. "Damn. Look at that. I love you more than I did a second ago." He kissed her again. "Okay, I was wrong. I could, and will, love you more every second of every day."

She laughed. "Want to hear the craziest thing about all of this?"

"There's more craziness?"

"I think it comes with dating me," she teased. "All I've wanted to do since the moment you told me you were falling in love with me was to say it back. I've been waiting for the perfect time because I wanted to make it as romantic and wonderful as it was when you said it. I thought that time would be tonight, just the two of us down here by the water, after your big day. I had this elaborate scheme planned, like you did for our first date. I was going to leave you clues to find me down here by the water, where I'd be waiting inside a circle I drew on the beach."

Dear God, I'm the luckiest man on earth. "A circle?"

"Beauty in evolution and imperfection." She climbed off his lap and drew a circle in the sand. His heart thundered as she took his hand, bringing him into the circle with her.

"My friend Google told me a circle is the symbol of imperfection." She wrapped her arms around his waist. "And we're the symbol of evolution."

He gazed into her loving eyes, drowning in her all over again.

"Sam?"

"Yeah?" he choked out of his emotionally clogged throat.

"I don't think you're breathing." She pressed her palm to his chest and smiled up at him. "I think you're waiting."

She knew him so well he didn't even try to respond.

"I love you, Sam, imperfections and all." She went up on her toes, hovering a breath away from his. "Sam?" She pressed her hand to his cheek.

He was so full of emotions, "Mm?" was all he could manage.

"You need to kiss me now."

Epilogue

Three weeks later…

"IT'S HARD TO believe this is where it all started for you and Faith." Sam's mother threaded her hand through his arm. They'd closed Mr. B's for the celebratory dinner with the Fishers after Krissy's dance recital, which was spectacular. Krissy danced like it was what she'd been born to do.

Sam hadn't been able to take his eyes off of Faith all night. She stood across the room talking with Leesa, Jewel, and Tempe and swaying to the music in her little black dress. She'd been stealing glances at him all night, sending a shock of heat with each one.

"It started long before that night, Mom. I just didn't realize it." Faith had moved into his cabin two weeks ago, and Lira was taking over the lease on her apartment. Sam had offered Lira the opportunity to work remotely for however long she wanted to, but she'd decided a clean break was better than living in the shadow of her hurtful past. Sam didn't blame her. After all, that's what Faith had done, and look how lucky he was because of it. He hoped Lira would find happiness in Peaceful Harbor, too.

His mother smiled up at him, her thick blond curls framing her happy face.

"I've never said much to you about your personal life, but I want you to know that I never judged you for how you chose to live. We all take different paths, Sammy. Yours led you to Faith."

"Thanks, Mom. That means a lot to me."

She glanced across the room. "She's wonderful, you know."

"I know." Faith glanced over, and he blew her a kiss. She touched her lips, as if she felt it land.

"You're wonderful, too, sweetheart." She kissed his cheek.

"You're a little biased," he teased as his father and Nate joined them.

His father draped an arm around their mother and said, "Three down, three to go."

"Two," Ty said. "I'm holding out for a mountain-climbing vixen with an eye for risk and a body made for—"

"Ty!" Their mother shook her head. "I don't want or need to hear the end of that sentence."

"What?" Ty asked with innocent eyes. "I'm leaving next week for a photography assignment in Spain, and I plan on enjoying the *culture* in as many ways as possible."

Nate jumped on that, and Sam took the opportunity to

cross the room and steal time with his favorite person.

Cole fell into step with him before he reached Faith. "I talked to Jon."

Sam stopped, turning his attention to Cole. "And?"

"He's cool with four weeks of vacation for Faith so she can travel with you, but we need at least two weeks' notice before any trip that's longer than four days so we can bring in a temp."

"You're the best. Thanks."

"No worries, but I have a feeling your girlfriend won't like you going around her."

He was right about that, but soon enough she'd have plenty of planning to do, and he just wanted to ease this one worry. "It was for a good cause. I think she'll forgive me."

FAITH'S PULSE QUICKENED with each of Sam's determined steps. Her world had changed so much in the past few weeks, and Sam had been with her every step of the way. The resource page she'd created for Women Against Cheaters was getting almost two thousand hits a day, and tomorrow she and Sam were going to a small-business meeting together to see if they could gain community support for the group in other ways. Work was as busy as ever, and her professional relationship with Cole hadn't suffered. If anything, they had an even stronger relationship because of it.

"Sammy's on the prowl," Tempest whispered to her. "How do you stand him looking at you like that?"

She hoped she never had to live a day when he *didn't* look at her that way.

"Ladies." Sam stepped between Tempest and Leesa and drew Faith into his arms. "Missed you." He kissed her tenderly.

Tempest sighed. "I don't know what love potion you've given him, but when I find a man, can you please inject him with whatever it is?"

Faith laughed, vaguely aware of the girls moving away and *very* aware of Sam's big body pressed against hers.

"You scared everyone away." She wrapped her arms around his neck, not unhappy that he scared them off, even if a little embarrassed. But she'd learned that was part of being with Sam, too. That hint of embarrassment came from his overwhelming love for her, and she wouldn't trade that for the world.

Sam didn't respond to her halfhearted complaint. She knew he wouldn't have cared if he'd scared off an army, just another thing she piled onto the mountain of things she loved about him.

They moved to the music, gazing into each other's eyes, and Faith was sure the touch of their bodies was throwing sparks for all to see. They fell into this position, dancing to a beat—*existent or not*—at least once a day, and it usually led to them ravenously devouring each other. Sometimes when they were cooking dinner or taking a walk, Sam would take her in his arms and sing while they danced, which was her favorite thing of all. She loved the way he sang straight from his heart, his emotions sailing directly into hers.

"Remember when you wouldn't dance with me?" he asked.

"I don't think I'll ever forget. Turning you down was the hardest thing I've ever done." The room was so quiet, save for the music and their bodies brushing against each other. She wondered if everyone was watching them, but Sam was blocking her view. *My Greedy Sam.*

"I'm glad I don't have to ask anymore."

"Me too."

"There are lots of things I don't have to ask about anymore." He pressed his lips to hers. "Like that." He nuzzled against her neck. "And this."

"Sam," she said with a giggle. "That drives me crazy."

He pressed his cheek to hers and said, "I know."

A river of shivers flowed down her spine. He leaned back far enough to look into her eyes, and the depth of emotions in his stilled her heart.

"There's one thing I still have to ask you."

"Really? I thought I'd given you carte blanche to my entire being."

"I want carte blanche to your entire future. Trips, babies, dancing beneath the stars. I want to get old and gray with you, and when we have too many wrinkles to count, they'll be our wrinkles, baby. Our imperfections, each one born from a life we spent loving each other."

Her throat closed as tears spilled down her cheeks.

"Marry me, Faith. Let me love you, embarrass you, and dance with you until the day you bury me six feet under. Then I'll wait for you on the other side, knowing that whatever else there is, we'll experience it together."

She swallowed a few times, maybe a dozen, trying to force words from her lungs, but her heart had swelled and her chest had constricted, and she could barely stand. She nodded vehemently.

"Baby, I—"

"Need to hear it?" she managed, a half laugh, half cry bursting free. "Like you'd ever let me say no? Yes, Sam. I want to be your wife. I want to have our babies, and take trips, and get wrinkly. But what I want most of all is to have you look at me like you are right now for the rest of my life."

Sam's mouth came possessively down over hers as he lifted her to her feet and spun her around.

"I love you, baby," he said, and it was then the rest of the room came into focus. The women were crying and smiling, hugging one another, while the men beamed and cheered.

"Just one more thing." Sam lowered her feet to the ground and reached into his pocket, pulled out a sparkling diamond engagement ring, and slid it on her trembling finger.

She couldn't take her eyes off of the circular diamond, surrounded by another perfect circle of round diamonds. A trail of round diamonds ran down the center of the wide band, bordered by intricate designs in white gold. Her vision blurred with fresh tears.

"Sam, it's beautiful. It's so *us*."

"Our circle forever, baby." He kissed her again, long and languorously, which made everyone hoot and holler.

"Smile, baby. You're on family camera." He pointed to the television above the bar, where her parents, Vivian, Charley, Mack, and Sam's sister, Shannon, were waving and congratulating them at once.

Thankfully, Sam held her around her waist, because her noodle legs were nearly useless.

"How? You've never even met my family." She waved to her parents. Her mother's eyes were wet, her nose pink from crying, and her father smiled proudly down at her. "I love you Mom. Dad."

"We love you, pumpkin," her father said.

"I couldn't ask you to marry me without speaking with your parents first," Sam explained. "Vivian, who would do anything for you, did this for me."

Faith covered her mouth, trying to keep the sobs from breaking free as she looked up at her best friend. Vivian's tears mirrored her own, and they both mouthed, *Love you*, at the same time.

Sam's mom was the first one to embrace Faith. "Congratulations, sweetheart. We're so happy to have you in our lives."

She was passed from one person to the next, in a flood of hugs and tears and *welcome to the familys*. Faith finally found her voice and talked with her family and Vivian over Skype. Before signing off, she and Sam planned a trip to Oak Falls to visit her family, and Vivian planned a visit to Peaceful Harbor. Faith had a feeling she'd see very little of Vivian on the trip, since she'd confided in Faith that she'd been keeping in touch with Tex. So much for her hiatus.

As the evening came to an end, Sam drew her close for one final dance at Mr. B's. "Now all we have to do is pick a date."

"Why do I have a feeling you've already got one in mind?"

Ready for more Bradens?

Fall in love with Shannon Braden and Steve Johnson in
CRUSHING ON LOVE

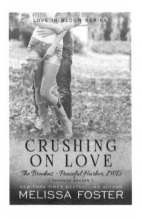

Steve Johnson is living his life's passion watching over the Colorado Mountains as a ranger and wildlife consultant. But his peaceful life is upended when overzealous and insanely beautiful Shannon Braden flits back into his life after returning from a brief trip home to Maryland. He thought his attraction to her was under control—after all, she's only in Colorado temporarily, and he doesn't do casual affairs.

Shannon's return to Colorado has as much to do with the game of cat and mouse she and Steve have been playing as it does the data she's been hired to collect. But despite her efforts to explore the undeniable heat simmering between them, Steve's intent on keeping his distance.

When a ranch abutting the national park goes up for sale, Steve will do whatever it takes to keep it from falling into the wrong hands. And when all his attempts fail, he's left with no alternative but to follow Shannon's guidance into the online world he abhors in order to raise the funds. The more time they spend together, the deeper their attraction becomes, and a game of cat and mouse turns into an unstoppable connection. But when Shannon's assignment comes to an end, will it mean an end to them, too?

Ready for your next binge read?

You met the Whiskeys in RIVER OF LOVE

Get to know them better and see why readers are calling TRU BLUE, the first book in The Whiskeys series, Melissa's best book yet!

He wore the skin of a killer, and bore the heart of a lover...

There's nothing Truman Gritt won't do to protect his family–Including spending years in jail for a crime he didn't commit. When he's finally released, the life he knew is turned upside down by his mother's overdose, and Truman steps in to raise the children she's left behind. Truman's hard, he's secretive, and he's trying to save a brother who's even more broken than he is. He's never needed help in his life, and when beautiful Gemma

Wright tries to step in, he's less than accepting. But Gemma has a way of slithering into people's lives and eventually she pierces through his ironclad heart. When Truman's dark past collides with his future, his loyalties will be tested, and he'll be faced with his toughest decision yet.

Have you met the REMINGTONS?

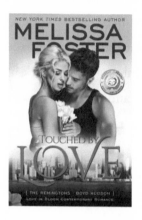

Fiercely independent Janie Jansen has always believed there were worse things in life than being blind, and she's spent her life proving it. She's moved away from her overprotective parents, built a life in New York City, and is one of the top technical editors in her company. That is, until an unfortunate accident turns her life upside down and she's forced to give up the very independence she's worked so hard to achieve.

Firefighter Boyd Hudson pushed past his tragic past and is weeks away from accomplishing his ultimate dream—being accepted into medical school. His intense focus on his goal while working three jobs has taken its toll. With a trail of failed relationships behind him, Boyd is painstakingly aware of his limitations and avoids girlfriends completely—a difficult task given his attraction to one of his co-workers.

When Boyd comes to Janie's rescue, she's forced to accept his help, and Janie discovers there's more to the sexy-sounding office flirt than one-liners. Their connection deepens as Janie heals, but it turns out that Janie isn't the only one who needs healing. Boyd's painful past comes back to haunt him, threatening their relationship and forcing Boyd to reevaluate everything he knows about himself.

Meet Mick Bad, your naughtiest book boyfriend

BAD BOYS AFTER DARK: MICK

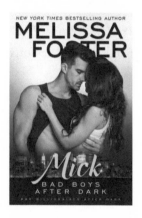

Amanda Jenner is done being a boring-man magnet and has finally taken control of her love life. As any smart paralegal would, she's researched the hell out of how to seduce a man. She's waxed, primped, and ready to put her newfound skills into action—and a masquerade bar crawl is the perfect venue for her solo coming-out party.

Entertainment attorney Mick Bad lives by two hard and fast rules. He never mixes business with pleasure, and he doesn't *do* relationships, which makes the anonymity of a masquerade bar crawl the perfect place for a onetime hookup.

Amanda thinks she's hit the jackpot when she bags a tall, dark, and sinfully delicious masked man—until she discovers the man she's made out with is her off-limits boss. Mick's already crossed a line he can never uncross, and one taste of sweet and sexy Amanda has only whet his appetite. When Mick offers to give Amanda a lesson in seduction—*no strings, no regrets, and for goodness' sake, come Monday, no quitting*—the tables turn, and Mick's totally unprepared for the lessons this sweet temptress provides.

Love the Bradens?

The Bradens are just one of several families in the Love in Bloom big family romance collection. Characters from each family series make appearances in future books, so you never miss an engagement, wedding, or birth. Love in Bloom features: Snow Sisters, The Bradens, The Remingtons, Seaside Summers, The Ryders, Wild Boys After Dark, and Harborside Nights.

View the complete Love in Bloom series
MelissaFoster.com/LIB

FREE Love in Bloom ebooks
MelissaFoster.com/3FREE

Reader Goodies: Series checklists, reading order, and more
MelissaFoster.com/RG

Keep track of your favorite characters with the essential Love in Bloom Series Guide
MelissaFoster.com/LIBSG

More Books By Melissa Foster

LOVE IN BLOOM SERIES

SNOW SISTERS
Sisters in Love
Sisters in Bloom
Sisters in White

THE BRADENS at Weston
Lovers at Heart, Reimagined
Destined for Love
Friendship on Fire
Sea of Love
Bursting with Love
Hearts at Play

THE BRADENS at Trusty
Taken by Love
Fated for Love
Romancing My Love
Flirting with Love
Dreaming of Love
Crashing into Love

THE BRADENS at Peaceful Harbor
Healed by Love
Surrender My Love
River of Love
Crushing on Love

Whisper of Love
Thrill of Love

THE BRADENS & MONTGOMERYS at Pleasant Hill – Oak Falls

Embracing Her Heart
Anything For Love
Trails of Love
Wild, Crazy Hearts
Making You Mine
Searching For Love

THE BRADEN NOVELLAS

Promise My Love
Our New Love
Daring Her Love
Story of Love
Love at Last
A Very Braden Christmas

THE REMINGTONS

Game of Love
Stroke of Love
Flames of Love
Slope of Love
Read, Write, Love
Touched by Love

SEASIDE SUMMERS

Seaside Dreams
Seaside Hearts
Seaside Sunsets

Seaside Secrets
Seaside Nights
Seaside Embrace
Seaside Lovers
Seaside Whispers
Seaside Serenade

BAYSIDE SUMMERS
Bayside Desires
Bayside Passions
Bayside Heat
Bayside Escape
Bayside Romance
Bayside Fantasies

THE RYDERS
Seized by Love
Claimed by Love
Chased by Love
Rescued by Love
Swept Into Love

THE WHISKEYS: DARK KNIGHTS AT PEACEFUL HARBOR
Tru Blue
Truly, Madly, Whiskey
Driving Whiskey Wild
Wicked Whiskey Love
Mad About Moon
Taming My Whiskey
The Gritty Truth

More Books by Melissa

Chasing Amanda (mystery/suspense)

Come Back to Me (mystery/suspense)

Have No Shame (historical fiction/romance)

Love, Lies & Mystery (3-book bundle)

Megan's Way (literary fiction)

Traces of Kara (psychological thriller)

Where Petals Fall (suspense)

Acknowledgments

Writing a book is not a solo endeavor, and I am indebted to my fans, friends, and family, who inspire and support me on a daily basis. Please continue to keep in touch. You never know when you'll end up in one of my books, as several members of my Street Team have already discovered.

If you don't yet follow me on Facebook, please do! We have such fun chatting about our lovable heroes and sassy heroines, and I always try to keep fans abreast of what's going on in our fictional boyfriends' worlds.
Facebook.com/MelissaFosterAuthor

Remember to sign up for my newsletter to keep up to date with new releases and special promotions and events and to receive an exclusive short story featuring Jack Remington and Savannah Braden.
MelissaFoster.com/Newsletter

For a family tree, publication schedules, series checklists, and more, please visit the special Reader Goodies page that I've set up for you!
MelissaFoster.com/Reader-Goodies

As always, heaps of gratitude to my amazing team of editors and proofreaders: Kristen Weber, Penina Lopez, Jenna Bagnini, Juliette Hill, Marlene Engel, and Lynn Mullan. And, of course, to my awesome family.

~Meet Melissa~

www.MelissaFoster.com

Melissa Foster is a *New York Times* and *USA Today* bestselling and award-winning author. Her books have been recommended by *USA Today's* book blog, *Hagerstown* magazine, *The Patriot*, and several other print venues. Melissa has painted and donated several murals to the Hospital for Sick Children in Washington, DC.

Visit Melissa on her website or chat with her on social media. Melissa enjoys discussing her books with book clubs and reader groups and welcomes an invitation to your event. Melissa's books are available through most online retailers in paperback, digital, and audio formats.

Melissa also writes sweet romance under the pen name, Addison Cole.

Made in United States
Troutdale, OR
06/09/2023